The Missing

The Missing

Jim Sabin

Cover designed by SelfPubBookCovers.com/Novalarty

This book is a work of fiction. Names, characters, places, and
incidents are either products of the author's imagination or are used
fictitiously. Any resemblance to actual persons, living or dead, events,
or locales is entirely coincidental.

Printed in the United States of America

First Printing: June 2025
Lucy K. Sabin, Oxford, OH
ISBN: 979-8-218-65055-1
Library of Congress Control Number: 2025936308

AUTHOR'S WIFE'S NOTES

My husband Jim worked on this novel for quite a few years. Sadly, he passed away from cancer at age 49 in late January of 2023 and never got to see it published. He loved his sons and the game of baseball, both of which you'll see reflected in this story.

I want to thank Jim's early beta reader, Linda Leszczuk. Unfortunately, she passed away about a year before Jim did, but I know her wisdom and generosity in sharing it really helped him. I'd also like to thank Jim's Columbus writing group, Buckeye Crime Writers, for bringing his book to fruition. Specifically, I'd like to thank Jenna Grinstead, Patrick Stuart, Andrew Welsh-Huggins, and Kandy Williams for taking the time to beta-read. In addition, a very big thank you to Eileen Curley Hammond for editing and formatting the book, as well as handholding me through the process of getting this book to print. I wouldn't have been able to do it without her, and I appreciate all the work done behind the scenes by the Buckeye Crime Writers group. Thank you for loving Jim so well and helping make his dream a reality—I think he'd be blown away by what you have all done for him.

If Jim were here, he'd also want to thank his mom and dad for their support of his writing journey, as well as his grandparents, and his brothers and their families. He loved his family, and they meant so much to him. Speaking of family brings me, of course, to his sons, Chris and Alex. Thank you for giving your dad so much purpose—he lit up with his love for you.

Personally, I'd like to thank Eileen Curley Hammond, again, for all her support. Eileen and I both thank Jim for such a wonderful final draft and his great note-taking and organization.

When finishing his book was first mentioned to me, it seemed unfathomable, but here we are. And the last words go to my husband, Jim. I love you so much, my lovely, and am so glad this was possible. Until we meet again.

Lucy Sabin

For Jim: You always dreamed of having a book published, and I'm so thankful that this dream is now a reality. Thank you for sharing part of your life with me; I'm grateful I got that chance. I'm proud of you and love you more than I can say.

For Chris and Alex: You were your dad's pride and joy. I hope you get a kick out of seeing his book in print and being able to share your dad's talent with those who never got to meet him in person.

CHAPTER ONE

R ed, white, and blue lights pulsed and clashed as I pulled my car to a stop on the side of Ohio Route 98. As always, the lights made me nauseous. They brought back memories of bad injuries and worse mistakes.

Tonight, they reflected off an array of chrome-plated surfaces, red and brown leaves, and dark tree trunks. Shadows flashed through the woods, banished moments after their creation by a new light from a different angle, only to blend into another as the swirling colors changed. With the moon barely a quarter full, they were a beacon.

I parked my car about thirty feet behind the closest fire truck, picked up my reporter's notebook and pen, and, with a sigh, left the recorder on the seat. It was great for interviewing coaches after games, but tonight, any voices would compete with running engines.

Not bothering to lock the car, I walked slowly toward the fire truck. Like the rest of the vehicles, it thrummed as if attempting to drown the shouts going back and forth between the firefighters and deputies. An officer watched me with narrowed eyes. He was there to direct traffic, though no traffic was getting down 98 any time soon.

I flashed my press pass, and he made a show of examining it. It featured my picture — dark hair, mustache, chocolate brown eyes, gold-rimmed glasses, and pertinent details — six-one, two hundred and twenty pounds along with my name, "David Kendrick, reporter, *Lynwood Post*," typed in block letters. Somehow, it took him at least thirty seconds to compare the badge to me, maybe he was trying to calculate my age—thirty-six—from the birthdate shown, though he already knew who I was.

"Stay out of the way," he growled.

"Always do." I was used to the attitude, but it still bothered me.

I walked alongside the fire engine, trying to attract as little attention as possible. Up ahead, I found at least part of the accident. A large pickup truck with dual-rear wheels and a trailer full of grain sat in the northbound lane, facing south. An officer shined a big Maglite into the vehicle.

The back door of one of the ambulances was open, and a young guy, maybe twentyish, perched on the floor, legs swung out onto the rear bumper, blanket draped over his shoulders. He had black, stringy hair and hadn't shaved in a while. He was talking to an officer who took notes on a clipboard. Three more cruisers, another fire truck, and one more ambulance completed the ensemble—all of which brought back too many unpleasant memories.

The stringy-haired man—the truck driver, I guessed—seemed to realize he was being watched and looked at me. He stared blankly for several seconds, and I realized he looked vaguely familiar. His pale skin contrasted with his black hair, and the dark circles under his eyes were pronounced. Perhaps he'd fallen asleep while driving.

As I was about to blink, he smiled. It wasn't a bright, sunny smile. Instead, it was a slow one—filled with victorious menace—the kind I used to give just before I hit a home run off an arrogant pitcher back in my playing days.

I shivered and turned away. Perhaps he'd hit his head or something, but I got the odd feeling he was enjoying himself. I wished I could place him.

The officer checking over the truck was now looking at me with contempt. He shook his head and mumbled something before turning away.

I suppressed the urge to flip him off. I'd been in my own crash many years ago, and the local police officers had never forgiven me for it. I understood why, but to still be getting grief after all these years was beyond silly.

My feet crunched through the gravel on the side of the road, mostly to get away from the belching fumes of the nearby fire truck. It was one of those cold, clear nights that normally smelled of crisp wood smoke, but the mingled odors of diesel exhaust, spilled gasoline, and well-used fire apparel overwhelmed any more pleasant smells. Stopping at the edge of the grass, I peered at where most of the action was happening, forty feet from the side of the road, against a massive tree trunk. Something was crumpled at its base, the remains of which bore a passing resemblance to a car.

For one thing, it was on its side, its roof against the tree, which had not yielded when it had been hit at an obviously high rate of speed. The roof was caved in, and the car's frame was bent. The front driver's side wheel well was in the air, but the wheel was missing, and the front end had been mashed. The bumper, too, was gone. It looked like the car had flipped multiple times before finding something stable enough to stop its momentum.

Firefighters and paramedics swarmed it, working to get to the poor soul or souls inside. Some officers watched while others searched the area for debris or plotted the car's path. A firefighter was perched on the car's back door, while another stood below him near the exposed undercarriage, holding a large device up to the bottom corner of the vehicle. Metal shrieked as it was cut.

3

I waited patiently for a few minutes, trying not to think about my own experience. I've been to a lot of crash scenes since, but they never got easier, especially when it was a nasty one.

"Going to make deadline?" Tim Jepson asked.

I jumped—I hadn't heard anyone approaching. Tim was one of the few police officers who didn't look at me with revulsion, so that placed him among my favorites. "Depends on how long they take to pull the poor sap out," I motioned toward the car. "I can't imagine anyone surviving."

"You never know. Safety features these days are pretty impressive. People can survive a lot now," Tim said.

I didn't answer right away. I wasn't sure if he'd meant something more by that comment or not. Finally, I decided to pretend he didn't. "Still, I'd better get something soon. Deadline's in fifteen, and Marla needs a little time to write whatever I call in."

"I'm sure she can handle it."

He was probably right. Marla Anderson was the night editor at the *Lynwood Post* and, before her promotion, had been the newspaper's cops reporter. She and I had done this routine more times than I cared to remember. The scanner sounded, and even though I was on the payroll to cover high school sports, I'd be sent to the scene. Then she'd work her magic, and a decent little story would appear on our website and in the print edition without me returning to the office.

It worked for Marla and the *Post*. Nobody ever bothered to ask if it worked for me. Maybe they didn't want to hear my answer.

"Better get a move on. What happened?" I asked

"Don't quote me, but looks like the truck driver fell asleep and went left of center," Tim said.

"Guess he's awake now."

"Yeah, but he claims he doesn't remember a thing. Doesn't seem to realize what's going on." Tim shrugged and looked over his shoulder toward the ambulance. "He has no idea what he's in for, that's for sure."

I followed his gaze. The guy was still in the ambulance, staring into space. At least he wasn't smiling anymore. I had no idea why they hadn't taken him away yet.

"Isn't he injured?" I asked.

"Doesn't seem to be. If he were, we'd have transported by now. That's just a warm place to keep him till we can interview him."

"Who can tell me all this for publication? Please don't say Reynolds." I'd seen the bookish sergeant standing near the crumpled car.

"I won't say it, but you're right in one." Tim pointed to Reynolds. He didn't have the authority to talk to the media as an officer, so it had to be a sergeant or above.

"Wonderful." I felt my shoulders sag. Sergeant Blaine Reynolds was a bland sort of fellow who looked like he'd be more at home in a library—sandy hair, wire-rimmed glasses, and features so dull most people had to meet him three times before they'd remember him. He also had an attitude like an old-time librarian, the stern one who'd rap on your table if you whispered too loudly or ooze condescension if you couldn't find a book in the arcane Dewey decimal system. The sergeant made no secret of the fact that he didn't like me.

"I know time's tight. Let me get him for you," Tim said. Without waiting for an answer, he stepped down the gravel side of the road, hopped the small, empty ditch running alongside it, and headed for my least favorite sergeant.

I took out my phone and texted Marla: "It's a bad one. Car vs. big pickup, car's flipped over and against a tree. They're extricating."

I hit send, then checked to see if Mom had texted me back. She'd sent me one earlier, which was unusual — she wasn't generally a texter. She hadn't sent another, but I opened the thread anyway, just to check: "Davey, can you come over after work tonight? I need to tell you some things. It's important. Let me know."

I had replied: "Be over by 11 at the latest."

I sighed — the clock in the corner of the screen now read 10:47. I sent a new message: "Sorry, Mom; breaking news. I'll be over when I can. Late, maybe 11:30 or 12."

I closed the phone and looked up as a firefighter came from behind the wrecked car.

"Hey, sarge, got a purse," he shouted over the racket made by the mechanical door spreader and tossed a bundle to Reynolds. "Just one person, so it's probably hers. Looks like there's a wallet."

Reynolds, his back to me, caught it, then rummaged through. As Tim approached, Reynolds turned toward the headlights from the road, and my breath left me with a whoosh.

It seemed like Reynolds removed the wallet from the oversized bag in slow motion. He placed the purse on the ground and flipped the wallet open, but I was transfixed by the bag. Its purple, red, and blue coloring was crystal clear in the headlights of one of the cruisers. There was more red than used to be on the bag, and the new spots glistened in the light.

I knew that bag well. Mom made it.

Somehow, I was on my knees, and the chilly night air seemed much, much colder. Part of my brain was years away, hearing distant shouts that had nothing to do with the scene before me.

6

And then I remembered that smile — that sick, vengeful smile on the face of that smug asshole in the back of the ambulance. I stood and turned. The truck driver was still there — watching me — a faint smirk on his face.

"Son of a bitch," I growled. At that moment, I was convinced that the guy knew exactly what he had done. Almost without thinking, I took a step toward him, and then I began to run. The truck driver didn't move — he just watched me.

Someone in a brown firefighter's turnout coat materialized in front of me. I shoved him and kept going. Twenty feet, ten… then someone else slammed into me from the side, got tangled in my legs, and took me down. I landed on the pavement hard, smacking and scraping my cheek, knees, and elbows.

"Get off!" I screamed. By lifting my head, I could see the trucker's feet resting on the silvery bumper of the ambulance. "God damn it, let go! He killed her!"

I bucked, but someone else was there now, maybe more than one, holding me down, pulling me away from the ambulance, scraping my knee joints against the cold pavement.

Men were yelling at me, and my arms were wrestled behind my back, cold steel snapping against my wrists.

Finally, a voice cut through. Someone said my name repeatedly — Tim's voice — "Dave, stop. Dave, stop. Dave, stop fighting."

I turned my head and tried to look up. Tim was kneeling between me and my quarry, one hand on my shoulder. Under that upraised arm, I could see him — the truck driver — slack-jawed, watching me. No. He was watching the scene, vacant, unfocused.

"Dave, what the hell are you doing?" Tim asked.

"Let me up," I said. "Please. He killed my mother."

He blinked. "He *what?*"

"That's her purse," I said. "Mom's purse."

"Hold on. Just hold on." He looked stunned.

Like I had a choice. Tim stood and walked out of my field of vision. I heard murmuring—but couldn't make out the words because everything else was so loud. My knees throbbed as they were pressed into the rough asphalt, and it was getting harder to breathe, whether from the pressure or the circumstance.

Then Reynolds's voice came through loud and clear, "Yeah, he's right. It's his mom."

My face hit the pavement again as fury and grief warred for control. A door slammed, and an engine revved. When the deputies finally let me up, the ambulance had gone. Tim unlocked the cuffs.

"Take him to jail, Tim. Take him and never let him out," I said through gritted teeth.

"Dave, it was an accident." Tim's voice was maddeningly calm.

"It was no accident, Tim. He killed her. He killed my mother. Don't you ever let him out where I can find him."

CHAPTER TWO

Tim led me to the back of the other ambulance and got one of the paramedics to work on my cheek. I hadn't realized how much it stung until the guy started wiping blood away. My phone buzzed, but for the moment, I ignored it. Marla wouldn't like what I had to say anyway. Numbly, I wondered if it had been damaged when I was tackled. Tim stayed in front of me as if he had been ordered not to let me leave. Another officer I didn't know hovered ten feet behind him, eyeing me with a mixture of contempt and pity.

"He killed her, Tim," I said for perhaps the twentieth time. "He killed her, and he smiled at me as if he was happy about it."

Tim responded with the same patience he'd used the last nineteen times. "Dave, listen. We don't know if she's gone. They're still working to get her out of the car, okay? She might have survived." His eyes told me he didn't believe that any more than I did, but he still had to say it. "Besides, it was an accident. The guy fell asleep. He didn't know what was going on."

"Then, why did he smile at me?"

"I don't know. Maybe he's in shock. The medics said he wasn't hurt, but you never know." He glanced over his shoulder toward the crash scene, which was hidden from me by the ambulance door. "We have a lot to sort here."

"Blue Honda Accord? License plate QUILTR1?" I asked.

Tim nodded. "Someone else might have borrowed her car."

"Tim, just stop. That's bullshit — you have her purse. We both know it's her."

I felt like I was watching the scene from above, outside my body. How had I not recognized Mom's car? Of course, with no front bumper, there was no license plate. The lights, those damned lights, had made the car look blue, purple, even green, at least what little of the paint job I could make out. Besides, it hadn't occurred to me that the car might be familiar.

I still felt guilty. I should have known.

"How long?" I murmured. "How long till she's out?"

"I don't know, Dave. The… the car's pretty torn up. They're using the tools." Or had been, at least. The shrieking of metal being cut had stopped.

My phone buzzed again, and I reached for my back pocket. My elbow ached, and not just from the scrapes, and my shoulder, cranky on good days, screamed at me. I pulled out my phone and swiped it with my thumb.

"Marla. Going to be a bit yet," I mumbled into the phone.

"We're on deadline, Dave. What do you have?"

I sighed, staring blankly back toward the pickup, whose darkened headlights bored into my soul.

"Two cars. One car, one pickup. Truck driver not hurt. Extracting the other one now," I said. "Call you when I have more." Without waiting for an answer, I hung up.

"You're working?" Tim stared.

I shrugged. "I guess."

"Stop that. She calls again; I'll handle it." Tim took the phone.

I looked at him, then back at the truck. It was a dull red, like maroon, or at least it appeared to be. The driver's side bumper was shoved in, and the grill was bent, but it didn't look nearly bad enough to have caused so much damage to the Honda. Of course, it hadn't flipped and hit a tree either. I shuddered.

My phone lit, and Tim raised it to his ear, but the words were lost. All I could focus on was that the front of that pickup was the last thing my mother had seen in this life.

———————

It felt like someone else lived my life for the next two days. I met the doctor, who confirmed what Tim and even Sergeant Reynolds had been reluctant to tell me. Mom died in the crash, probably instantly, but they had done everything they could for her. Standard lines, I'd heard them a million times on medical shows, cop shows, and sitcoms. They'd never been said to me, though, which made it all the more real.

My injuries still hurt from being tackled—my right shoulder and elbow were stiff, and they joined bruised and swollen knees. Paired with scrapes on my cheek, they gave me a distinct Frankenstein effect as I dealt with the funeral home, mom's lawyer, her insurance agent, and random well-wishers whose messages all seemed copied from the same book.

I emailed the fire chief and apologized for knocking over one of his guys. I wouldn't normally do something like that, but the fire department, of which my father had once been a member, had tried to be there for us after he was gone. It was the least I could do.

I did not send a similar message to the police chief. Tim told me the pickup truck driver had been charged, dragged into court for an initial appearance, and released pending the next court date. I resisted the urge to find his address.

I tried to work Wednesday night, the night after the crash. I was there all of fifteen minutes before Walt, the editor, called me into his office and told me I needed to go home. He told me to take sick time and get myself together. He even offered a bottle of whiskey, but I knew that would be a bad idea. Besides, I had long ago vowed never to drink whiskey again—rum, beer, any number of other options, but not whiskey. I declined the drink and accepted the sick time.

On Thursday, I steeled myself to go to Mom's house to organize things. Snickerdoodle cookies resting on racks greeted me in the kitchen along with the faint aroma of cinnamon. I selected one and sank onto a chair. My favorite. She must have made them the day of the accident, knowing I would be there. I bit into it—slightly stale but buttery goodness, all the same.

I filled a cookie jar from the pantry, carefully stacking them inside. I would savor each and every one of the last ones she'd made. Then, I started as I realized an hour had passed since I stepped across the threshold.

I needed to select an outfit for her funeral, but I dreaded going into her room. It seemed so final. I straightened my shoulders and marched up the stairs. This task took a half hour because I kept tearing up and walking out. I finally grabbed something and brought it to the funeral home.

That done, I drove back to her house, ordered a pizza, and watched the Tigers play the A's. The Tigers won, and three days earlier, I'd have been on top of the world. But in my reality, the game was little more than background noise to the thoughts swirling in my head.

Instead, I sat puffy-eyed, fighting heartburn from the entire pizza and several cookies I had eaten. I switched off the TV and wandered upstairs to the house's only bathroom, relieved myself, and washed up. The scrape on my face stung, and I examined it closely in the small mirror. I looked terrible. Scabs covered half of my cheek, which was too large to cover with standard-sized band-aids from the pharmacy. No wonder Walt sent me home. I leaned close, wondering if any of the cuts would leave scars.

Soon, my gaze wandered further. My hairline was drifting north, and my dark hair was starting to show a bit of gray. Even in October, my face still looked tanned, a trait I attributed to long hours of playing baseball in the sun as a kid and more spent in batting cages and on golf courses as an adult. I ran a calloused hand through my hair, glad it was still thick at least. I preferred gray hair to bald, but at thirty-six, I wasn't ready to sign up for either.

My eyes looked as alien as my scraped cheek. Puffiness made them look smaller, and they looked blank. I couldn't even summon tears to give them emotion.

Finally, I looked away, turned off the light, and went downstairs. At least sitting on the couch, I couldn't see my own eyes.

CHAPTER THREE

I woke, gasping for air, heart racing. Then, I looked around wildly, trying to figure out where I was. The room was dark, but faint flickers of light danced here and there about the room. I was on a couch, and it wasn't my own. Tim's? Some hotel's?

I was still at Mom's. This room should have been as familiar to me as my bedroom, but, at the moment, it felt as alien as a hammock in the Amazon. The room felt cold and bare, as if it, and the house, knew that no one lived there anymore, the way pets moped when their owners were out. I was transient, so I didn't count. I hadn't spent a night in this house in years. Given the nightmare that woke me, perhaps I should have continued the streak.

Then again, it might not have mattered. It was still Thursday, just before midnight, two days after Mom's crash, and she'd made an appearance in a dream every time I'd dared to doze off.

Though dead in this world, in dreamland, Mom was alive, well, and baking cookies. The first couple of dreams had been as much memory as imagination. In one, Mom baked cookies before Christmas, and in another, she played canasta with her sister, my Aunt Joan. It was a Tuesday night, and she'd been going over lesson plans. Mom had taught kindergarten at Lynwood Elementary and sometimes liked to talk through her lessons with someone who wasn't a teacher for perspective. The scenes were at once familiar and unique. I don't remember any of them happening with this particular set of details, but they certainly could have—they were so normal.

I'd been at home in my one-bedroom apartment on Hanover Street, half a mile or so away, for those dreams. Tonight, it felt as though she'd been waiting for me. For this episode, Mom talked to me about death.

She'd been sitting in her navy-blue recliner—despite myself, I looked toward the shadowed corner and shivered, half-expecting to see her there—and had started talking about making arrangements in case she died.

"There's going to come a time when I won't be here, Davey," she'd started, as calmly as if telling me that lunch would be served at one. "My time will come, and I'll move on, and you'll have to go on without me."

In the dream, of course, she was alive, so I'd tried to deflect with my customary good cheer. "Mom, don't be stupid. You're fine. You have a long way to go." I waved my hand as if to end the conversation. In the dream, it felt prophetic, and I wanted it to stop.

She ignored me. She told me where to find her insurance paperwork, her will, her banking information—even her passwords for various websites, such as Amazon and Facebook. "Just shut that down for me, Davey," she said of the social media account. She was the only person I allowed to call me Davey. "I don't want it sitting out there in cyberspace like some sort of macabre memorial. Did you know it reminded me last week that it was Joan's birthday? She's been dead for four years!"

She was good at tangents. I suppose she had to be, dealing with kids all the time.

Some of the things she mentioned in the dream I had already found. The will and insurance documents were in a filing cabinet in her little craft room off the dining area and kitchen, and the passwords I'd discovered in a kitchen drawer scribbled in a little black address book that predated the need for online passwords by a few decades.

I hadn't run across her banking records yet. This was the first time I'd allowed myself to spend more than a few minutes in the house. I'd arrived around two in the afternoon to pack up a life no longer lived.

She said other things in the dream that didn't make much sense. She told me to make sure I kept the windows clean and to vacuum the carpet. She asked me to take care of myself and my wife and children. Her hopes for my future were higher than mine. And she told me to read well, whatever that meant.

The dream felt so real. She droned on about the need to prepare me for her death, and then she got up and walked toward the front hall, saying she needed to get some coffee from the kitchen. And when I had, in the dream, gone after her, she disappeared. The kitchen was empty, dusty, and disused. The door to the outside was closed, but the basement door stood open, and beyond it was impenetrable blackness. Something scared the shit out of me, and that's when I woke up.

The street lamp across the road provided faint, dancing illumination as it pierced the half-bare tree limbs on its way to the window. Tentatively, I reached over and turned on the table lamp. Pulling the switch made my wrist twinge, but not as badly as it felt the day after the crash.

I stood and hobbled on sore knees, retracing my steps from the dream—first into the wide foyer that served as an extra sitting room, then into the dining room with its massive table and heavy wooden chairs. I peered into the craft room on the right, flipping on the light, then walked around the dining room table toward the dark kitchen.

Everything was where it should be. The basement door was closed, as was the door to the outside, and when I switched on the overhead light to the kitchen, it looked as I had left it. A pizza box lay on the counter, and my plate and glass were still in the sink. My neatnik mom would not have been impressed.

I stood in the middle of the room, unable to shake the feeling that Mom was somehow about to walk in. The thought should have warmed me, but it didn't. It terrified me. I pictured her as a zombie, smiling awfully and offering me a glass of lemonade.

A shiver ran up my spine, and I left the kitchen, walked into her craft room, and switched on yet another light. The filing cabinet on the right side of the room was open. I closed the drawer, then turned to the ancient rolltop desk against the far wall, under the window. I sank onto the chair in front of it and ran a finger along the wooden grooves.

I'd never opened this desk. It was Dad's, and though Mom had never told me to stay out of it, I had never been interested. After years of avoiding it, I felt as though I'd be punished for opening it, so it stayed closed. I'd seen Mom work there, but it felt off-limits to me.

I sighed. Now wasn't the time for my silly rules. I grasped the knob and rolled the top up.

The rattling echoed, and when it slid open, the silence seemed deeper than before. I cast an inadvertent glance, making sure I was still alone. I was. No one else had the key to the house.

I turned back to the desk. In the dream, Mom said the bank files were in the drawer and that the key was taped to the underside of the top of the desk. I reached into the shadowed interior, felt around, and nearly jumped when my fingers brushed cold metal. I pressed my thumbnail under its edge, and a small key dropped, cellophane tape covering its head. I pulled the tape off and examined the skeleton key. It had an elaborate, curled head that looped back on itself and teeth jutting in two directions. For some reason, I had expected a standard key, like one for a modern filing cabinet, but this desk had probably been old when the house was built a century or two ago.

Though the desk seemed sturdy, I was careful when I inserted the key into the lock and turned it. The drawer opened smoothly, and I found a series of folders inside. The third one from the front was filled with documents from Lynwood Bank. A cold chill returned. How could I have possibly known, even subconsciously, that these documents were kept here? Had my dream been real? I might have seen Mom grab the key before, but finding the documents spooked the hell out of me.

There was nowhere else to look, I told myself firmly. *You wondered where they were, and your brain figured it out while you slept.*

I left the folders where they were, closed the drawer, tucked the key back inside the rolltop, and rattled it closed. Then I went through the house, turned off the lights, grabbed my jacket, and rushed out the door. I refused to look back at the house as I walked to my car, jumped in, and drove away.

I probably shouldn't have spent so much time there alone when her death was so fresh. But there wasn't really anyone else I'd wanted to join me. I could have asked one of my poker buddies, but I had wanted to do this alone, although I struggled to remember exactly why that had been important to me.

CHAPTER FOUR

Weldman and Dirk's Funeral Home, like many businesses in Lynwood, would have looked out of place had it been located in just about any other city. To my knowledge, it was the only funeral home with a gift shop attached and a horse-drawn hearse option for funerals.

The funeral home occupied a massive, two-story brick building with white trim and huge columns that supported the porch roof. To the left was a loading zone and entrance from the parking lot. In the rear was the funeral home's other business—Haunted Lynwood Carriage Tours and Gifts. The front of the gift shop resembled a doctor's office more than a gift shop. However, posters in the windows advertising ghost walks, paranormal tours, and "Haunted Lynwood memorabilia" gave it away.

Next to that was the garage that housed the hearses. One of them, the horse-drawn wagon, was out today, and a man was carefully cleaning the glossy sides. The wagon had been built as a hearse originally, but it had been modified with rows of removable seats and a bench behind the driver's area where a tour guide would sit, microphone in hand, telling paying customers just how mysterious and bloody Lynwood's past had been—and how many of its victims were still around to prove it. The wagon was long, black, and shiny, with chrome accents glinting in the sunlight. On the corners and on wheels, sinister-looking knives—dirks—were welded on, branding the funeral home without the need for a garish and, no doubt tasteless, sign.

Usually, I found this amusing, but on the day of Mom's funeral, it irritated me like a mosquito bite on the end of your elbow that you bumped every five minutes. However, Mom, apparently as prepared for her death as she had been in my dream, had pre-paid for her funeral, so Weldman and Dirk's it was.

Lynwood had long since given in to the various legends of ghosts and other spooks and did a brisk trade making money off them. Haunted Lynwood Carriage Tours and Gifts was one of half a dozen businesses that served as jumping-off points for haunted tours, though it was the only one that could bring a horse-drawn hearse to the table. Some guides carried iPads with ghostly images queued up, while others relied on their powers of storytelling to draw in their marks. I'd gone on a few ghost walks over the years and found them to range from interesting from a historical perspective to downright silly.

The "Dirk" half of Weldman and Dirk's—Dirk Coleman, a portly, grandfatherly guy in his mid-fifties, greeted me at the door. As he had all week, he exuded kindness and grace, with a practiced deadpan that made it difficult to tell when he was being serious.

"Good morning, Mr. Kendrick." He shook my hand and offered to take my jacket. I declined. "I believe everything is arranged as you and your mother specified, but I encourage you to review the details to be certain."

He said this as if Mom and I had come in just yesterday.

"Thanks. I'm sure it's all fine," I said. "Honestly, I just want to be done, you know?"

"Of course." He glanced at the coffin at one end of the room. I could see Mom's made-up face, and for a moment, I wondered if she was going to get up and check the details herself.

"Also, the carriage will be put away shortly, so your guests won't be tempted to go for a tour," he said, and I thought I detected the hint of a smile. "Someone spilled a soda last night, so we had to clean it. Tours every night this time of year, after all."

"Of course." I wondered if he was making conversation or promoting the business. "I guess kids get spooked by the stories, huh?"

"They do, but this was a dad more spooked by whatever he had mixed with the soda before getting on board," he said, face neutral. "Ah, well, these things happen."

"I can only imagine."

Dirk took his leave, and I walked to the front of the room. Mom's body lay there looking as nice as a dead person could look, and again, I expected her to move, wink at me as if to say she was enjoying the show, and wouldn't they be surprised when she popped up and sang. The image was so powerful I actually laughed, a noise that echoed around the lonely room of death as if trying to find an escape.

"I hope this is how you wanted it, Mom," I said. "You know I'm not good at planning things, but I'm trusting that you and Dirk worked it all out."

When she didn't reply, I pressed on. "I guess that's why you called him in the first place, right? Because you knew I'd be useless at this part. I can't even organize a backyard barbecue, let alone a funeral for one of the most popular teachers in the city's history."

I wondered how many people had stood in this spot, talking to their dead relatives. I hoped I wasn't the only one.

"Anyway. The people will be here soon. The service is in an hour. I don't know how many are coming, but Dirk said to expect a lot, so I hope I got the dress you wanted."

Pressure was building in my eyes, and I had to blink, which forced the tears I vowed to keep to myself. I ignored it and put my trembling hand over her very still ones. "I love you, Mom. I'll find out what you wanted to tell me. Don't worry about it."

There was movement behind me, and I withdrew my hand and wiped my cheeks before turning.

Rusty Radinsky was the first one to arrive. He was the sports editor of the *Lynwood Post* and my boss, but we'd worked and collaborated for so long that I didn't think of him that way. Rusty was a few years older and had joined the *Post* about six months before I started freelancing for the paper. He hired me full-time a year later. That was sixteen years ago.

We stood chatting quietly for a few minutes as others trickled in. Tim Jepson arrived shortly after Rusty. Then, suddenly, there was a line at the guest book that went out the door. The forty-five minutes preceding the actual service passed in a blink. I was the reluctant recipient of dozens of hugs, well-wishes, and promises that Mom was in a better place. It was remarkably easy keeping my composure, since I spent at least half the time trying to remember who people were or whether those who identified themselves as her students or parents of her students were people I was supposed to know.

There were others I did know, of course. Several senior fire department members, who had worked with my dad, came. Tony Gianini, a captain now, had sworn in with my dad, and when Dad went missing, had led a group that checked on Mom and me when I was a kid. His hug was the most bone-crushing of the lot.

"I'm sorry you have to go through this again, Dave," he said. "I know it's different, but still, so sudden. I had just talked to her, and to think she was gone so soon after... it's heartbreaking."

"Thanks, Tony," I said. "It's quite a shock, and I'm not sure what to do next."

"I lost both my parents in the past few years. I had time to prepare, but you're never actually ready." He put a hand on my shoulder, an almost fatherly gesture he'd been doing since I was six. "Call me if you need anything, right? Anything at all?"

"Yeah. I will. Thanks."

He was quickly swept away in the crush, but I couldn't help but watch him go. As a child, I resented the fire department but later realized it wasn't their fault. At one point, I was convinced that the department knew what happened to my father long before I did, but Tony ultimately convinced me that wasn't the case. Not before I showed what a brat I could be, of course.

The next hand on my shoulder was heavier, if not stronger, than Tony's. I turned to find its owner, Ezekiel Heyward, dressed even sharper than usual in a three-piece suit. His trademark silver necklace with an amber pendant dangled from his neck, and his bald pate shone while his ever-present secretary, John West, a balding, older, Black man in a trim suit, hung behind him.

"Hell of a thing to happen, David. How are you holding up?" Heyward asked.

"Um. As well as I can, I guess," I said. "Thanks for coming. I didn't realize you knew Mom."

"Oh, yes, we go way back," he said. "Been out of touch for a little while, is all. Listen, I know this isn't the place, but I left you something at your office. A gift, of sorts, to help you through this rough time."

I knew immediately what he meant. Ezekiel Heyward was the owner and president of Fontana's Whiskey, a distillery on the north end that served as Lynwood's largest employer and claim to fame, perhaps even more than the ghosts. "Spirits and spirits," one of the company's ad slogans read. Heyward was famous for gifting bottles of his whiskey to politicians, business owners, and others with whom he wanted to curry favor, and some part of me wondered what he wanted.

"Your buddy tucked it away, so don't let him keep it. You need anything, you call me, okay?" Heyward patted my arm.

I didn't have the heart to tell him I don't drink whiskey anymore. I nodded politely and shook his hand. His secretary, John, guided him to the seats, which were starting to fill up.

A few more people offered platitudes, and then the pastor, Josiah Francis, stood beside the casket. Those still standing either found seats or took places lining the walls. My seat was reserved up front, and I sat gratefully.

Francis was tall, maybe six feet six, lean, and with a scholarly air about him. Unlike many pastors I'd met, he seemed to have as many questions as answers and was more than willing to talk about anything—even the Bible—as a scholarly exercise, not as a teaching moment. I wasn't big on religion, but Mom had frequently invited Francis and his wife over for dinner. He drew on those conversations as he spoke, recalling Mom's love for the children she taught, her struggles with guiding them the right way, and her strength in the face of adversity in losing my father, all while raising a wonderful son.

When he finished, he asked the audience to share memories. At first, the room was silent, and I wondered if they were waiting for me, but I couldn't make my legs move. Finally, the elementary school principal took the podium and spoke almost as eloquently as Francis had. Seven more people felt the need to share their thoughts on what a wonderful woman my mother was, and I was suddenly glad Dirk Coleman had suggested recording the funeral, an idea I initially found macabre.

And then it was over, and the five men who had agreed to serve as pallbearers joined me at the front of the room and helped carry Mom's casket, now closed, to the back of a traditional hearse for the ride to the cemetery. Rusty drove me to the grave site, where Francis said more beautiful things I could barely process, and then the mourners scattered to their cars like dandelion seeds in the wind.

CHAPTER FIVE

I begged off Rusty's offer of a ride back to the funeral home—told him I needed to clear my head. As I walked, I forced myself not to think about Ralph Walther, the truck driver. Yesterday, I learned his vitals from Jenny Johnson, the overly perky new reporter we'd hired at the *Post* who worked the cops and courts beat. She'd updated the crash story the day after it happened. Ralph Walther, 24, of rural Lynwood, taken to the Truman County Medical Center, treated, and released. It was right below the line that said Elaine Rae Kendrick, 60, of Lynwood, had died at the hospital following the crash.

And, of course, my name was there. "David Kendrick, a reporter for the *Post* who was covering the crash, was taken to Truman County Medical Center with unrelated injuries. He is the son of Elaine Rae Kendrick."

I fumed over that for a bit, of course. I could easily imagine an officer leaving my name out of the report, but I guessed Reynolds wrote the report and enjoyed including it a little too much. He'd say it was required if anyone asked, and technically, he'd be correct, but in a small town like this, I'm sure people got away with more.

And, of course, Jenny just had to include it in her brief. I'm sure the clicks were through the roof. But she'd made up for it the next day with a glowing story about Mom's career as a kindergarten teacher.

But mostly, I spent my time obsessing about Ralph Walther until I realized I needed to think about something else before I hunted the little prick down. Jenny's story said Ralph fell asleep at the wheel, and maybe he had, but that grin—that rictus grin—it was almost like he was happy my mother was dead. Like he had intended it. The police cited him for failure to control, a misdemeanor. I hoped it was a placeholder until they could get vehicular manslaughter lined up. An irrational part of me felt like that charge would never happen.

I didn't know Walther, but I knew of him, or at least his family, which is why he looked familiar. The Walthers owned a farm on the north side of town, growing corn and soybeans and raising cows and probably a host of other barnyard critters. Harry Walther, who by his age I assumed was Ralph's grandfather, had been a county commissioner until a few years ago. Like most town leaders, I'd met Harry Walther a few times in passing and had interviewed him once.

Since I didn't know Ralph personally, my rage shifted toward the so-called justice system.

Killing someone in a car crash was rarely punished the way people, particularly relatives of the victims, felt it should. I knew that personally. My crash on 98 resulted in the death of someone I cared about. I ended up spending only thirty days in jail. Even I thought that was too little, but it was what my lawyer bargained for and that's what the judge decided. The thought of grinning Ralph Walther walking free before Christmas made it hard to concentrate on anything else.

My car crash is why I'm not popular with the Lynwood Police Department. People might forgive small mistakes but not huge ones. Those they never forget—or let me forget. And the fatal one I made years ago would never go away.

I needed to stop thinking about it before I started snapping at people. I have a much better hold on my temper than I once did, but grief and a lack of sleep had me on edge.

I slid into my car and drove to Betty's Burger Barn on the east side of town. Mom might have wanted some kind of wake or reception, but I couldn't face organizing something like that.

Betty's was right out of a Fifties movie. There was a long soda counter at one end paired with shiny red plastic stools lined with silvery chrome, a row of booths on one wall, and table and chair sets sprinkled throughout the rest. Red, white, and black tiles formed a jaunty floor, while a jukebox stood in the corner. Until last year, the juke had been vintage, playing old 45s, but people finally got tired of the same tracks, and the owner had sprung for one of the newer digital models, with anything you wanted available to download. Today, someone picked Kenny Rogers's song, "The Gambler," which I was sure had been on one of the old 45s.

I parked myself in the booth furthest from the door and the soda counter. Maybe a dozen others were there, which was a lot for three in the afternoon. Everyone was in groups of twos or threes except me, and most of them glanced at me with pity written on their faces at one point or another. I ignored them or tried to.

I usually hung out at Betty's because I liked the atmosphere and friendly people. But today, I didn't feel like being alone, and, at the same time, I didn't feel like talking to anyone. As a bonus, Betty's burgers were just that damned good.

My thoughts turned to plotting impotent revenge on Ralph Walther, debating the merits of punching that smiling mouth or hitting him with his own truck. As I pondered, I glanced at my plate and realized I finished my burger without tasting it. I consoled myself with the few sips left of my chocolate milkshake when she walked in.

I had only seen Allison Knight a few times in the past several years, though I knew she was around somewhere. She was my major crush in high school, but by the time I stumbled my way through asking her

28

out, I discovered she had just begun dating another guy. Luke Van Buren played first base on the high school baseball team while I played third, and he hit behind me. He managed to get ahead of me with Allison, and now she was Allison Van Buren, though I couldn't bear to think of her that way.

Luke knew how I had felt about Allison at the time, so I was furious at his betrayal. He tried to excuse his behavior by telling me he thought I would never work up the nerve. From that moment on, aside from what was necessary on the diamond, I stopped speaking to him. I never thought it would be a permanent thing, but I underestimated my stubbornness on that front. And, since I shunned him, I didn't talk to Allison, either.

I knew they lived on the south-side of town and had a child. She worked in a little auto parts factory, and he worked at Fontana's, Ezekiel Heyward's distillery. But she was here now, a young boy of about eight trailing, and no sign of Luke. Not that such things should matter.

She approached the counter, and a tall, skinny redhead who looked like he was still in high school waved his hand, miming that she could sit anywhere she liked.

She turned and said something to her child. Our eyes met, and I immediately became interested in the bottom of my shake. When I looked up, the pair had chosen a table not far from the door.

Allison was a knockout, and that hadn't changed, but something else had. Her lips were tight and narrow, not in her normally open smile that made you feel like she couldn't wait to hear what you had to say. Her wavy blonde hair was caught in a ponytail, and her vibrant blue eyes were puffy and red-rimmed as if she'd been crying. She was also dressed up, which she'd hated doing in school. She wore a dark skirt and white blouse like one might wear to church.

The boy, too, looked unhappy. I'd only seen him once or twice, so I had no idea what normal was, but I figured most eight-year-old kids would be happy at the prospect of a greasy meal followed by a root beer float or a milkshake. He wore slacks and a button-down shirt with the top two buttons undone, as if he couldn't take the restriction, and gave most of his attention to the floor.

Maybe the music will help, I thought wryly, as somebody who must have been fond of the 80s selected Dexys Midnight Runners' "Come on Eileen" from the jukebox. I stirred ketchup with a French fry and tapped my foot. It didn't work. I had paperwork for Mom's estate, a lawyer to meet, a hospital bill and insurance to wrangle, and a house to clean and sell. At least. And instead, I was sitting here obsessing about Ralph Walther, trying to enjoy pop music, and desperately trying not to stare at my old crush.

"Dave?" Allison put her hand on my shoulder. "I'm sorry about what happened."

My chest constricted, and I nearly knocked over my glass.

Allison blushed. "I didn't mean to bother you."

"No, ah, it's ok. Um, and thanks," I stammered. "I haven't really processed it yet."

She nodded. Behind her, the boy doodled on his menu with a crayon and watched us. "I mean, it's bad enough, but to actually be there right after the accident... I don't know how you managed it."

"Neither do I. It's... well, it was awful." I felt awkward.

She nodded.

"How are you?" I asked. "I haven't seen you in a while."

"Just checking some things out." She glanced over her shoulder at the boy. He looked toward the counter, tapping his crayon rapidly and wiggling his feet. She lowered her voice. "We're moving," she said. "Trying to find a place. After what happened."

"What happened?"

"Oh." She ran a finger over her ear as if to push her hair back but came up empty because her hair was in a ponytail. "My, ah, Luke... I figured you'd heard. Of course, you've had other things on your mind, haven't you?" Her lip quivered. "Luke died the other day."

My ears felt hot, and my heart sank. Though I hadn't known, I felt like I should have. Perhaps if I'd been in the office. "My God... I'm sorry, Allison. How?"

"I don't know. I mean, I know, but I don't know why." Her shoulders slumped, and she glanced back at the boy to ensure he wasn't paying attention. "Luke killed himself. Said he had to."

I stared at her. I couldn't help it. I wanted to stand and hug her, but I knew the restaurant was quieter than it had been. I glanced, and sure enough, several people were watching, not bothering to pretend they weren't. The boy seemed to catch on and turned our way.

"I... that's awful," I managed. "How could he do that to you?" That was apparently the wrong thing to say. Her eyes immediately welled.

"Anyway. I just wanted to say I'm sorry about your mom." Without waiting for a reply, she turned, returned to her table, and whispered something to the boy. She hugged him and headed for the small restroom in the back.

I sighed, shook my head, and leaned it against the booth, stealing a glance at her son. He watched me, twirling a blue crayon in his left hand like a drumstick. I smiled a little, hoping it seemed sympathetic and gestured toward the counter. The redhead held a tray of heaping plates and milkshakes. The boy seemed to forget I existed as he took in the feast, though I noticed the crayon never stopped twirling until the tray hit the table.

CHAPTER SIX

I strolled to the counter to pay my check, thinking if I was standing, it would give me an excuse to talk to Allison again on the way out, but she was still in the bathroom by the time I paid. On impulse, I paid for theirs too. I couldn't walk by and ignore the boy, particularly since we made eye contact when I turned to leave.

He finished chewing, swallowed, and watched me, head tilted to one side. His hair was dark like his dad's, but his eyes were the same shade of green as Allison's. "Hi," he said. "You know my mom?"

I nodded. "Knew her back in school. Nicest girl there. My name's Dave." I held out my hand, and he shook it.

"Chase." He kicked the leg of his chair. "Your mom was nice—she was my teacher. That really sucks."

"Yeah," I echoed, momentarily thrown. "I heard about your dad. That sucks too."

He stuck a fry in his mouth, then sipped his shake. "It does," he said finally. "I guess he did it for us. That makes me mad."

I had no idea what to say to that. I glanced over my shoulder—still no Allison.

"Maybe it will make sense someday," I said. "Things have a funny way of doing that."

"Sure." He rolled his eyes.

"Yeah. That might be bullshit," I told him. He stopped chewing and just stared at me.

"It's all bullshit," he said. "My dad, Mrs. K... all of it." He shrugged as if it didn't matter, but not convincingly.

I scanned the room again. The diners had mostly turned away, though a couple nearby appeared to still be attentive.

"Well, listen," I said. "You take care of your mom, Chase. And if you ever want to talk about bullshit, come find me."

He cocked his head, looking far older than he was for a moment. "Yeah, okay. Thanks."

I nodded and glanced toward the restroom door. Still closed. "Okay," I said. "See you later."

I headed for the door, walked into the hazy sunshine, and got into the car.

I barely remembered driving back to Hanover Street, and it wasn't until I let myself into my second-floor apartment that I managed to stop shaking. The news of Luke's death really shouldn't have affected me the way it did. I was conflicted. Sad because he died without us resolving our differences, but hopeful because Allison was now free.

"She just lost her husband, you moron," I said to empty air. Luckily, I had enough sense not to answer. I dropped my jacket over a chair and stepped around the table into the tiny kitchen. A few ounces of rum joined the ice cubes and a splash of Pepsi in my glass, and I took the concoction to the couch, where I brewed and sipped too fast.

So many trains of thought were whistling for attention. How was I to deal with losing Mom? What should I do about Ralph Walther? Did he kill Mom on purpose, or was I just being irrational? Why would Luke kill himself, leaving that beautiful family? How could I talk to Allison again without seeming like an opportunist? And how could I have made her cry?

I had answers for none of those questions but somehow considered them until the room grew dark. The most straightforward and least productive problem was Ralph. Could he have caused the crash on purpose? And if he didn't, why did he give me that creepy smile?

Another thought nagged. What was Mom doing out at that time of night? And driving in from out of town? She didn't leave Lynwood very often, and then it was only for day shopping trips to one of Columbus' megamalls. She loved Lynwood, especially for its little quirks, and even after she had Dad officially declared dead, she hadn't wanted to move. She had never wanted me to go away anywhere either, even when I was playing ball. Of course, I had every intention of leaving. I had scholarship offers and pro scouts checking out my game, and it was only a matter of time before one team or another whisked me out of Lynwood.

Or so I'd thought. During my senior year, I committed to play third base at Ohio State, and Mom was supportive but sad too. She didn't seem to want me away from home and probably knew she would lose me forever if I went. Then, just days after graduation, I got picked in the tenth round of the Major League Baseball draft. I knew the scouts liked me, but it never occurred to me that they liked me that much. They offered me a signing bonus, and my Buckeye dreams faded into oblivion.

The next day, I decided we should celebrate. I was dating Erin Adams, at the time, who had graduated from high school with me, and I took her to Columbus for a night on the town. She was initially nervous, having never been outside Lynwood—but I talked her into it. We went to Ohio State's campus and wandered in and out of a few of the bars on High Street until we found one with bartenders who didn't check ID, discovered beer and whiskey, and generally had a blast.

Then I tried to drive us back to Lynwood and crashed.

My memories are somewhat scattered. I remember getting off Interstate 70 and heading north on 98 toward Lynwood. Headlights came the other way, drifting into my lane, and Erin screamed and grabbed the wheel. The next thing I knew, I was hanging upside down in the seat, with shattered glass and blood everywhere. The car had rolled, and everything hurt. The door had crumpled against my arm, and I was cold and wet—I lost control in more ways than one. And Erin, who had insisted she didn't need a seatbelt, lay awkwardly on the crumpled ceiling, not moving.

Enough space remained on the passenger side to allow the flashing lights of the responding vehicles to reflect wildly off every piece of glass. It was months before I stopped seeing them every time I closed my eyes.

I told the police that there had been another car, but they didn't believe me. They uncovered that I'd been drinking and blamed my lack of memory on that, not the fact that my head was hit hard. I had a variety of injuries, most notably to my shoulder, which never quite recovered.

Neither did Erin. She was pronounced dead at the scene.

And my baseball career was over. The team that drafted me, quite understandably, decided they didn't want to sign an injured player with a fatal alcohol-related accident on his record, even though it was later determined I was under the legal limit.

Somehow, I came through the ordeal with only a month in jail, even though Erin's Lynwood police officer father had been so furious he had to be restrained in the courtroom.

Even today, although my so-called debt to society had long been paid, many people, especially in the police department, felt my punishment had been insufficient.

I didn't blame them—I had expected worse, and while I knew the crash had been caused by a combination of factors—another driver swerving and Erin grabbing the wheel, I was the driver—I should have been in control of the car. I couldn't forgive myself for driving after drinking. I found myself playing a game of what if—what if my reaction had been swifter—what if I had pushed her hands from the wheel—what if we had left the bar earlier? If I'd been fully sober, would the result have been different?

I tried to shake the memories, but it wasn't working. I walked to the kitchen, grabbed my cocktail ingredients and a bag of chips, and returned to the couch. I mixed another drink, then another, and tried to drown my maudlin thoughts.

CHAPTER SEVEN

I'm not sure what came next qualified as "waking up." The world felt wobbly, and I knew opening my eyes would be painful. I wasn't sure where I was, though the word "couch" sang around my brain like some lunatic mosquito. Or cicada. Eventually, the sound turned into a high-pitched whine, then gradually relaxed into something resembling church music. But not pretty church music — loud, clangy music that might once have been played in a church but now belonged to an elevator in an amusement park.

About the time I realized the noise wasn't coming from inside my head, it stopped, only to be replaced by a more distant sound, a faint whisper punctuated by rattling I assumed was blood rushing through my brain. I lay there for a minute until another chime pierced the fog. I finally dared to open my eyes and found a dim light glowing from across the living room ceiling. I stared dumbly at it for a moment, and it blinked out. I waited to see if it would return, but it didn't. The room stayed dark.

With what felt like a supreme act of will, I turned my head. There was just enough light drifting into the room around the edge of the heavy red blackout curtain for me to make out the almost empty rum bottle sitting on the coffee table, a glass devoid of even melted ice, and, next to that, my phone. Beyond the table was the crammed bookshelf and an oversized tube TV that you probably couldn't even buy anymore.

The chime. The light. It was my phone. And that other sound was rain, water drumming against the window and roof.

I started to sit but flopped back when the room swam. I'd had more rum than intended, or so I told myself. I took a deep breath, sat up again more slowly, and stretched to snag my phone before flopping back against the fake-suede cushion. With one thumb, I activated the phone's screen, wincing against the sudden light.

It was ten after two in the morning. With difficulty, I did the math and realized I had picked up the bottle nearly eight hours ago and had sat in the dark drinking and ruminating for god knows how long. Eventually, I dimly remembered stumbling to the bathroom, then back here, taking another sip, and lying down. I had no idea when that was.

And somebody called. I hit the phone icon, then recent calls. Typical—it was from someone not on my phone list. A local number, but not one I recognized in my half-inebriated, half-hung-over state. The chime had been from voice mail, so I hit that button next.

I wondered if the caller had been half as drunk as I was and misdialed. I decided to find out.

At first, the message was empty hissing. Then, after seven seconds, a man's voice: "Uh. Hi. This is Ralph. Ralph Walther. Listen, I just wanted to tell you that, um… look, I know what happened, and I know how it looks, but I don't… it wasn't me, okay?" The voice sounded confused, slurred. "Obviously, it *was* me, or I wouldn't have been there. But it felt like someone else was driving, and I couldn't stop it. I just know…" He paused, and I could hear his ragged breathing. "Jesus, I don't know what I know. I was taking the load back to the farmhouse. Half a mile. Next thing I know, I'm in a hospital with the cops telling me I killed somebody. I swear, Mr. Kendrick, it wasn't me. So… yeah. That's it. I'm sorry. I thought I should call you and try to explain."

The message ended. I stared at the phone in disbelief. My hand trembled, and my head pounded, but the fog was gone. I played the message two more times, but it always ended in the same place, even though I wanted more.

I dropped the phone onto the couch. First, the guy wrecks his truck and kills my mother. Then he had the nerve to call me in the middle of the night and say he didn't remember doing it. He was drunk, had to be, but there was something else in his voice. Fear? Well, that made sense. If I had my way, he was going to prison for a long while. Of course, if I had my way, I'd get a shot at him with my Louisville Slugger first, but I didn't suppose that would happen.

With a groan, I reached toward the lamp at the end of the couch. Ignoring the sharp twinge in my shoulder, I switched it on, blinking against the stabbing light. I managed to stand and take the bottle and glass into the kitchen, filling the cup with water and taking a deep gulp. It helped a little. I topped it off, grabbed two pain relievers, and stumbled back toward the living room.

A voice in the back of my head — the same one that hadn't wanted me to open the rum — screamed at me now as I punched the "phone" icon. I ignored the voice and hit Ralph's number. It rang four times before a robotic voice told me the person I was trying to reach was not available. I groaned — the bastard could call me at two in the morning but didn't want to be bothered the other way.

I raged into his voicemail. "Listen, asshole, I don't know what the hell you think you're doing. The police told me to let them deal with you, and I am. But if you start bugging me, I swear I'll beat you right out of this world. So, fuck off."

I stared at the phone and then remembered to hang up. After a minute, the screen went dark. I shook, I was so angry.

I swallowed the pain relievers, drained the glass, and then slammed it onto the coffee table. I stormed to the window, drew the curtain back, and glared at the parking lot and street below. Rain sluiced, blurring everything.

The window was cool as I pressed my forehead to it and looked left and right. I knew Ralph Walther was down there somewhere — standing in the parking lot or the street — staring at me. But all I could see was the usual array of cars in the sickly yellow glow from the parking lot — the same light that prompted me to buy the curtains. Nothing was moving but rain.

Soon, my breath fogged the glass, and I stepped back and shut the curtains.

"It's been a hell of a day," I half-croaked — the funeral, Allison, rum, and now this. My stomach rumbled — I hadn't eaten anything but a handful of chips since the burger — but I ignored it, switched off the lamp, and went into the small bedroom off the living room. I figured if I fell asleep fast enough, I wouldn't worry about food or anything else.

I was right.

———————

The next morning — and by morning, I meant two in the afternoon — found me back on the couch. I grabbed Mom's address book from the box of her things on the coffee table and opened my laptop to the searchable Truman County auditor's website. Mom had written her friends' names and phone numbers but not their addresses, and I didn't want to make blind phone calls. In-person visits would be better.

Besides the odd dream and discovery of records Thursday night, the other thing that nagged at me was why Mom was out Tuesday night in the first place, but even more than where she had been, I was bothered by her text message. What had she wanted to tell me? Why couldn't it have waited until morning?

I tried to turn on her phone, but the battery was drained. After I plugged it in for a few minutes, it had enough juice for me to turn it on.

A few seconds after that, the phone pinged, and I jumped. It happened again, and two messages came up — new texts from me — my replies to her Tuesday night request.

Mom never saw them. She asked me to come over, crashed, and died.

I couldn't help it. I dropped the phone into the box and cried harder than I've cried in my entire life, the kind of irrational, chest-heaving sobs that somehow wrack the whole body and leave it aching. I thought I had been grieving at the funeral, and I had gotten emotional, of course, but not like this. For long minutes, I sat there, shuddering and crying, until I wondered how there could be any moisture left in my puffy eyes.

Finally, I got control of myself, or at least stopped crying, and drew in deep, rattling breaths.

Mom's phone pinged again. My breath caught as I stared at it. It was face down, but the screen light glowed. I hesitated, then picked it up and turned it over. The latest alert came into view. It was a local text, not from a number associated with a name on Mom's phone. Instead of words, there were two emojis. One was a frowning face with tears flowing from its eyes. The other was an overly cheerful clown face with large teeth visible in a big smile.

With a chill, I lifted my phone and opened call history. Sure enough, Ralph's number and the one on Mom's phone were identical.

CHAPTER EIGHT

By Monday afternoon, my mood had devolved from blood-boiling fury to despair and a general grumpiness. Usually, I would get out of bed at eleven, be at the *Post* around one, work until eleven, and then stay up till two or three in the morning. It worked for me.

This morning, my phone rang at five after nine, thanks to Ronnie Thompson. Ronnie was the lawyer handling Mom's estate, and he wanted to meet to go over a "few things." I'd showered, dressed, and arrived at his office before ten. Those "few things" took nearly two hours.

To reward myself, I went through Betty's drive-through for another burger and drove to the *Lynwood Post* on autopilot. After working there for close to seventeen years, I didn't really need to pay attention to where I was going anyway.

My reflexes were tested in Lynwood's town square, or what the locals affectionately called Shapesville. Where most towns had a plain square, Lynwood upped the ante with a square surrounded by a circle encapsulated by another square, hence the nickname. The center of it was a square, four-sided park, which was ringed by a traffic roundabout and that was surrounded by a square pedestrian sidewalk and businesses. Two main roads—Montcalm and Greenbriar streets—entered square Shapesville at the center of each of the outer square's sides, and the narrow alleys at the square's four corners led to parking lots tucked behind the buildings and generally out of view of the square itself.

I had to go almost all the way around Shapesville to get to the *Post*'s parking lot, and I was halfway around when a child of about six wandered from the park toward the garish gift shop across the street. My attention was on the cars waiting to enter from Montcalm's eastern exit, so I saw the girl at the last moment and slammed on my brakes. The burger bag hit the floor, and the girl screamed, but fortunately, the brakes held, as did those of the pickup truck behind me, and everybody went home happy, including the girl's frantic mother.

Shaken back to the present, I made it the rest of the way to the *Post*'s parking lot. I retrieved my burger and soda, punched in the key code to unlock the back door of the building, and stepped onto the darkened loading dock. Dim safety lighting showed the yawning gap where the printing press had once thrummed with daily editions of the *Post*. The aroma of ink still lingered.

My footsteps echoed as I walked across that graveyard to the design room where staffers had literally put the paper together — cutting articles and pasting them precisely onto the pages to be mass-produced. Today, computers perform that work, so the space was converted into a combination morgue, storage area, and breakroom. For birthdays and holidays, Walt Quinlan, the *Post*'s editor, rearranged the larger tables, ordered a cake from a bakery down the street, and had lunch catered from one of the various delis and restaurants in town.

Today had been one of those days. Two advertising reps sat at the end of one of the tables, chatting over crumb-strewn party plates. I remembered that one of them had a birthday today, but at that moment, I couldn't remember which — or even if it had been someone else. I thought about frantically scrolling on my phone to see who, but couldn't summon the energy, so I skirted the edge of the room, hoping they'd be too lost in their conversation to notice me.

"Dave!"

So much for that. The two women looked at me, pasting concern over their previously bubbly pleasure. I might have laughed, but the amusement I felt was dulled, like everything else.

"Hi, Karen... Dawn." I waved. "It's your birthday today, isn't it?"

"Yes, twenty-nine again." Karen Linscott, the younger of the two, rewarded me with a sheepish smile. I smiled back, mostly because I was glad it was one of the two women whose birthday it was.

"So, how are you holding up?" asked Dawn.

"Just staying busy, I guess. Lots to do." I gestured toward the newsroom. "Haven't talked to Walt since it happened, so that's next on my list."

"Well, come back when you're done and get some cake, okay?" She gave me the smile she used to make sales at the counter.

"I'll do that. Happy birthday." I ducked into the newsroom.

As usual, the small space was busy. The *Post* had six reporters and Walt, who was the only one with an office. The newsroom had six desks placed side-by-side and face-to-face—three on one side and three on the other. On the right, two news reporters had desks at either end, while the middle desk was reserved for Marla Anderson. She didn't come in until after two.

On the left, the sports editor sat closest to Walt's office, and another news reporter had the far end. My desk was right in the middle, home to a dizzying array of high school sports preview booklets, baseball cards of players whose names or exploits had amused me even if they'd never been stars, stacks of rosters of Truman County's various fall and winter high school sports teams, and general clutter. My goal was to keep everything chaotic enough to put my hands on whatever I wanted and to make sure the rest of the staff would cringe at the thought of finding anything and, thus, leave my desk alone.

At the moment, Jenny Johnson, a news reporter, and Rusty Radinsky, the sports editor were both on the phone. Rusty saw me and gave an exaggerated eye-roll.

The other two news reporters, Ray Cooper and Jamie Yost, were in Walt's office. The door was open a crack, and their voices droned. At the same time, the emergency scanner chattered about sending out the fire department on a lift assist, and even more voices were yammering over the six-foot barrier separating the newsroom from the advertising section.

I stood there for a minute, feeling at home, then sat and turned on the computer. I was sure the stack of emails would be endless, but I relished doing something as mindless as de-cluttering my inbox.

I spent three minutes clearing out twelve of the two hundred or so unread emails when Rusty extricated himself from his phone call.

"These people are never satisfied, are they?" Rusty's oft-repeated refrain was as warm and familiar as one of Mom's home-cooked meals, though I'd never tell him that.

"Of course not," I gave the ritual response. "Not until you start publishing straight play-by-plays, including mentions of every good effort and glossing over every bad one."

"Maybe I will—see how they like it," he grumbled. After a moment, we both laughed.

"So, I haven't missed anything, is what you're telling me."

"Nah, same old crap." Rusty's chair creaked as he leaned back. "LHS played decent but still lost on Friday. Camden actually won for a change but lost its running back, the McLaren kid, probably for the year. So, they're done. At this rate, we won't have any playoff teams this year."

"Well, early start on winter sports, I guess. Too bad about McLaren." I meant it. While he was no great shakes as a college prospect, he was one of the nicest kids I'd ever interviewed. Smart too.

"Yeah." Rusty seemed to appraise me for a moment. "Sure you're ready to be back?"

"Gotta happen eventually." I shrugged. "Might be good to try on normal life again."

"True, but I'm sure Walt would give you more time."

"I don't know about that. Besides, I'm going a bit crazy, staring at the same walls and trying to figure out what the hell to do next." I picked up the stack of mail someone had thoughtfully left in the detritus next to my keyboard and started sorting, just for an excuse to do something.

Rusty didn't say anything for a long moment until I wondered if his attention had drifted off. "You need any help figuring it out, you let me know, okay?" he finally said. "Lost my parents a few years back. My brother and sister helped, but I've been through it. You don't have anybody like that."

I nodded, blindly staring at an envelope in my hand. I realized I had frozen and dropped the envelope in the trash can.

"Thanks, Rusty. I have a lawyer and all, but he's not exactly the picture of empathy. And probably charges me every time I glance at his letterhead."

"Oh, brother. Lawyers. Maybe talking to angry parents isn't so bad."

"Maybe not." My first genuine smile formed. Yeah, it was time to come back, all right.

"That reminds me." He opened a lower drawer and pulled out a paper bag. "Felt like I ought to conceal it, but the Fontana's guy dropped this off for you. He must have really liked your mom."

"Why?" I took the bag and pulled out the bottle of whiskey I knew would be there.

"He brought the good stuff." He tapped the black label. "Fontana's Finest."

"I don't follow." My nose wrinkled.

"Most people get a bottle of Fontana's Best. I have a couple myself. But he only gives the high-end stuff to special people. Like the mayor or the governor." He smiled.

Walt's voice boomed from the office door, where he was seeing Ray and Jamie out. As usual, it was just a touch too loud, meant to draw in everyone in the room. He had a voice that carried — from a church to a bar during a concert — without much effort. Standing six and a half feet tall and built like a linebacker, Walt was entirely too big for his tiny office.

"I guess he doesn't always save it for people who can do something for him, after all." Walt pointed at the bottle. "It's good to see you, Dave."

"Hey, Walt," I said. "Good to be back."

"Come on in." He stepped to one side. I walked past and sat as he shut the door.

"So, how are you doing?" He sank onto the one halfway-decent chair in the building.

"Honestly? I'm looking forward to the day when that isn't the first thing people ask me." I shrugged. "I'm surviving. I'm figuring things out. But it sucks being me at the moment."

He nodded. "Yeah, it's a bitch, isn't it? There's never a good answer, but you're insensitive if you don't ask." He leaned forward and parked his massive forearms on the desk. "I won't ask again, okay, but if things get too much, you've got to let me know."

I told him I would. "Yeah, I just need to try on real life again, you know? Get back to rosters and games and things."

"Best thing for you."

"And I'm trying to figure out what Mom wanted that night too."

"What do you mean?"

"She texted me—told me she needed to tell me something. I was on my way to her place when I got sidetracked by the scanner."

"Huh." Walt raised an eyebrow, leaned back in his chair, and then changed the subject. "Listen, have the cops talked to you yet? I heard a rumbling they were thinking of charging you with disorderly conduct over the crash scene. What happened out there?"

"Charging me? For what?" I blurted. "I never touched the guy."

"Reynolds came here on Friday, asking if you were back in the office. Said he had to talk to you. Said you'd tried to attack somebody."

The thought of the bookish sergeant asking about me made my skin crawl.

"I... hang on," I said, suddenly suspicious. "Are you just asking me, or are you asking as a journalist?"

Walt shook his head. "Not for publication. I'm just wondering how long I have you back and if you need a hand holding anything off. And," he paused, "wondering if we need to involve our legal team in case the victim decides to press charges."

"The victim?" I practically shouted. "He called that asshole the victim?"

"Calm down, Dave. Bad choice of words." Walt assured me. "I'm not saying the guy's a victim. Reynolds made it sound like you'd tried to attack someone, is all."

Shaking, I forced myself to let go of the arm of the chair I was in. Then, I took a deep breath.

"I didn't touch him," I finally managed. "I wanted to, yes. He... he knew what he'd done, and he seemed to think it was funny. When I realized who was in the car... yeah, I lost it." I realized this was the first time I had told anyone about what happened in detail, and it was making me angry all over again. "So, yeah, when I put it together, I wanted to kill him. I went toward him. The cops tackled me."

"You didn't hit one of the firefighters?"

I thought for a minute. Had I?

"I don't know, maybe? It all happened pretty fast."

"Reynolds said you shoved one of the firefighters into his truck before they stopped you."

I sat back, trying to think. I dimly remembered someone between me and Walther, but I couldn't picture his face. It had to have been a police officer or a firefighter. No one else had been there.

"I suppose it's possible. I don't think I hurt anyone. They were trying to stop me, and I didn't want to be stopped." I looked down at the floor. "I know it was dumb, now, but at the time, I wasn't thinking straight."

"Nobody would be," Walt said. "And that's what I told Reynolds. Said that if he tried to charge you for overreacting while your mother was dying, he'd have more than you to worry about."

I saw the determination on his face.

"Thanks, Walt," I said. "When did you say he came in?"

"Friday."

The day of the funeral. There's no way Reynolds hadn't known when the funeral was. Half of Lynwood had been there, and police had escorted the funeral procession. "Friday," I repeated. "Well, I haven't exactly been hiding. He can find me if he tries."

"I'm sure." Walt hesitated. "Listen, if he does, or if you see this guy Walther, promise me you'll keep it together, okay?"

"Yeah, I will," I said, hopeful I'd be able to honor that pledge.

CHAPTER NINE

Over the next few hours, I caught up on my emails, got my week's assignments from Rusty, and fended off various well-wishers. Throughout, Reynolds' visit nagged at me. I managed to convince myself that if he had any intention of charging me, he'd have just arrested me, not gone to Walt. So, what was he playing at?

Still, it wasn't until ten o'clock that it occurred to me that Jenny probably had a copy of the police report. She kept the most recent ones in a plastic tray on her desk. I told Marla and Rusty I had some catching up to do, retrieved the stack, and took it into the break room in the back. I stopped by the fridge, which contained the remnants of the birthday cake, and helped myself to a generous piece, settling in at one of the tables. Then, I started at the bottom of the stack of reports since the crash had happened nearly a week before.

Jenny had a system for the police reports. Besides keeping all of them in case something was needed later, she also affixed a sticky note to highlight the interesting ones. There were about half a dozen of those. Skimming, I found two missing persons reports, two crashes, and a suicide.

I flipped to the crashes, and Mom's was near the bottom. Most of the details were burned into my memory, so I skipped to the last page, where there was an addendum. In Reynolds' narrative, he stated that I shouted I was going to kill Ralph Walther and that I had "attacked" a firefighter, Leo Hopkins, before attempting to get to Walther. The report said that Hopkins had suffered a bruised shoulder and was "considering charges."

At least he hadn't referred to Walther as the victim.

I shook my head. First, I couldn't understand where they'd gotten the idea that I had attacked anyone. Granted, I probably *would* have attacked Walther, but I hadn't gotten the chance. The firefighter had just been in the way. Second, I couldn't imagine Leo considering charges. While I wasn't popular with the police officers in town, the firefighters tended to look at me with pity because my father had been one of their own. Of course, none of the younger guys knew him personally, but the brotherhood was strong, and when I was a kid, various firefighters felt the need to look out for me, even when I didn't want them to.

I hadn't always been very kind to them in return. They reminded me of what I had lost.

I forced myself to read the entire report. Reynolds had kept the rest of it pretty straightforward. He wrote that Ralph Walther drifted left of center and claimed he didn't remember the crash. Based on that, Reynolds decided that Walther had fallen asleep. Mom had apparently drifted too, probably trying to get off the road to avoid being hit, but to no avail. The driver's side of the truck collided head-on with her driver's side. Charges were pending.

And that was it. It seemed a painfully short summary of something that ended a life, but I suppose there wasn't much more to say.

My eyes glazed. I didn't want to go back into the newsroom, and since I was supposed to be "catching up," I decided to peruse some of the other reports. I flipped to the first of the missing persons reports. They weren't uncommon in Lynwood.

Lynwood had long had a reputation for disappearances. Logically, of course, I knew that every town had its runaways and occasional mysteries, but the legend became magnified in a hurry when coupled with Lynwood's ghostly reputation.

Of course, my own father had vanished into thin air one night in 1994, which meant I tended to take the rumors more seriously than most. Usually, the reports were of a teenager who decided to stay out late and frantic parents worried they'd left town or something. Or been abducted.

The first report wasn't a teenager though. Robin Elliott was thirty, married, and disappeared from her backyard on Oct. 4, a Friday. She was reported missing by her husband, Mike Elliott, the following day. He told police they had been fighting and that Robin did chores when she was angry. She took the trash out at about nine p.m. and had not returned. Mike said he assumed she went for a walk to clear her head, and he'd gone to bed when Robin didn't come back right away. When he woke up in the morning, she still hadn't returned.

According to the report, Robin had left her keys, phone, purse, and jacket behind, though it was only about forty-five degrees that night. As expected, the trash was in the outside container, but she was gone. The reporting officer told the spouse that authorities would check with her relatives, but nothing further indicated whether that had been done.

The next one was even stranger. Steve Cervelli, twenty-three, had gone missing on Oct. 10. Police had responded to a loud music disturbance and found Cervelli's car in the middle of a residential street. It was running, with the driver's door open and stereo cranked. I wondered what kind of music constituted a "noise" disturbance.

The police found no sign of Cervelli. His phone was in the car, along with a carry-out meal from the McDonald's on the edge of town where he worked. He left work an hour before his car was found, but he never made it home. The reporting officer noted that Cervelli had a history of drug issues. They impounded the vehicle and moved on.

I wondered if follow-up investigations were being conducted. I assumed there were, but then again, adults are allowed to disappear for a while if they want.

I checked the crash report—two cars, one injury, no big deal. Then, I went to the suicide report.

The person who reported her husband's suicide was Allison Van Buren.

CHAPTER TEN

O f course, the report for Luke Van Buren's suicide would be here, but it hadn't even occurred to me. The top sheet listed Allison and Luke's names, as well as Chase's. It termed the nature of the call as "suspicion of mental." A box marked "medical transport" was checked.

The time of the call was 23:12. Just after eleven o'clock. While I had been standing on the side of Route 98, on the verge of learning that my mother was dead, Allison had been about to lose her husband.

I turned to the next page. Dread filled my gut with cold lead. It grew even colder when I read the short narrative.

"Caller stated the victim was threatening to harm himself. Upon arrival, we determined he shot himself with a firearm. EMS transport."

That was it. No grisly details, no comforting words, just that he shot himself. I supposed there would be a supplemental report somewhere, but this surface-level version was chillingly impersonal.

I don't know how long I stared blankly at the page. My mind whirled as I tried to picture what the scene looked like, tried to square it with the guy I'd known in high school. I couldn't do it.

Luke was the team prankster; he once coated a bucket of baseballs in cooking grease and left it on the mound, so when our pitcher took warm-up tosses, the balls slipped from his hand. Another time, one of the outfielders complained about the mosquitoes, so Luke soaked his cap with bug spray before the next game and hid his backup cap. And you never knew when a firecracker was going to go off somewhere. It got old after a while but never failed to crack Luke up.

The thing was, he never did it maliciously. He was trying to loosen things up, and it worked more often than not. He'd always been a likable guy. I stopped talking to him once he started going out with Allison, but that was just me being childish. I never could have imagined that he'd be the type to commit suicide.

When I finally stood, I had to stretch both legs to get the circulation moving again. I took the stack of reports back to the newsroom, but before dropping them into Jenny's wire basket, I took the suicide report and Mom's crash report to the copier. I stuck the copies into my bag and closed the computer.

"I think I'm going to check out a bit early if you don't mind," I told Rusty.

"Sure, bud," he said. "Get some sleep, okay?"

"Yeah, will do," I mumbled. I packed up the laptop and left.

As I walked through the orange-lit parking lot, I half expected to find Blaine Reynolds sitting in a cruiser or perhaps Ralph Walther in his freshly battered pickup truck, but the lot was deserted.

I didn't go straight home. At first, I intended to drive by Mom's house to check on the place, but I decided against it. I also didn't want to face the quiet of my apartment, so I headed toward the south side and a bar I occasionally frequented. By the time I got there, I didn't want company. So, I passed it by and just drove.

I made it to the north end and had just braked at a stop sign on Lancaster Street when I saw it. A big pickup—a Ford with dual rear wheels—idled at the cross street. I waited since it was there first, but it didn't move. I started to wave him on, but then I realized the truck was red, possibly the same shade as the one that hit Mom's car.

I squinted, but the streetlight's glare prevented me from seeing into the cab. We both idled for what seemed an eternity. Finally, I inched forward, hoping to get a clearer view. The truck didn't move, but I still couldn't see its driver.

I let out a breath I didn't realize I'd been holding. This had to be my imagination. Hadn't I been looking for this very truck earlier tonight? But no, this couldn't be it; the bumper had no damage.

I shook my head as if doing so would settle my nerves. It didn't work. Then, giving up on the other driver, I pushed the gas pedal firmly and drove into the intersection.

My resolve to not look at the truck again broke. Halfway through the intersection, I looked left, and there, in the driver's seat, was Ralph Walther, wearing that same manic grin he'd shown at the crash scene.

And finally, the truck moved.

There was a squeal of tires as the truck lurched, and by pure reflex, I floored it and shot across the intersection. A second later, it filled my rear-view mirror, headlights blazing, so close I couldn't see the grill until there was more distance between us. I had the Olds up to sixty before I let off the gas pedal, then hazarded a glance at the rearview.

The pickup was following me, though I had left it well behind. At the next intersection, I turned hard right, and the laptop bag rolled toward me and almost bounced over the center console. I sped down the street and checked my rearview once more.

No sign of the truck. He hadn't been going as fast as me and either had passed through the intersection before I checked, which seemed unlikely, or he stopped. I didn't slow down until I realized I was likely to hit somebody myself or get pulled over. I slowed, but my heart continued to race for several more minutes.

I finally pulled into a grocery store parking lot and drove to the front, scanning wildly around me for any sign of the maniac in the truck. Half a dozen cars dotted the lot at this hour, with another row well off to the side, probably the employees' cars. None of them was a pickup truck of any size.

I left the engine running and rolled down the window, gripping the wheel with both hands. Had that really been Walther? Had he tried to hit me, or had I just not seen him moving when I crossed the intersection? Was he chasing me? The grin, at least, was the same as the one Walther had flashed at the crash scene. It had to be him.

Didn't it?

It took several minutes for me to stop shaking. The calmer I became, the more I realized I must have been mistaken. Some part of me was confident it had been Walther, but the rational side of me knew it was unlikely. I didn't even know the man. Why would he deliberately try to hurt me? But then, as far as I knew, he didn't know my mom either. So, had he meant to kill her? Or did he not know who she was?

None of it made sense, and my brain was still in too much shock to try to unravel it. My arm didn't feel fully attached to my body as I put the car into drive and eased back toward the street. This time, I headed straight for my apartment on Hanover, my eyes darting in every direction along the way.

As I pulled in, it occurred to me that I could compare tonight's memory to the genuine article soon enough. Ralph Walther's hearing was the following morning.

CHAPTER ELEVEN

Walther's hearing was scheduled for ten. As I guessed, he made an initial appearance the day after the crash and was released on his own recognizance as he didn't have a prior record. I arrived at nine-thirty, dressed in the same suit I'd worn to Mom's funeral, the only one I owned. While the judge dispensed with a variety of misdemeanor hearings, I scanned the crowd, most of whom were here to face the judge for some minor offense or other, but there was no sign of Walther.

One by one, the defendants answered when their names were called, heard whatever the judge had to say, and left, often with an attorney in tow. The crowd dwindled as those who had been summoned to court and those there to see them crept out.

The proceedings continued past ten, and I started to get antsy. Finally, the prosecutor ran out of defendants.

"Your honor, we'd like to call Ralph S. Walther on the charges of vehicular manslaughter and failure to maintain reasonable control." The city prosecutor turned toward the dwindled audience with a little more flair than was truly necessary, then, ignoring the defense attorney who stood at the mention of Walther's name, turned back toward the judge, her graying hair swirling. "It seems he couldn't be bothered to attend."

"Your honor, we'd like to request an extension until tomorrow for my client's appearance," the defense attorney said. "He was unexpectedly detained this morning."

"Detained?" The judge was a blonde woman in her mid-fifties who had missed the memo that the job was supposed to age her beyond the look of a forty-year-old. She now wore a faint smirk and a quirked eyebrow. "How was he detained, counselor?"

"I'm still gathering details on that, your honor."

"Counselor, do you have any idea where your client is?" Her tone suggested this was not the first time the defense attorney had tried this.

The man hesitated, then gave in. "I do not, your honor."

"When was the last time you spoke with him?"

"Uh... Friday, October the eleventh," he finally said.

I wanted to object—say that I'd seen Walther the previous night—but I was no longer sure, plus I wasn't part of the proceedings. Instead, I sat in stunned silence as the judge issued a warrant for Walther's arrest, determined that nothing else was on the docket for the day, and adjourned the session.

I didn't see or hear anything about Walther over the next few weeks. I did see Reynolds a couple of times, but only from a distance, and he didn't notice me. I happily returned the favor, spending most mornings at Mom's house, packing up the things I might want to keep.

Eventually, I would have to decide on the house. I wasn't ready to move into it, even though that would be the smart thing to do financially. I've always rented, so it's not like I had an investment in another property. And it would be great not to have to pay rent. The house was paid off, taxes were significantly less than my rent, and I'd have a lot more room. I certainly wasn't ready to sell it because it might be the right time for me to move in someday.

I was doing okay financially, and Mom left a modest inheritance, but I didn't want the property to sit empty. Renting it seemed like the right idea for now. So, I put all of Mom's personal stuff into one of the upstairs bedrooms — the one she used as a spillover for any crafts that didn't fit in the little office downstairs — and installed a deadbolt. A three-bedroom rental would still be an attractive option for families, and it would also be handy to be able to store tools I might need to maintain the property on-site rather than clutter my apartment.

Most of my evenings were spent at work, settling back into the routine of covering high school sports, mainly football, and collecting police reports. I bumped into Tim several times on my rounds, and we made small talk. Each time, I asked him whether Ralph Walther had been arrested. And every time, the answer was the same — an apologetic "no."

"His family is either good at lying, or they have no idea where he is," he confided one night, swearing me to secrecy. "I questioned them myself. They seem worried about where he is — even filed a missing person's report."

Getting things in order, I posted a for-rent sign on Mom's house and listed it in the classifieds in the paper just as the holiday season got off to a roaring start.

In Lynwood, "holiday season" meant mid-to-late October, capped by the annual Halloween festival. Lynwood officials shut down Shapesville for Halloween and November First, which this year fell on Thursday and Friday. Schools were off too. The only thing that didn't change was the high school football schedule. Some things trumped even holidays.

November First wasn't just a day of recovery, though many used it that way. In 1863, the 198th Ohio Infantry mustered in Shapesville to serve the Union in the Civil War. More than half of the men in Lynwood had volunteered, and a fair number hadn't returned. Certainly, those who did were changed men. The 198th saw plenty of action. One group, Company F, was ambushed in Virginia. The survivors were rounded up and put on a train to Andersonville, the infamous prisoner-of-war camp run by the Confederacy in Georgia.

The train stopped in South Carolina, and a number of the men—including the company's commander, my great-great-great-great grandfather, Capt. Alan Eugene Kendrick managed to escape. Some of the men were recaptured, but Alan managed to take refuge with a group of enslaved people despite being badly wounded. The story was famous in Lynwood—the enslaved people nursed the northerner back to health, and when he recovered enough to attempt the trip home, he brought a friend with him. Isaac Cooper was enslaved on the plantation where Alan recuperated, and the two managed to make their way to Ohio, arriving shortly after the war ended. Only a dozen other men from the 100-man company came back alive.

Less than two years later, Alan Kendrick's wife and three of his four children were murdered, and Alan, as well as Isaac Cooper, disappeared that day. His surviving son, Levi Kendrick, was away on business and came home to find the scene of the slaughter, or so legend held, and declared that Cooper was the culprit. On the strength of that declaration, while the mob hunted for Cooper, they found a Black man and lynched him. Then, they learned the man they killed wasn't Cooper. It was a stain on Lynwood's past.

Even with that dark mark, the town memorialized these Union soldiers every year on the first of November. Reenactors set up tents and dressed accordingly, although, to be frank, their efforts were usually haphazard, thanks to the Halloween party the night before. During the celebration, speeches were made, names were read, and survivor stories were told. Alan's name came up occasionally, but only in passing.

Over the last thirty years, the November First celebration faded into the background. The Halloween party was the big thing now. There were ghost walks all year, of course, but in October, it ramped up, and it was impossible to drive around Shapesville without dodging a group or two. The horse-drawn hearse from Weldman and Dirk's, usually only used on weekends, was in Shapesville every night leading up to Halloween. It hauled families and thrill-seekers alike out of the square and past some of Lynwood's oldest houses and buildings while stories of spooks and séances and murder and mayhem were repeated with gleeful solemnity. And the gift shops, led by Jethro Miller, made killings of their own.

I tried to avoid the whole thing, but I got pulled in each year somehow. This year, the culprit was Walt, who decided I was just the man to do an in-depth feature on Jethro's gift shop.

CHAPTER TWELVE

L ocated directly across Shapesville from the *Post*, "A Haunting Memory" was characteristically busy when I arrived a week before Halloween. The store doubled as an ice cream parlor, bookstore, and ghost hunter's haven. Shelves behind the counter were packed with devices that would beep if a "ghost" was present, send out laser beams for ghosts to disturb, and play white noise that ghosts could talk through, along with more mundane gear like flashlights, video cameras, and voice recorders. I'd gotten my voice recorder there a few years before, and I only used it to interview coaches, not the undead.

The front half of the store was bedecked with a riot of t-shirts depicting the city's Civil War ties, spooky photos of "haunted" buildings like the Wilson Hotel, which was next door to the *Post*, and the Lynwood Opera House about half a mile to the west. There were Civil War and ghost-themed candies, chess boards, jackets, and figurines stacked almost at random. Just beyond the main counter was the ice cream parlor, which looked right out of the Fifties, like Betty's, but with less authenticity.

Then there were the books in the back—the history of Lynwood, tales of the Ohio 198th, and stories about Ohio's contribution to the Civil War. One was dedicated to the founding of Fontana's, the ever-expanding, successful whiskey distillery owned by Ezekiel Heyward. Another tracked the descendants of some of the survivors of the war. We Kendricks were omitted. There were also stacks of the four volumes of local legends penned by the store's owner.

Jethro Miller greeted me at the front counter with an enthusiasm I found uncomfortable for a man I considered no more than an acquaintance.

"Dave, I'm so excited you're the one doing this story. You get it, man. Your history's the same as mine," he said as he led me to a booth in the ice cream parlor, and we sat.

"Well, kind of," I said. Jethro's ancestors had also served in the 198th with a unit that had seen far less action and mostly returned unscathed. The Miller clan had done very well for themselves since turning out a variety of lawyers, doctors, and other upper-crust professionals.

Jethro's hair was white and unkempt, his teeth were in dire need of repair, and lines creased his cheeks and forehead. He wasn't ashamed of any of it, which I admired.

"We're both Civil War descendants, lived here all our lives. Close enough, man." He clapped me on the shoulder. "And we've both had people disappear. My grandfather walked out one day, and poof, no one's seen him since. Just like your dad."

"I'm not sure I knew that," I said.

"Really? Huh. I thought I told you. Well, I mention a lot of things to a lot of people. Can't keep track!" he cackled. "Hey, you still like those root beer floats?"

"Yeah, but..."

"Great." He waved at the waitress and held up two fingers.

"You know I need to pay for that myself, right?" I said through gritted teeth.

"On the house, brother."

"I mean…" I shrugged and dropped it. Journalism ethics dictated I not accept a gift, but the few dollars weren't worth the argument with a guy I'm writing about.

He didn't seem to notice my dilemma. "So, look, it's the thirtieth anniversary of the store, and people say it's kind of the reason Halloween took off around here, right?"

I nodded. "Lynwood's always had a bit of a reputation, but it wasn't a big deal back then."

"No! It wasn't! And it should have been!" Jethro's eyes were as bright as whitecaps on a sunny day. "I mean, people have gone missing from this town like crazy. Amelia Earhart needed a whole ocean to get lost in, but Lynwood people do it in their own backyards. It's nuts!"

"What makes you think our rate of disappearances is higher than anywhere else?" I knew I was taking the bait, but I couldn't help myself. I remembered to switch on my recorder as he got started.

"Back in the 80s, we saw headlines. Your dad, for one. That kid… what was his name? Jimmy Nelson. Made the news in Columbus that one did. They happened all the time!"

I nodded, wondering how two people had somehow managed to become an epidemic.

"Just go through your archives, man. Every year, you find people disappearing." He gestured behind him to a wall in the bookstore area. Newspaper clippings dominated like an Area 51 conspiracy theory board. "I've been collecting those. Sixty-eight people have never been found. And that's just since I started paying attention back in eighty-eight. But there are more, lots more. I mean, your own Civil War guy and his slave buddy, they even disappeared, didn't they?"

"That's the story," I said.

"Well, sure. The guy comes back from the Civil War with a slave in tow, and a year or so later, somebody kills most of his family, and he and the slave disappear."

"It wasn't his slave, you know." I felt strangely defensive.

Jethro waved a hand as if it didn't matter. "Point is, nobody ever found 'em. His son found the bodies of the rest of them, and that was it. Poof." He clapped his hands for emphasis.

"But there's no proof of what happened. It's just another legend, isn't it?" I asked. "I mean, there are a ton of them."

"Of course." As he put his hand over my recorder, his foul breath chased his words, and I had to fight not to cringe. "You know they used the old quarry as a dumping ground, right?"

"A what?"

"A dumping ground. Bodies got dumped there. Columbus and Cleveland's gang-bangers brought them there because they knew nobody ever checked. And some of the bodies... let's just say they weren't intact." He pointed to his head. "If they were alive, they wouldn't have been wearing hats anymore, if you get my drift. Anyway, they had to find somewhere new because of the development." He leaned back in the booth as if he made his point.

I felt the interview had gone off the rails and wondered how to get it back. "How do you know?"

Jethro tapped his temple. "I have sources too. Can't reveal 'em. You know Fontana's ripped off their recipe from them, right?"

"What? From whom?" I regretted asking as soon as the words left my mouth.

"Slaves," he said matter-of-factly. "Stole the recipe and killed them to cover it up. That's why that guy got lynched when they went looking for your great-great-grandpappy's friend."

"Uh-huh." Another year, another variation to the story, but it gave me a chance to get back on track. "So, you started telling these stories as Lynwood's history."

"I went to a gift shop in Gettysburg when I was a boy. Loved the place. Always wanted to run one. When this space came open, I jumped on the chance."

"But nobody knew the legends then."

"Of course not, but they knew about the 198th. I found some reenactors and convinced them to start doing their thing on November First, instead of the boring memorial ceremony they used to do. Remember that?"

I shrugged.

"Anyway, it was much more entertaining and started bringing more people in. And then I started writing my book on the ghosts of Lynwood."

"Where did you get the stories?"

"Same way you do, my friend. Interviews." Jethro paused as the root beer floats were delivered, took a sip, and continued. "I found a little independent publisher who agreed to print some copies of my book and sold them in the store. It was an article in the *Post* about the book that got things going. And once that happened, people told me more stories."

There were four volumes of Jethro Miller's *Ghostly Tales of Lynwood* in the series, and they were practically required reading for anyone who liked history.

"You studied history in college?" I asked.

"Bachelor's and master's degrees, Ohio State," he said proudly. "Did my master's thesis on some of the buildings here, including the old opera house. Aren't many of those in the state still running, you know."

"Aren't you worried that some of these ghost stories aren't real?"

Again, he shrugged. "The history behind the buildings is real. And every story I wrote has some sort of documentation. There were four people killed in a fire at the Wilson. After arguing with her boyfriend, an actress fell from a catwalk in the opera house. And that guy did get lynched right there on the square. Nobody made those things up."

"No, I suppose they didn't."

"All I did was call attention to it. And when sales started to drop, I started the ghost tours as a way to keep it fresh. And the rest is history."

"Does it bother you that all these other places make money on it now? The restaurants, the Wilson, all the tours and things?"

"Of course not! Lynwood's booming! I don't want to go back to the tired old town Lynwood was—half the storefronts empty and the rest sagging in on themselves? No way, man."

I worked on the root beer float for a minute, figuring out how to ask the next question. I spoke slowly, choosing my words carefully. "Does it bother you that people might see this whole thing as manufactured? We're on all these lists—more ghosts per capita than Savannah, Georgia, and the place people go to disappear. Three of the buildings in Shapesville have been on paranormal TV shows. Heyward Manor is considered the most haunted house in the state, even though, as far as I know, nobody has ever figured out who supposedly died there."

"It's fun, and it's good for our economy. I can't speak for the Heyward, you know? I didn't include it in my books for that reason. It's a neat old place, on the National Historic Register and all, but old Zeke doesn't let people in, so they just filled in the blanks, I guess."

Jethro's straw made a sucking sound as he reached the end of his milkshake.

"Does Zeke even know why the place has the reputation?"

"I asked him about it, but he shut me down. Said he didn't want me making up stories about the place."

"So what's next for the shop, A Haunting Memory, and for you, Jethro Miller?"

"I have a new volume coming out. Ten new stories of Lynwood's past and how they impact the present," he said. "I have good eyewitness testimony from people you'd never expect and fun backgrounds for the locations. This might be my best volume yet. And get this — this time — Heyward Manor gets a primo mention."

I should have guessed — he didn't want an anniversary story — he was looking for a book promotion. I sighed. "Any highlights you can share?"

"I can tell you that two locations are right here in Shapesville. The Waggoner and the Elks Lodge."

"The Waggoner? But that's only fifteen years old!"

"There were things there before that building. And things still happen there."

"I thought it was an empty lot."

"Sure, since 1958. But there used to be another hotel there, and its history would have made the shenanigans at the Wilson pale in comparison."

I got the book's details and then wrapped up the interview, equal parts annoyed and mildly intrigued. I wondered if Walt knew about the book, but it didn't matter — he'd want the story anyway. With Halloween just around the corner, I didn't blame him. While Miller's motives were questionable, he was right in that Lynwood owed much of its success to the legends his books promoted. Civil War reenactments didn't draw crowds that could sustain a sleepy town, at least not in central Ohio.

I made my way across Shapesville, studying the Elks Lodge, just south of A Haunting Memory, and the Waggoner Restaurant, directly across the square from the Elks. I wondered how soon they, too, would end up on a TV show.

CHAPTER THIRTEEN

The Halloween parade always occurred at noon, meaning I had to park half a mile or more away from Shapesville when going to the office. And I always had to work on Halloween. We all did. Not only was it the social event of the year, but it was also the night most likely to end with a dozen arrests, thanks to people drinking or just causing general mischief.

Every year, the parade participants gathered at Fontana's, one of the few places in town with a parking lot big enough for the crowd. The costumed parade participants, a motley collection of marching bands, youth football teams, veterans, service groups, and politicians, were accompanied by fire engines and police cruisers as they made their way south on Greenbriar, counterclockwise around the square, and out to the east along Montcalm, where they'd carry on for a mile or more until they reached the county fairgrounds.

The parade used to muster at the fairgrounds, but then someone thought of bringing in food trucks from around the state and hiring a few carnival rides and games to keep people entertained. They reversed the direction of the marchers so the kids could play at the fairgrounds for a while, ensuring they would be nice and tired when their parents were ready to turn them over to grandparents and sulky teenagers so the parents could join the revelry downtown, the next stop for the food trucks after the fairgrounds closed.

I watched some of the parade go by from the *Post*'s second-story window, which had a spectacular view of the square. The grand marshal this year was none other than Ezekiel Heyward, decked out in a three-piece suit that would have made Mr. Monopoly proud. He waved enthusiastically from the back of a Cadillac convertible, his necklace bouncing on his ample chest. John West drove the car, looking as stately as an English butler.

The Lynwood Fire Department was next, with its glittering ladder truck and ambulance followed closely by their brethren from surrounding townships. I watched long enough to catch one of the county schools' marching bands, students' faces painted as pale as ghosts, before returning to the desk.

"C'mon, Dave, there's got to be another hour to watch," Rusty said, not trying to hide his grin.

"I don't get what people see in parades," I said. "I mean, the kids get to see some cool trucks. And it's the only time they can run in the street to pick up candy without getting run over. But really, is it worth it?"

"Don't forget the costumes."

"Those get better at night." I chuckled.

"Of course they do." Rusty winked. "But they're still funny."

Each year, we had set roles. Rusty, the longest-tenured staffer after Walt, would hang out in Shapesville, usually at or near the table where the DJ kept the square rocking until two or three in the morning. Between being the sports editor, doing a weekly radio show, and having a TV spot every week during football season, Rusty was a celebrity in town, and for that one night, he loved it.

And I, along with Ray Cooper, the features writer, floated around the party, looking for juicy anecdotes for the next day's paper. These could be anything—a particularly funny or impressive costume, an attention-grabbing display, or a DJ who got a good response. Ray enjoyed it and would keep going long into the night. I found it barely tolerable, particularly after doing it for a decade, and tried to find the best tidbits fast so I could both top Ray and leave.

At seven, I wandered onto the square—it was early enough that people weren't drunk but late enough that the crowds had arrived. I spotted Tim and his wife, Reggie, but Tim pointed toward the Waggoner and mouthed the word "reservations." I motioned like I was taking a drink—and mouthed, "Have one for me."

I grabbed a burrito from a food truck and sat on a bench in the middle of Shapesville, which was a riot of color. A Haunting Moment looked like it was about to burst at the seams with customers, and I envisioned Jethro Miller strutting, chatting happily with anyone who would listen. The Waggoner, as well as the Booth, the sports pub across the square, had lines out the doors, and I wondered how Tim had managed to get reservations—or the night off, for that matter.

The roads were closed, and people in costumes roamed the streets, openly carrying beer and other spirits. "Spirits for the spirits," one of the old Fontana's commercials used to say, and "Spirits for everyone." That was certainly true tonight.

I finished eating and decided to walk around the square. I spotted three ghost tour guides stationed near the exits to Shapesville, each gathering crowds but not bothering to shout over the music before leading them away from the noise—one of the guides dressed convincingly as a Union soldier, complete with battle wounds. The iPad he held somewhat ruined the effect. I got his attention long enough to pull a few paragraphs together. It turned out the iPad showed a ghost video one of his clients had captured the year before during one of his walks. It was a blurry smudge drifting in front of a house, but it was convincing enough to give me a little chill.

Further down Montcalm, the Weldman and Dirk's wagon waited, and though I couldn't be sure, I thought I spied Dirk Coleman standing atop, waving his arms in time with his mouth as people took their seats. I started in that direction, but the wagon moved before I got anywhere close.

I had almost completed the circuit, making my way between a face-painting booth and a tarot card reader, when I saw her. Allison Van Buren was talking to a couple I didn't recognize, partly because the man was wearing a full luchador wrestling costume, complete with a mask. The woman standing next to him had long, hot-pink hair that didn't look real and wore a skin-tight outfit probably patterned off some pro wrestler.

Allison was rather colorful too. She had a goofy hat with a bell on top tucked between two pointy ears and wore a long red skirt, red tights, and bright green shoes. Her white top was garnished with a green vest, and the entire ensemble was completed by a strand of battery-operated Christmas lights draped over her shoulders. I couldn't help but laugh.

She saw me and waved. "Hi, Dave! Where's your costume?"

"I'm working, so I don't usually dress up. Are you a Christmas elf?"

"Santa's got to grant vacation sometime!" She winked.

"How are you?"

"Okay, I guess." She gestured to the couple next to her. "These are my friends, Pedro and Lisa."

"Nice to meet you." I shook their hands. "Robbed any banks lately?"

"Never heard that one before," Pedro quipped.

I stayed and chatted, even though I felt awkward—two people I didn't know and one I was having a hard time feeling comfortable around. After ten minutes, I excused myself, blaming work. I thought, or perhaps just hoped, that Allison looked disappointed.

As Halloween parties went, this one was tame. There were only twenty arrests, which was down from previous years, and just a few reports of vandalism. The notable exception was the guy who walked out of the Booth, headed south on Greenbriar, and then walked right in front of a car. Police said he was alone, having left his friends just after ten o'clock, saying he'd be right back. Instead, he landed in Lynwood Hospital.

Jenny Johnson, the only reporter who worked the day shift on Halloween and the day after, gave me the particulars the following afternoon. She had already written a recap of the arrest but left the report with me to chase.

The hospitalized guy made it through Friday, but when I called on Saturday, the dispatcher told me the guy died—Tommy Dawsey, age twenty-eight, of Lynwood. According to his Facebook and LinkedIn pages, he was married, had two kids, and worked in the warehouse at Fontana's. I put it all in the online report. They must have known pretty soon after the crash he wasn't going to make it because his obituary rolled in that afternoon. It confirmed everything I'd found but didn't list his job.

Half an hour after my story posted, Ezekiel Heyward waltzed in with his sidekick John West trailing.

"Dave, it's good to see you," Heyward said, but the sentiment didn't reach his eyes. "Glad you're here. Wanted to see if you can fix something for me."

"Me?" I asked. "What's that?"

"Well, your story on this poor kid, Tommy, says he worked for me."

"He did, didn't he?"

"Well, yes, but that's hardly relevant, is it?"

I looked at him, confused. "I'm not sure what you mean."

"Well, it's an unfortunate thing, of course, but I can't see why where he worked matters for the story. It makes us look bad—a drunk employee wandering the streets."

I took a deep breath and then let it out. "I'm sorry, Mr. Heyward, but it's common practice to include details about a person's life in cases like this. So they're not just names, you know?"

"I get that. But I'd appreciate it if you would take out where he worked." It might have been a request, but it sounded like an order.

I glanced at Rusty, not quite sure how I was going to get out of this. I caught West's eye, too, and he gave a nearly imperceptible shrug as if in apology.

"We can't just take things out," Rusty offered. "We have to clear it with the boss. He's not here until Monday."

"I'm afraid this can't wait, son. You'll have printed it by then, and you can't take that back, can you?" Heyward sneered.

"We could run a correction, but it sounds like that's not the case since he did work for you." Rusty examined his nails.

"But it's inappropriate!" Heyward exploded.

"Let me call Walt. It's up to him," Rusty lifted the phone and dialed.

After Rusty explained the situation to Walt, Heyward gestured impatiently for the phone. "I was just telling your boys, Walt, how they should take our name out of this unfortunate story about Tommy," He nodded a couple of times, then handed the phone back to Rusty.

"How do you want to handle this, boss?" Rusty's eyes widened, but he said "okay" and hung up.

"We'll take it out, Mr. Heyward," he mumbled.

"Thank you kindly, young man." He nodded. "Dave." Heyward turned on his heel and walked toward the front door without another word. West ran ahead to open it, and they were gone.

"What the hell happened?" I asked after I checked to make sure the door was locked.

"Said it wasn't worth the battle." He shrugged. "You were right, but it's above my pay grade."

CHAPTER FOURTEEN

More than a week passed, and there was still no interest from anyone in renting Mom's house. Then, on Veterans Day, a Tuesday, my phone jangled. It was Walt, sounding more businesslike than usual. "David, glad I caught you. How soon can you get here?"

Rubbing my eyes, I mumbled something about not being scheduled until one.

"I know, but we have a big story cooking. Jamie's on vacation, Rusty's not picking up, and I need all hands-on-deck. Can you be here by ten?"

Groaning, I checked my bedside alarm—nine-fifteen. "Yeah, I guess. What's up?"

"Not sure yet. Police are all over Lynwood Elementary, and they're fanning out. They're not saying anything—Jenny and Sam are there, and Ray's working the police department. We need more eyes at the school."

"I'll be there in a jiff."

He ended the call without a goodbye.

————————

Lynwood didn't have a large police force, maybe eighteen to twenty-two sworn officers with over a dozen blue-and-white police vehicles that ranged from a couple of battered Crown Victorias to a pair of shiny new SUVs. At least half of them were parked either in the Lynwood Elementary parking lot or on the surrounding streets, joined by four of the state's gleaming white patrol SUVs that were probably supposed to conjure images of knights on white horses but instead came off as bland and boring. Two state cars bore the "K-9" legend on the back doors.

I had plenty of time to assess the police presence as I had to park three blocks away. Besides the impressive array of law enforcement, there were three news vans from various Columbus television stations. The effort wasn't confined to the ground, either—a black helicopter with yellow markings, probably from Franklin County, buzzed back and forth to the north while a blue-and-white news chopper circled the school, almost managing to keep a respectful distance from the police chopper.

I approached the school from the side, which was a wise move. At the front, a throng of worried-looking parents clamored, being held at bay by a single police officer.

Jenny wore a black jacket and jeans and stood between a pair of heavily branded television reporters from competing networks. The three were either comparing notes or trying to distract one another, and I couldn't tell which. There was no sign of the third network. Just before I reached them, I spotted Sam Thomasini, our photographer, off to the left, camera raised. Thirty-two, she had black hair in a no-nonsense short bob and wore khakis and a blue blouse.

Sam was toward the back of the school at the corner of the parking lot, which had been blocked with yellow caution tape. I veered in her direction instead. "Got a permit for that thing?" I growled and was rewarded when she jumped.

"Damn it, Dave, I thought I was going to get to yell at somebody," she grumbled. "What took you so long?"

"Walt didn't tell me the whole town was here. If he had, I'd have ridden my bike," I said, though it only now occurred to me that it might have been a great idea to do just that.

"The parents are rabid—Jenny talked to them earlier," she said, not taking her eyes from the lens. "Nobody's telling them—or us—what's going on."

"That'll make them feel better." I looked toward where she was shooting—behind the school. "What's so interesting back there?"

"That's where they took the dogs and where the higher-ups keep going." She clicked a few more frames and lowered the camera. "I have no idea if I'm getting anything, but maybe I'll get lucky. I don't know, maybe there's a loading dock."

"There is, but you can see most of where any truck would park. The staff parking's back there too, and a playground." Mom made it a point to always keep her distance from me, but sometimes I'd skip the bus and catch a ride with her.

"Can't even see the playground from here." Sam leaned left and craned her neck.

"You could see it from the other side better," I said. "Come on. You can fill me in on what's happening."

She glared at the offending corner, blocking her view. "Might as well—can't see shit from here."

We walked along the tape toward the front half of the building, a low, red-brick relic from the sixties, when the multi-level schoolhouse had gone out of vogue in this corner of the state.

"We heard about it on Facebook first," Sam said. "Parents were freaking out about the police cars being here and wanted answers. They're just as ticked at us for not being on top of things as they are at the school and cops for keeping quiet."

"Can't blame them, can you? I mean, they all remember Sandy Hook and Uvalde."

"I guess not, but still. We're in the same boat as them."

"You tell the mob that. I'll wait over there."

She snickered. "Hey, Jen, we're going around the other side. Call if you need me. I won't hear a text."

Jenny looked up and waved. Two more TV reporters had joined her.

"So, what have the police said?" I asked.

"Very little. All they'll tell us is what's not happening." She sniffed. "So far, they've said the kids are safe, and there's no shooter, so that's something. But they also say they won't release the children until it's safe to do so, which doesn't square."

We walked around the parents, reached the corner, and turned. The third TV crew was nearby, interviewing a particularly animated dad. A couple of the other parents approached us, but Sam held up a hand. "We're just as in the dark as you folks, and we're working on it." That earned us a dirty look as they harangued the police officer charged with keeping order.

"Have they said if they're going to do a press briefing at some point?"

"Won't say when or where," Sam groaned. "Which means if Jenny calls, I'm going to have to run. And something is happening over there too." She pointed up the street toward where the police chopper was circling with more blue-and-red flashing lights on the ground.

We finished walking in silence as the playground came into view. There wasn't much to see—it and the basketball court against the side of the school were empty. A few cars dotted the school parking lot, and a pair of officers walked back and forth, shining flashlights on the ground despite a clear sky.

Sam's camera clicked. "That the staff lot?"

"Yeah. Building's a U-shape, with the staff entrance on one of the inner legs."

"How come you know so much? Oh, yeah, your mom used to work here, didn't she?"

"And I went to school here." Sam was one of the few people I knew who hadn't grown up in Lynwood. She'd gone to school in Columbus, decided city life wasn't for her, and Walt had snapped her up.

"You bring your backup camera?" It hung from her shoulder, but it felt polite to ask.

"Why?"

"Thought I might take it for a walk." I nodded to where she had been pointing a few minutes ago.

She grimaced. "You know it's my personal one, right?"

"I'll be careful, I promise. Just set it for dummies, and I'll be fine." I knew how to find good angles but had no idea what to do with the camera's settings.

"One of these days, you'll learn how to use it." She rolled her eyes, having said that many times in her three years at the *Post*.

"One of these days," I agreed as she made a few adjustments and handed it to me. "Call me if anything goes weird."

"You too. And I want that back in one piece."

I saluted, turned on my heel, and started up the street to the north. That area certainly seemed more active than the school, at least on the outside.

CHAPTER FIFTEEN

The November breeze nipped at my fingers as I walked north along Tremont. A thin layer of clouds had drifted in since I arrived, blocking the sun and rendering my light jacket a poor defense against the chill. To counter, I picked up my pace. The nearest police officers were several blocks up.

Stately, older homes lined the right side of the street, across from a narrow swale of grass and a row of scrubby trees that didn't quite conceal the creek behind them on the left. The searchers concentrated there, walking the tree line and peering grimly toward the stream. It had been relatively dry for the past couple of weeks, so it wasn't overflowing, but it was still deep enough to cause trouble for someone who didn't know how to swim. One of the helicopters buzzing overhead rattled my eardrums.

I continued walking. An ambulance was parked three blocks up a side street, with two jittery medics sitting inside, waiting to be summoned. Then, half a block further, was a German shepherd leading a state trooper, sniffing excitedly. If there was an order to the search I couldn't see it. In the distance, people were shouting, but the voices were clipped—like instructions were being given, versus that something had been found. I lifted the camera and stopped long enough to take pictures of the trooper and the dog.

The helicopter's path took it over the creek, bringing relative quiet. There may have been searchers on the other side, but I couldn't see through the trees on that bank.

"Felicia?" someone called. "Felicia, can you hear us? Can you make a sound if you hear us?"

Had a child wandered away from the school? Or maybe not made it in the first place? It seemed odd that the search hadn't started earlier if that was the case.

I couldn't remember Mom mentioning a child named Felicia, but she had been retired for a couple of years before she died.

After another half a block, I stopped. Tremont would end soon anyway, and it didn't appear the searchers were going further than that. I counted eight or nine officers poking around the tree line.

Once I'd snapped a few more photos, including a closer one of another state trooper and his German shepherd, I swapped the camera for the phone and sent Samantha and Jenny a text, letting them know there was a search in progress. I put the phone in my pocket and found a police officer marching toward me. I swore under my breath—leave it to me to find Sargeant Blaine Reynolds in a sea of cops.

"What do you think you're doing?" He frowned like he'd caught me talking out loud when I should have been whispering. His wire-frame glasses looked damp as though they'd fogged.

"My job. Same as you. Kindred spirits, we." I couldn't stop myself.

"Media are to stay at the school. We'll brief you later."

"Don't worry, we're covered there. Who are you looking for?"

"None of your business." His left eyelid twitched. "Go back to the school."

"I heard you were looking for me," I said.

"I know where to find you when I need to." He leaned closer as if to challenge me.

"I just heard... well, it doesn't matter. It's a public street, and I'm just doing my job. Any idea when the briefing will be, by the way?"

"If you don't return to the school, I will have to arrest you for obstruction." His voice was hard.

My mouth dropped. "Your guys don't even know I'm here. You're not searching the road."

He reached for the radio on his shoulder. "Lieutenant?"

"Hey, Sarge!" I yelled at the state trooper with the dog. "You guys searching the street, or am I good here?"

Reynolds' radio made a noise, but he didn't answer, instead turning to look at the trooper.

"Road should be fine. Something wrong?" he asked Reynolds.

When Reynolds looked at me, his face was lined with anger. "Never mind, Lieutenant," he barked into his radio. He released the button and told the trooper, "No problem here." After the man went back to his search, Reynolds glared. "Don't ever pull that shit again, Kendrick."

"I'll try to remember, officer," I emphasized the last word, knowing the use of the wrong rank would irritate him further.

"Stay on the street." He stomped away.

I let him get about twenty feet before I called out, "By the way, have you guys found Walther yet?"

He froze mid-step but didn't turn around. Then, he continued on his way.

I chuckled. I'd been about to return to the school, but now that I'd made a nuisance of myself, I decided to stick around.

A few minutes later, I was glad I did. One of the officers at the end of the road shouted, and several others, including Reynolds, sprinted toward him. I walked more slowly, taking pictures. About fifty feet away, I lowered the camera in case they'd found a body. They milled around a pickup truck parked in front of a house near the end of the street.

I snapped a few more photos but couldn't see what all the fuss was about. One of them opened the driver's side door, and Reynolds strapped on gloves, leaned into the vehicle, and poked around for a few moments. Finally, he closed the door and spoke into his radio.

Reynolds walked to the home the truck was parked in front of — the woman who answered the bell shook her head and shut the door. There was additional radio communication, and then two officers moved around the side of the house and returned a minute later, shaking their heads.

I texted Jenny and Sam — they wanted to join me, but I texted back: "Not yet."

I was across the street by this time — even with the pickup. There was a Walther Farms logo on it, and for a split second, I thought it was Ralph Walther's truck, but no — this one was painted white.

The police excitement quickly died down, at least there. I stayed for another hour, my fingers growing numb, as the searchers pushed further downstream, past anything I could claim was public property.

Finally, shortly after noon, Jenny texted. "Might as well come back. Chief says a teacher walked away from school at the same time someone suspicious was lurking around."

That was weird. All this for someone who might have decided to take a sick day without telling anyone?

I texted: "Be there shortly. Can't see much from here anyway."

I walked back, robot-like from standing so long, and found Jenny lingering in the parking lot with the last of the crews packing their gear.

"Hey, surprised you're still here," I said.

"Just making sure there's nothing else to see," She glanced meaningfully at the camera crew. In other words, making sure they didn't find something we didn't.

Jenny briefed Walt and me in the newsroom twenty minutes later. The missing person was Felicia Erickson, a sixth-grade teacher. Now that I knew her full name, I realized Mom had mentioned her several times — I had thought a kid was missing, not an adult. Felicia told her class she needed to retrieve her lesson plan from her car and never returned.

When one of the kids finally reported that she was gone, the school's security officer found Felicia's car in the lot, trunk open, but with no sign of the teacher. The officer then checked the school's security footage.

"That's when the Chief got vague," Jenny said. "The video showed Felicia open her trunk, then turn around and walk toward the playground. She walked right out of the camera frame. And there was someone else there too."

"Who? What did they do?" Walt asked.

"Don't know. Chief Adams said a man who shouldn't have been there was nearby, and his presence made them think Felicia was in trouble — that she didn't just walk away. But he wouldn't say if the guy abducted her or even left with her. He kept talking about Felicia, saying she didn't have a coat, was wearing high heels, and wasn't dressed as if she was planning to walk through a field to disappear."

"That's weird as hell," Walt said. "What do you have, Dave?"

I told him about the search along the river, the pickup truck police had found, and Reynolds attempting to chase me away. He frowned at the last but didn't say anything.

89

"For now, let's focus on the teacher," Walt said. "We don't know enough about the other guy yet. Get her description out there, make that the lead. Do we have a photo?"

"There's one on the school's site. I can link to that," Jenny said.

"Do that, but we'll need a picture for print. Okay, let's get it done."

We worked the rest of the day without any updates from the police. One of our informants said they finally called off the search at dusk, having gone well down the creek as well as into a nearby neighborhood.

The school district sent children home at one o'clock, and I did a story on why they'd kept the kids there so long. That made me focus more on the strange man because the stranger, whoever he was, caused the delay.

I didn't have time to puzzle over it then. Football season had given way to basketball, and I had a game to cover.

CHAPTER SIXTEEN

The mysterious disappearance was the town's topic of conversation over the next few days. Rumors, spread online and through more conventional means, grew wilder by the day. By the end of the week, most had decided that Felicia Erickson had been abducted from her classroom in front of a gaggle of screaming children, and the police and school district were covering it up.

The school district, of course, wasn't doing anything to dispel the rumors—they referred everything to the police. And the police department didn't do itself any favors by releasing a description of Felicia, but also of a "mysterious stranger" they identified as a John Doe. The description was laughable—white male, between 35 and 55, average height, average build, dark hair, possible facial hair. In short, two-thirds of the male population of Lynwood fit the description.

But for some reason, even though the stranger was on video, police refused to release an image.

That afternoon, Walt urged Jenny and Sam to track down Felicia's family to see if they'd talk. I couldn't hear the replies because only Walt's voice was loud enough to carry through the closed door, but when they came out, I could tell they were frustrated.

I didn't have time to worry about it. I had a game to get to at Lynwood High School. Although the school allowed games the day Felicia disappeared, events had been canceled afterward. This would be the district's first public event since the disappearance, and while there was every chance things would go smoothly, I was concerned something weird would happen.

It did. Lynwood won. Its basketball team was even worse than the football team, but they pulled off just enough lucky shots to edge the Riverdale Warriors.

The second odd thing came after the game ended. I had just wrapped up a postgame interview with the basketball coach and was leaving the locker room when someone called out, "Hey, Dave!"

I turned. The team's assistant coach, George Barlow, trotted from across the room.

"What's up?" I stepped back in to let the door close.

"Glad I caught you. Got a minute?"

I checked my watch. "Just—deadline and all."

He led me toward a corner of the room away from the still-celebrating players. "Listen, you cover cops sometimes, too, right?"

"I do."

"Well..." He took a deep breath. "I've known you a long time. You've always been fair and honest."

"What's going on?" George had been an assistant coach for ten years, but beyond that, he'd been a neighbor of my mom's since I was eight.

"I'm good friends with the Ericksons. Felicia Erickson." His words came out in a rush. "And I know somebody from the paper has been trying to talk to her husband Keith, but he's pretty freaked out right now and doesn't know this reporter. And neither do I. But I know you, and I trust you, and..." He took another deep breath. "And I got Keith to agree to talk to you, but only if I were there."

I blinked, momentarily at a loss for words. "He'd talk to me?"

"Because I vouched for you. And I want Felicia found, and I think the paper can help. You can help."

"Well… sure. I mean, I have to clear it with my boss, but yeah, I imagine he'd be fine with that."

"Call me tomorrow, okay? We'll work it out then."

───────────────

For what seemed like the twentieth time in the past month and a half, the jangling of the phone woke me the following day. Resolving for at least the tenth time to get a decent ringtone on the thing, I fumbled for it, brought it to my face, and tried to read the name. It was just a number, and my brain was too fuzzy to recognize it.

"Hello?" I hoped I sounded robust and awake.

"Hey, David. Sorry, did I wake you?" A man asked. So much for robust.

"I was just getting up anyway. Sorry, who's this?"

"George Barlow. You were going to call me about the interview to let me know if you could do it."

"You were next on my list." I rubbed my eyes. "I'd be happy to. When is Keith available?"

"We were wondering if you could do noon."

I nodded, then realized he couldn't see it. "Sure, noon's good most days. When were you thinking?"

"Well… today, actually," George said, sounding surprised I had asked.

That's typical. My first Saturday off in a month, and now I'm working. A glance at the clock told me it was already ten-thirty.

"Yeah, I can do it today." I suppressed a groan. He gave me the address, thanked me, and then hung up.

Grumbling, I walked to the kitchen and switched on the coffeemaker. Then I sent a quick text to Sam, asking her to meet me at the Erickson's house. That done, I was halfway to the bathroom for a quick shower when the jangling started again.

"Geez, George, I said I'd do it," I turned back toward the bedroom. Sure enough, it was another unfamiliar number.

"Hello," I snapped.

"Oh… hi. Is this David? Sorry, is this a bad time?"

It was a woman's voice, one that sounded familiar, but I couldn't place it.

"Sorry, just running around. It's okay," I lied. "What can I do for you?"

"I was calling about your house. Your ad, I mean," she said. "You have a place for rent?"

"Oh. Yeah, I do." I'd been so busy I had nearly forgotten placing the ad—it had been running for two weeks with no hits.

"It seems perfect—it's just for two of us. We only need two bedrooms—your place is bigger, but to be honest, we're in a hurry, so that's okay."

"When do you want to come see it?"

"Are you free today?"

I blinked. Two in one day? "Um, sure. I have an appointment at noon that'll take me… oh, a couple of hours, I guess. How about around three?"

"Three's great," she said.

I gave her Mom's address. I hoped I'd have enough time to get over there and mow the lawn, at least, before she showed up.

Shaking my head, I hung up and hurried to get ready. Halfway through the shower, I realized I hadn't even asked who she was.

CHAPTER SEVENTEEN

The Erickson house was a modest affair—a split-level in one of the town's newer neighborhoods on the west side of Lynwood. Many of the houses looked the same at first glance, but closer inspection revealed random differences—wind chimes hanging from a porch here, pumpkins still displayed there. A fake skeleton sat in a rocking chair on the porch next to the Ericksons' house. I wondered if the sight of it bothered Keith Erickson.

Sam pulled in just after I did, so we walked to the door together.

"What's this guy like?" she murmured.

"No idea. Coach Barlow at LHS set it up." I rang the bell.

I wasn't sure what I expected Keith Erickson to look like, but this wasn't it. Felicia was a blonde, vivacious type I tended to associate with TV anchors and cheerleaders, and Keith was the exact opposite. Lumpy and overweight, his dark hair exploded from his scalp and chin with equal fervor, creating a mountain man image that somehow didn't work with his short stature and pasty skin. His eyes were bloodshot and general appearance unkempt. He wasn't holding up well.

"Are you David?" His voice trembled.

"Yes. And this is Sam. Coach Barlow, George, said you were hoping to talk to us?"

"Yeah. Yeah." He seemed to be persuading himself that this was true. "I did. Please, come in. George is already here."

He stepped back and led us into a sitting room on the ground floor. An entertainment center sporting a large TV was lined with dozens of comic-book superhero movies and had a row of heavy books lining the bottom shelf. I recognized a few titles — one of my childhood friends had been into Dungeons and Dragons, and it looked like Keith still was.

The far end of the room was littered with toys. A dollhouse stood in a corner, stuffed animals were scattered, and what looked like a child's chemistry set covered a pink-and-white plastic table.

Keith led the way up the stairs into the dining area. An oak dining table took up half the room, and a curio cabinet stood in the corner next to a wide, open doorway that led to a kitchen. A computer desk, printer, and a dizzying array of cables and other electronic gear were on the opposite wall.

George was in the kitchen. He waved and promised coffee.

Keith took one of the chairs around the table, which was littered with an empty pizza box, as well as red and blue posters bearing Felicia's photo. "I thought the colors might make them stand out more." He stacked the posters, pushed them aside, and then tossed the pizza box onto the kitchen counter.

"Please, no fuss for us, okay?" I sat. "Do you mind if Sam takes a few pictures while we talk?"

"Um. I guess that's okay." Keith squirmed.

"Just pretend I'm not here," Sam said.

Keith snorted. "Sure."

I put a voice recorder on the table. "Mind if I use this? Helps me keep everything straight,"

He hesitated before nodding his agreement, and I quickly glanced at Sam, signaling that I was not sure how well this would go.

George placed coffee mugs on the table and then returned with the coffee pot, sugar, and cream. "Thanks so much for doing this, Dave." He sat next to Keith. "I know it's not normally your thing."

"No problem. And in return, thank you for talking to us," I turned to Keith. "I can't imagine what you're going through right now."

He didn't reply, so I pressed on. "Have the police been able to tell you anything about what's going on—where they think Felicia might be?"

Again, no answer. I looked at Sam.

"Keith?" she asked. "Maybe you should tell us about Felicia first. How did you meet her."

He sniffed, and a smile fought its way onto his face. "We met in college. Michigan State. We moved here about nine years ago when Felicia was offered the teaching job." His mouth twitched as he seemed to gaze back in time.

"I was sitting by this river that runs through campus," he said. "A clueless sophomore with no direction. I had a few friends, but none that were close, and I was... well, I was depressed. And was staring at the river, and suddenly she was behind me, asking if I was okay."

His eyes glistened. "She said, and I'll never forget this, 'I know the river's pretty, but I don't think you're looking at it.' She was the most beautiful thing I'd ever seen. I thought she had mistaken me for someone else. I'd never had a girlfriend or anything, and she was just... well, out of my league, you know?"

I nodded encouragingly, and he continued.

"So I said, 'I'm just thinking, sorry.' And she wanted to know why I was apologizing and asked if she could sit with me. I couldn't believe it. I just nodded, and she sat. I didn't know what to say, so I was silent, and after a few minutes, she asked my name. We talked for three hours.

"Years later, I asked why she had stopped that day. It turns out she had gone to this suicide awareness program, which encouraged people to reach out if they saw someone who might be in trouble."

He wiped tears from his eyes and looked at me with new intensity. "I wasn't suicidal or anything—at least, I don't think I was—but Felicia saved my life that day. She made me feel, for the first time, like maybe someone cared and that what I felt was okay, even if I didn't understand it. As our friendship and relationship grew, I became more confident and willing to speak my mind to other people."

Keith chuckled. "It didn't hurt that I had the prettiest girlfriend on campus, either."

"I need her here to talk to me now." He caressed one of the posters.

"Have the police been able to tell you where she's gone?" I asked.

"All they keep saying is it looked like she just, I don't know, walked away. Went to her car, opened it, changed her mind, and just..." He shrugged. "Just left, I guess."

"But where did she go?"

"I don't know—and it's driving me crazy. They said Felicia walked up the street for a while, by the river, but they don't know where she went after that."

"Did she take anything with her?" I prodded.

"Her keys, I guess. That's it. Her purse was still in the classroom, so she had no money or phone."

"She had to have gone somewhere. People don't just disappear into thin air."

"That's what these are for." Keith waved at the posters. "I've been everywhere: gas stations, stores, restaurants, anywhere I can think of. We even went over to Columbus. Someone has to have seen her."

"We?"

"I… my daughter, Jessica. She's been staying at my parents' house a lot, but she wants to help."

"How old is she?" My heart sank.

"Seven." Keith's eyes, already puffy, were glistening now. "She's afraid to go to school again. She keeps saying she can… she can hear her mom's voice at night."

At this, he lost control and put his head in his hands. It felt indecent, watching the man grieve in his own house. I looked awkwardly at Sam, who lowered her camera.

"That's awful, Keith," she said. "But more publicity will help find her."

"I hope so. I can't do this without her." He wiped his eyes. "You always think you'd know what to do in a crisis, that it'd be an adventure, and that if you do all the right things at the right time, you'd save the day." He grabbed a roll of paper towels from the seat next to him, tore one off, and blew his nose, a great honk that surprised me even though I saw it coming.

"But now I'm in crisis and have no better idea what to do than my seven-year-old. Felicia was my whole world."

I glanced at the recorder. It didn't feel right taping this, but now that he'd started, Keith pressed on.

"The cops keep saying she walked away, but when I ask about the stranger they saw, they just say they're not sure how he's connected. Or even if he's connected."

Glad he'd brought it up first, I seized upon it. "Do they know who he is, then? This 'mysterious stranger?'"

"Isn't that the stupidest thing you ever heard?" he shot back. "To put in a press release that a 'mysterious stranger'" —he used air quotes for emphasis—"was seen lurking around the school. As if that's helpful, and not going to terrify the hell out of everyone. Including us."

"It is odd," I agreed. "What else have they told you about him?"

"Not much." He shrugged. "Same thing they put in the press release they gave me a copy of. White, between thirty-five and fifty-five, medium build, medium height, shaggy hair. I mean, hell, I fit that description."

Given his build, I thought that was a bit generous, but let it pass.

"And they said he was standing under a tree near the car, the one over by the parking lot. He walked toward Felicia, but they lost sight of him before she walked away."

"Lost sight of him? He walked out of view of the camera?"

"Well, that's what I thought they meant, but I can't see how that would be."

"Why not?"

"Well... have you ever been behind the building?"

"More times than I can count. My mom used to teach there, and I went to school in that building."

"Oh... right, of course... Mrs. Kendrick. She was Jessica's kindergarten teacher." He squirmed in his chair. "Yeah, I wasn't thinking, sorry... I'm sorry about what happened."

"It's okay. Thanks," I said.

Sam jumped in before we could get derailed. "So what about behind the building?"

"Oh. Right." Keith shook his head. "Well, the camera is up on the corner of the building, shooting down toward the parking lot. I know; I installed it myself."

Seeing my look of surprise, he smiled. "That's my business. Well, one of them. I do computer repairs, virus cleanup, cybersecurity, security systems—that sort of thing. I own a shop downtown."

A switch flipped in my brain. "Kee Systems?"

"Yep. Keith E. Erickson, proprietor." He gave a practiced flourish.

"I always wondered why Kee was spelled that way. Now I know," I said.

"Yep. So, I installed those cameras at Lynwood Elementary three or four years ago before my little girl went there. That camera covers the entire parking lot and half of the playground area. And then, there's another that covers the playground too. I wanted them to overlap in case anything ever happened. And the thing is, if somebody walked away from that tree and toward Felicia's car, they'd be walking toward the center of the camera frame, not toward the edge."

"That is strange," I said as Sam started taking pictures again.

"Exactly. But the police say he never shows up on the camera covering the playground, even though they see Felicia walking across it and over to the street. The playground camera probably doesn't quite get to the tree this guy was under."

"But if he wasn't with her, he couldn't have forced her to walk away," I said, trying to work it out.

"You wouldn't think," Keith said. "But then, where did he go? And why do police think he's connected? It doesn't make any sense."

"None of it does." I agreed.

"It's just like those other cases," he said. "I mean, nobody knows where they went, either. It's crazy."

"Those old cases Jethro Miller talks about?" I asked.

"No—more recent. That housewife and the druggie. Robin Elliott and Steve Cervelli. They disappeared last month." He pointed to the paper lying on the table. "You guys reported it. I read about them in the *Post*."

"Wait a second." Cervelli's name, at least, sounded familiar, and then it hit me. I hadn't read about it in the paper, but I'd seen a police report the day I returned to work. "Wait... was he the one whose car was found in the middle of the road?"

"Yeah, that's the one. And the lady who took off from her house one night. I've been wondering if her husband is somehow connected."

"Keith, be careful here." George put his hand on Keith's arm, but Keith shrugged it off.

"Why do you say that?" I asked.

"Well, Cervelli's a piece of work." Keith shrugged. "Had a prior for domestic violence and a couple of assaults."

"You know him?" I prodded.

"No, but it's all public record. After Felicia went missing, I went back through the papers because I remembered reading about the other disappearances. I found those two and asked the cops if they were connected, but they said no. I didn't know what else to do, so I kept digging. Cervelli had been arrested for possession of marijuana and heroin a couple of times, so I thought maybe some drug dealer was after him. But then I found Mike Elliott's background, which got me thinking."

Keith leaned forward. "Look, don't put this in the article, okay? Because I don't have any proof and don't want to piss someone off. But think about it. Every time you see one of those shows with serial killers on TV—"

George cringed.

"—they say to go back to the first case," Keith continued, "because that one was somehow personal for the killer, right? So, let's say Mike Elliott kills his wife, and that makes him feel all-powerful or something. So, why not do it again? Maybe he's got some ties to drugs too. Maybe he feels Cervelli wronged him."

Keith stabbed the flyer with his finger. "They both happened a few days apart. Nobody gets caught. So now, maybe… maybe he's decided he can get away with… this stuff." His voice cracked as he realized he'd been about to suggest his wife had been murdered.

I nodded slowly. "But the police said there's no connection, right?"

"That's what they said. But they also said they lost sight of this mystery man, and they had the same sort of vague answers when I asked them for more details."

"Huh. We'll have to check that out," I said.

"Dave, please don't tell anybody this came from Keith," George said. "The police are hard enough to deal with, and I don't want him getting into trouble."

"I won't mention it," I promised.

CHAPTER EIGHTEEN

K eith Erickson's theory rattled in my brain as I drove east toward downtown. On one hand, it sounded ludicrous—a serial kidnapper, or worse, in Lynwood? Even if we did have somebody like that, why wouldn't they pick on the much more fertile ground in Columbus? Why Lynwood?

On the other hand, I remembered the other two missing people he mentioned. I had read the reports myself and had forgotten them after reading the sad, short report on Luke Van Buren's apparent suicide, but they both seemed just as light on detail as the Erickson case. I didn't know what to make of that—base police reports rarely had much substance in them, and I hadn't asked for anything further.

The interview went quicker than I expected—it was still not quite one o'clock—so I convinced Sam to go for a ride past the Elliott house. She dropped her car at the Post, and I called Jenny to see if she had looked further into the missing persons cases—she hadn't.

Sam hopped in. and I punched in Elliott's address from the police report into my phone. The couple lived on Derwent Street, about six blocks south and east of downtown. While not a great distance, the quality of the neighborhood deteriorated rapidly south of Montcalm. Derwent was lined with houses so close together and rickety that from the right angle, they appeared to be holding each other up.

"You sure about this?" Sam asked. "Walt didn't say anything about checking out these other cases."

"I know. But it's interesting, isn't it? Two women seem to walk away, with no hint of where or why. One of them's a federal case, and the other gets ignored? Why?"

"Because one walked away from a school."

"Sure. That's one factor. And it scared a bunch of parents. This one didn't, so nobody cares. It feels wrong."

Sam apparently didn't have a counter for that because she opened the door. We let ourselves in through the rusted chain-link gate, climbed two short steps, and knocked on the screen door.

No one came, and I was about to give up when we heard a thump. Sam and I looked at each other. When nothing else happened, I knocked again.

This time, we heard footsteps, and the inner door swung open. On initial glance, the guy looked scrawny, but his bare arms were corded with muscle. He wore a dirty white tank top and jeans stained with what looked like oil or some other automotive fluid. "Not buying anything," the man barked. His hair was unkempt, and it looked like he hadn't shaved for days.

"Not selling," I said. "Are you Mike Elliott?"

"Nobody else lives here, do they?"

"I'm Dave, and this is Sam. We're with the *Post*," I said, holding up my press badge, which he ignored. "We're following up about Robin."

He started, and for a moment, I thought he would slam the door in my face.

"Look, we saw her report, and now somebody else has gone missing. Do you mind telling us what happened?"

For a long moment, none of us moved. Finally, Mike mumbled something and started to close the door.

"Mr. Elliott, wait, I didn't catch that!"

"I said, go away." This time, he did slam the door.

Sam jumped. "Well, that was helpful."

After dropping Sam off, I pulled into Mom's gravel driveway and shut off the engine, then just sat, looking at the house. Finally, I roused, climbed out of the car, and picked my way through fallen leaves to the front door. Cool, crisp November air gave way to the musty interior of an empty house. I hadn't been inside for a week, but it still surprised me. I kicked off my shoes and opened all the windows on the first floor.

I had an hour before my potential renter would show up, and I spent a good portion of it wiping down surfaces and making sure I had locked everything important away. I double-checked the deadbolt I had installed upstairs and then returned to the craft room, planning to get Mom's stuff out of the rolltop desk.

It was open.

I stood in the doorway, staring. The unbelievably loud, clattery rolltop stood open. Just like the window next to it, the one I flung wide just a short while ago when I arrived.

The desk hadn't been open then. I was sure of it. I would have noticed. I stepped back and scanned the room, but there was no sign of anyone.

The shadowy corners inside the desk seemed deeper as I tiptoed across the little room. I half-expected it to slam shut on my fingers. Even though I'd been upstairs for a few minutes, I couldn't fathom how the desk could have been opened without my hearing it.

Or if anyone had snuck in, for that matter.

"Hello?" I called out, turning back toward the dining room. My voice seemed to fade and disappear. No one answered.

I sat at the desk. The key was right where I left it, metal cold to the touch, but perhaps that was my imagination. I unlocked the desk drawer and slid it out, and even that sounded far too loud for me to miss.

I lifted half a dozen folders out of the drawer and carried them into the dining room, stacking them where I could quickly grab them when I left. The desk was too big to haul upstairs and lock away, so it would either have to stay here or be moved when someone rented the place. Either way, I might as well get Mom's important papers now, in case I had a tenant soon.

I went back in, locked the drawer, and had just reached for the rolltop when a chiming sound made me jump as if the desk had bitten me.

"Holy shit," I murmured. The chiming died, and I stepped back into the dining room. Sure enough, there was a car, a little blue Beetle, parked behind my battered Oldsmobile. The chime was nothing more dangerous than the doorbell.

"Be right there!" I called and went in the other direction, to the kitchen. There was no beer, so I filled a glass of water and drained it, praying my heart rate would return to normal. I left the glass on the counter and walked to the front door, glancing toward the craft room as I went, half expecting the rolltop to have closed, but it just sat there, yawning at me.

Shaking my head at my jumpiness, I opened the door and was shocked again.

"Hi, Dave," Allison Van Buren said. "Thanks for letting us see the house."

"Allison," I said. "Hi. I didn't realize that was you on the phone."

"Oh... sorry, did I not say?" She glanced down, and it was only then that I noticed Chase standing beside her. "Should we not have come?"

"No, it's fine. I didn't connect the dots. Come in, please," I stammered. I hoped I had covered my surprise, but I caught Chase rolling his eyes and knew I'd failed miserably.

If she noticed, she was too polite to say anything. Allison and Chase stepped over the threshold, and I wondered if the place had had enough time to air out.

"I was surprised you weren't moving in here yourself," she said. "Such a big place. Did I hear you live in an apartment?"

"Maybe I will, someday, but I'm not ready yet. Too many ghosts." I'd meant it as a joke, but suddenly the vision of that open rolltop loomed large. "Can I show you around?"

I spent the next fifteen minutes leading them through the house I'd grown up in, trying not to notice that Allison had only gained a few pounds since her high school days. Chase's presence helped, though I still felt awkward when I showed her my old bedroom. The teenager in me couldn't believe that the former Allison Knight was in the place where she'd featured in so many fantasies.

"I can't believe how neat everything is," Allison said as we headed back downstairs toward the basement. "Did you do all this?"

"Mom ran a pretty tight ship. Even with her gone, I can't help but follow her standards," I said, lamenting the dirty glass I left on the counter. "The only room she...," my voice trailed off as we passed the craft room. The desk sat serenely, stately as ever, and most decidedly closed.

"Dave?" Allison said. "Everything okay?"

"Huh? Oh. Yeah, um... everything's fine."

Chase stepped in front of me, following my line of sight. "What's going on? I don't see anything."

"Oh." I looked from Allison to Chase, then Allison again. "It's just, I thought I'd left that desk open, but now I see it's closed."

"Maybe the wind blew it shut," Chase suggested.

"Yeah. Maybe." My heart raced, but I wasn't about to let Allison or Chase see me on the edge of a panic. "Anyway. The basement." I turned and strode purposefully past Allison into the kitchen, opened the basement door, and started down.

"So, how much are you asking for rent?" Allison asked as we reached the bottom.

"I figure $500 a month will cover expenses," I said.

"Really? That's all?"

"Yeah." I'd been planning for higher but was prepared to be talked down to $500. I knew she wouldn't be here if she weren't trying to get away from the house she and Luke had shared and wasn't going to make her haggle.

"Well, it's too big for us, but I can't pass up that price." She gave the basement a cursory look.

"Great. We can sort out the paperwork soon, then." I hadn't had lease papers drawn up yet. My lawyer was about to get another job.

When we came back up, the desk remained closed. I had the distinct impression that Allison would have signed immediately, even if the place had been a dump.

"One last thing, there is a garage if you'd like to see that," I said. "I haven't been in it for months, and the lock is broken, but you're welcome to use it."

"No need. We'll take it," Allison said.

"Great." It was the first time it occurred to me that Allison might be spending some time in my old bedroom, and I had to remind myself, again, that I wasn't sixteen anymore. "Tell you what," I added, pressing past that vision, "I don't have a lease or anything put together yet, but I should by Monday or Tuesday. When did you want to move in?"

"To be honest? As soon as possible. We're staying with Pedro and Lisa right now, and it's..." She glanced at Chase.

"There's people everywhere. Their house isn't very big," Chase blurted. "This place is nice. I like it."

"Okay. Well, it's ready, apart from the lease. And I trust you. You can move in tomorrow if you want."

"That might be pushing it, but, yeah, the sooner, the better." Allison patted Chase on the back. "But we can wait for the lease."

"I'll call as soon as it's ready."

They walked to the street and climbed into the little blue Volkswagen. I took out my phone, scrolled to Allison's number, and input her name, telling myself it was just business.

The breeze kicked up and sent leaves skittering across the path, and I figured I'd better get the yard ready. I took the leaf blower that was leaning against the garage and turned it on.

After a few back-and-forths across the yard, I went behind the garage to get started on the massive piles that collected there over the past few weeks. About half had been cleared when I uncovered something underneath the stack against the garage wall.

There, lying behind the two trash cans, was a dead man in the fall detritus.

I might have found Ralph Walther.

CHAPTER NINETEEN

The man was on his back and looked like he had stretched out to nap a month ago. His eyes were missing, and his face was shriveled as though someone had stuck a vacuum cleaner into his mouth and left it on too long.

His lips were open in a horrible, obscene sort of grin, and even though his eye sockets were empty, he appeared to be staring at me while one desiccated hand clutched a liquor bottle. The man wore a zipped-tight raincoat, jeans, and work boots. And on top of his head perched a baseball cap bearing the legend "Walther Farms."

I couldn't remember the last time I'd seen Blaine Reynolds so happy. He sat across the table from me in the police interview room, and the fabric of his uniform slacks rubbed against his chair as his leg twitched. It made the rest of his body quiver as if he were sitting in a bounce house that was being pumped full of air. I would have laughed under normal circumstances.

He clutched a notebook in one hand and a pen in the other. I thought it was for appearances. Fluorescent light glimmered off his glasses, drawing the eye away from his tight, mocking smile, and rain poured on the roof, punctuated by the occasional rumble of thunder — it had to be loud to be heard in this inside room.

"Tell me again how you 'found' him." He air quoted.

This was the second time I had been in this room. Both times, someone had died. Neither time had it been my fault. The police hadn't believed me last time, and I saw no reason to think they'd believe me now.

"I told you already. I was using the leaf blower to try to clean up the yard. And he was there, under the leaves."

"Mm-hmm." He pretended to write it down, though I had said this at least six times before.

My back was stiff. The cold metal chair, designed to persuade criminals to give up their stories, was compressing my spine. I tried to stretch without giving Reynolds the satisfaction of showing my discomfort but only got a slight crack for my feeble efforts.

"When's the last time you saw him before that?"

"The night of the crash." I felt like we were practicing lines for a school play.

Reynolds tapped his pen on the black linoleum top of the heavy metal table. Over his shoulder, I could see my reflection in the mirror — the one-way glass. I looked tired. On the other side, there probably were more officers trying to decide if I was telling the truth and enjoying watching me squirm under Reynolds' interrogation.

They'd kept me in the room for an age after bringing me to the station, and Reynolds had been in and out many times over the long duration I'd been there. I knew I should have asked for a lawyer. I also knew — or at least, I was pretty sure — they should have offered one. But they hadn't placed me under arrest, and since I knew I hadn't done anything wrong, I figured I'd be better off answering their questions so I could go home.

"Are you sure that was the last time you saw him?" Same script. Reynolds leaned back on his chair.

"Come on, sergeant. I know you're enjoying yourself, but how many times do we need to go over the same ground? Yes, Walther was driving the truck that killed my mom. No, I didn't like him very much. No, I didn't kill him. Can I go home now?"

"Still searching the house. Heard they had to bust open a locked door. What a shame." Reynolds smiled.

Great. They'd be searching for days. I hoped they liked sewing machines and old lady clothes.

"I don't live there, you know. In fact, I was just about to rent it out." I winced, knowing this would open a new line of questioning.

He leaned forward. "And who were you going to rent it to?"

"Nobody's signed anything yet, so it doesn't matter."

"Let me be the judge of that."

I sighed. It would only take one neighbor to mention there'd been another car at the house.

"I had a possible tenant come by today. That's why I was at the house. I showed her and her boy around, and she said she'd take it. She left, I went to clean up the yard, and I found Walther. The rest, you know."

He pounced. "Who was it?"

"Name's Allison. She's got nothing to do with this, and she's had a hard enough time lately, so leave her alone, okay?"

"And miss out on a corroborating witness? I don't think so. Allison, who?"

"Van Buren." I shook my head.

He wrote her name. "Funny you didn't mention it before."

"Like I said, she's had a rough month. Lost her husband, you may remember."

"I remember." He smiled as though I reminded him that his favorite show was about to start. "You claim you haven't seen Walther

113

since the crash. When was the last time you talked to him? Was it when you tried to attack him?"

He hadn't asked that before, and it threw me off.

"Talked to him? Um." Fatigue slowed my brain as I tried to remember. "I don't know that I've ever had a conversation with him. I mean, I yelled at him the night of the crash, but that's about it."

"Really?" He smiled that prim little smile of his. "Not even on the phone?"

"Phone? No, why…" I trailed off. I hadn't talked to him on the phone. But we had traded voicemails, hadn't we?

Reynolds lifted a plastic bag from the chair beside him as if reading my mind. I remembered him carrying something in, but it hadn't registered. Now I could see there was a cell phone inside.

"This is Mr. Walther's cell phone. Want to guess what we found on it?"

When I first arrived at the station and was left in an interrogation room, panic nearly overwhelmed me. Hours of waiting and repetitive questions had dulled my anxiety, but now it came back in full force. Between what I shouted at the crime scene and whatever I'd said in a drunken rage to his voicemail, I had a feeling I was going to be suspect number one.

Reynolds slid the bag to the center of the table and, through the plastic, punched a button. The screen came to life, and he activated voicemail.

"Listen, asshole, I don't know what the hell you think you're doing." My tinny voice echoed in the small room. "The police told me to let them deal with you, and I am. But if you start bugging me, I swear I'll beat you right out of this world. So, fuck off."

"Do I need to play it again?" Reynolds asked.

"No."

"Care to explain?"

"Not really." I knew that was the wrong answer, but I was starting to think I might need a lawyer after all.

"You threaten to kill a man. That man turns up dead in the yard you inherited. And you don't feel like explaining." He tapped his pen again.

I took a deep breath, then another. I leaned forward, putting my forearms on the hard table. "Okay. Walther called me. It was the night of the funeral, and the bastard called me. He left a message, claiming he didn't remember the crash, babbling that he wasn't really there, even though he knew he had been there. It didn't make any sense."

I took another deep breath. "And, like I said, it was the same day as the funeral, and it pissed me off. So, I called him back, got his voicemail, and left that message. And that was it. I haven't seen or heard from him since."

"And yet, you've done a good job of making sure people knew you hadn't seen him, haven't you?" Reynolds asked. "You even asked me a few days ago if we'd found him yet."

"Because I've been waiting for you to put him in prison for killing my mother!" I shouted, knowing that raising my voice wasn't a good idea, but I had had enough. "Why would I ask you to look for him if I'd killed him and dumped him on my own property? Why would I show somebody that property and make arrangements for her to move in while there's a dead person in the yard—and then report that I'd found that body? Does that make any sense?"

He stared at me.

I continued. "The answer is, it doesn't. Yes, I hated the guy. Everybody knows that. But I didn't go looking for him, let alone kill him. If I'd have killed him, I could think of a hell of a lot better places to hide his body than my backyard, barely out of sight of a road, of a house."

"Do you put a lot of thought into where to hide bodies, then?" he asked silkily.

"What?" I rubbed my forehead. "No, of course not."

"Because Ralph wasn't the only missing person, you know. There are others. Know anything about that?"

I jerked my head in surprise. "What? No. I know what we've been reporting, but that's it." I rubbed my forehead again and wondered how often I'd done that since entering this room. "I don't even know why you're asking that."

"You want us to believe it's a coincidence? Ralph Walther's been missing for weeks and turns up dead on your property. Other people are missing, too, some far longer than Walther. Are we going to find anyone else on your property? Or do you have better bolt holes for them that we haven't found yet?"

"You've got to be kidding," I said. The faint buzz of the fluorescent bulbs grew more insistent. "Those aren't connected to this. You've got to know that."

"Why?"

The simplicity of the question slammed me back in my seat. "Because... hell, I don't know. Motive? Opportunity? Anything?" This interview was getting worse all the time.

"Where were you the morning of Nov. 12?"

"You know where I was. I was at the school, covering the search."

"I mean before the police were called. When Felicia Erickson disappeared." He looked angry now.

"I was at home. Walt woke me up to call me in."

"Can anyone confirm that?"

"Well, Walt can. He called me." I said it slowly to make sure he understood.

"Can anyone confirm you were actually at home?"

"I live alone."

"What about the night of October 10th?"

I thought back; Mom's funeral had been on October 11th. "I was making funeral preparations."

"How late?"

"I don't know. Seven or eight, I guess."

The lights flickered, and we both glanced up. A roar of thunder a minute later explained the electrical disturbance.

"And after that?"

"Home. Watching a game, probably. I don't remember. Why?"

"And what about October 4th?" His pad was out, and he was writing on it.

I thought back. "That was a Friday, right?"

"Yes."

"I was at a football game," I said, relief rushing my words. "Lynwood game. They lost 28-0. I was in the press box for the game, in the locker room after, and then in the newsroom, writing my story and making phone calls until at least midnight. Anybody working that night can vouch for me."

He wrote something else down, then pulled the phone back and stood.

"Look, you can't keep me here all night," I said.

"We'll see." He left the room, pushing the door hard until it clanged shut and locked.

The last time I was in this room was that night in '06, the day after being drafted—the day of my accident.

The room hadn't changed much. Besides the faded silver of the reflective mirror, the drab green walls reminded me of an Army cot. The table might have been the same one from eighteen years ago. Scuffs marred every inch of its surface, but it still looked sturdy enough to hold up a circus elephant. The light, too, was the same. The only difference was the ceiling.

I sat in the same spot that night, waiting for another interrogation. I stared at one thing in particular—a dark brown blob I imagined was dried blood—near the corner above the window. It was gone now, having been painted sometime in the intervening years, but I could see it in my mind's eye as clearly as I could back then.

It was another twenty minutes before the door opened again, but it wasn't Blaine Reynolds this time. I would have preferred him.

The chief of police stood behind the chair Reynolds had vacated and leaned on it, weathered hands gripping the back so tightly his knuckles shone white.

"Why am I not surprised you ended up back here?" he growled.

I didn't answer. There wasn't much I could say to this man.

Police Chief Cameron Adams looked angry, but I'd seen him angrier. Once. Eighteen years ago.

The night my girlfriend—his daughter—died.

CHAPTER TWENTY

Adams had been a sergeant in 2005 and hadn't participated in the questioning due to his involvement. He never believed my story about the other car. Looking back, the similarity between my crash and my mother's had never been so obvious. I don't know how it hadn't occurred to me before, but now wasn't the time to ruminate.

"How did you do it this time?" Adams asked, his voice deadly calm.

"I didn't," I muttered.

"I've heard that before. What's the excuse? Sun get in your eyes?"

"I don't know how Ralph died. I don't know why he was at my mother's house. I didn't kill him."

"And you didn't toss him out by the trash cans either?"

"I didn't." I wished Adams would sit down. I glanced at the empty water glass Reynolds had given me earlier, but it didn't magically refill.

"Where did you kill him?"

I forced myself to meet his eyes.

"I didn't kill him. I don't own a gun, I don't own a knife, and I haven't punched anyone since high school."

"You have a baseball bat."

"Well, yeah, but I haven't hit anyone with that either."

"We're searching your apartment. And your car. And your momma's house."

"Don't forget the garage. You won't find anything."

"We'll see. Meantime, you can spend the night with some of our other friends."

My shoulders slumped. "Okay. I guess I need my lawyer now. You have no evidence to arrest me."

"Suit yourself." The door opened, and Reynolds, looking even more twitchy, beckoned to Adams, then he closed the door after them both.

"What?" Adams roared. Then there was rumbling, other words I couldn't make out, and finally, silence.

A minute later, Reynolds opened the door. "You can go." His face, pinched in the best of times, looked positively squished.

"I'm sorry, what?"

He jerked his head toward the door, and I stood and walked stiff-legged. He slid to one side to let me through.

The county prosecutor was waiting for me. He said, "Don't leave town. You're still under investigation. And you'll need to find somewhere else to stay — your house and apartment are off-limits."

"Right." I had no idea where I would stay, but that was a problem I could solve from the outside. "And my things?"

"At the front desk."

He seemed to have used his stock of words for the day and led me down a hall, where I waited as he retrieved the box of my belongings. I lifted my watch, keys, wallet, and cell phone from the box, then let him lead me through a heavy steel door into the lobby. He slammed the door behind me without another word, and I walked through the front doors into a frosty evening.

———————

Sleep proved elusive as I turned over on a too-stiff hotel bed, lumpy pillow tucked under my head. Whenever I closed my eyes, I saw Ralph Walther's ruined face. When I kept them open, I obsessed over the glee in Reynolds' voice as he tried to link me not just to Walther's death but to the disappearance of the others.

My phone battery was nearly dead, and my charger was home, so I didn't bother to check messages. There would be enough time for that in the morning. I wondered if I'd be welcome at work after having been hauled in on suspicion of murder. Probably not.

A million questions swam through my head, chasing each other like minnows eluding a net. What happened to Ralph Walther? Why was he at my mother's house? Had someone planted his body there to frame me? And why the hell had the police let me go minutes after promising me a night in jail?

I was too tired to puzzle anything out, yet sleep eluded as the night wore on, and my brain found older questions to ponder.

What had Mom wanted to tell me? And was it related to what happened to Ralph Walther. Somehow, I felt it was, though I had no idea how.

I must have drifted off because the morning sun beat through the hotel's cheap curtains far sooner than expected. I was stiff from the long hours in the interview room's metal chair, followed by a bed that wasn't much softer. A shower helped, but the unnaturally round patties of scrambled egg, odd-tasting sausage, and thin orange juice in the lobby breakfast bar made me queasy. It was barely nine when I checked out, and my first stop was Mom's house.

I called Ronnie on the way and filled him in. He made me swear to contact him if the police spoke to me again. I wasn't sure his legal skills were up to a murder case, if it came to that, but at least it felt like someone was on my side.

I knew I'd better call Walt soon too. But not yet.

The house looked more forlorn than usual. Police tape does that to a place. It was across the front porch, circling the entire yard from the front corners of the house to the garage. A lone Lynwood Police cruiser was parked in the driveway. I pulled up in front of the house, in the same space Allison had used less than twenty-four hours ago, and got out.

Tim exited the cruiser at the same time. "There you are. You okay, man?"

I gave a half smile, not sure how friendly I should be with anyone in the department right now, even Tim. "I'm all right. I'm guessing I can't go in yet?"

"Crime scene, and all." He shrugged. "Probably tomorrow. Don't tell anyone I said this, but I'm not sure there's evidence of a crime."

"You mean, besides the presence of a half-rotted corpse?"

He chuckled. "Well, there's that. We don't know how he died yet. Could've been exposure."

Somehow, that thought creeped me out more than the idea that someone had dumped him, trying to frame me.

"I don't know how these things work. How long do they keep the house like this? Or my apartment?"

"I think they're done with your apartment." He strode toward me.

"Really?" Somehow, I figured Adams would keep both of my potential places of residence blocked for as long as possible.

Tim shrugged and leaned against my car. "Again, it's not for me to say, but I don't think they found anything there."

I wanted to trust him. I really did. And yet, it felt like he was being awfully free with information. "Why are you telling me this? Couldn't you get in trouble?"

"I know you. You're not a murderer." He leaned against my car. "I volunteered to sit here for a while. We're taking shifts, but I was hoping to be here when you got back. Some of the others…." He shrugged again. "They're enjoying seeing you squirm."

I snorted. "No shit. Adams has always had it in for me, which, to be honest, I get. But I never expected the entire department to be that way."

"Tight brotherhood. And he's the chief. His dad was pretty well-liked too, was assistant chief years ago. They've got a lot of friends."

"You're part of that brotherhood."

"I am. But Adams doesn't walk on water, you know what I mean?" He shifted and pushed from my Olds, looking past the house. I wondered if he thought someone was listening. "But he has connections. Some guys go along with him because they learned that the hard way."

I wasn't sure what to say. "So, how will I know when I can get back in the house?"

"Somebody'll tell your lawyer. Probably the prosecutor's office. Don't know who you know at the district attorney's, pal, but that's why you weren't sleeping with us last night."

"I don't know anyone who'd like me there, but I'm glad."

"Well, watch your back, okay? Adams was plenty pissed. Reynolds, too, for that matter. He's always been annoying, but he was insufferable at roll call this morning. If there's anything out there on you, he'll find it."

"That's nothing new. I thought Reynolds would arrest me at my mom's crash scene."

"He wanted to. Fire Captain talked him out of it."

I blinked, shocked. "Who?"

"Gianini. He's getting on in years, but he's pretty persuasive when he wants to be and has a lot of friends himself."

That threw me. I hadn't even seen Tony Gianini, my father's old friend, at the scene, though I supposed he could have been in the command truck or down by the car.

"Well, I guess I owe Tony one." I paused. "Would it be inappropriate to ask you to keep me posted? I have a feeling whatever detective they assign to this case will only tell me what's absolutely necessary."

"As much as I can. They know we're friendly, so they might not tell me much either."

"Thanks." I shivered and wished I could get my coat from inside the house. "Can I ask you something?"

Tim shrugged. "You can ask. Doesn't mean I'll answer."

"How did Walther get here? He lived across town, didn't he?"

"Reynolds didn't tell you? His truck was in your garage."

My eyes widened. I wasn't sure what shocked me more — that the truck had been found in Mom's garage or that Tim was volunteering the information.

"You didn't notice it?"

"I haven't been in the garage since right after Mom died. The lock is broken, so I don't keep anything valuable out there except the mower, and I haven't had to mow."

I thought he wouldn't believe me, but he nodded. "You'll get asked about it."

"Yeah."

It had been more than five weeks since the crash. Had Walther gone from Lancaster Street to my mom's house the night I thought he'd been following me? Assuming it was him? And how had he died? I still didn't know that.

"I need more sleep," I said finally. "I'll be in touch, okay?"

"Sure. Take it easy." Tim rubbed his bare hands, chapped from the cold.

I said goodbye and got back in my car. I had no idea what to do next.

CHAPTER TWENTY-ONE

The police were not kind to the interior of my apartment. The sofa cushions were piled on the floor, leaning against the coffee table, and the sofa itself stood two feet from the wall. My clothes were in piles around my bedroom, and the drawers were left open and empty. Every piece of furniture had been moved, leaving new gouges in the walls from where investigators had been careless, guaranteeing me no shot at getting my security deposit back.

I reassembled the place over the next two hours but could still see subtle differences. I've heard that burglary victims never feel the same in their own space after someone violated it, and now I had an idea of what that must be like, even though the police had done mine.

Finally, I fell into bed, pulled up the covers, and slept like the dead. By the following day, my entire outlook on life had changed, and I had a plan. Or, rather, I had decided on how to approach Walt. Baby steps.

My grand plan was to arrive early and encourage Walt and Jenny to investigate whether the other disappearances were linked. Now, I not only had Keith Erickson's theories to go on and Mike Elliott's refusal to talk, but I also had direct questioning from the police to back it up.

I had no idea if Walt would fire me on the spot, suspend me, or hug me, but I decided not to worry about that. I also wondered if I could convince him there really was a connection.

That, as it turned out, was no problem at all.

Walt tried to call me in early again, but I was already pulling into the *Post*'s parking lot. I had stopped for a dozen donuts, hoping to butter up the colleagues, and made a show of dropping them on the spare desk in the newsroom, but no one noticed.

Jenny, the crime reporter, was nowhere to be seen. Jamie and Ray were on the phones, looking tense, and Sam was in Walt's office. I knocked on the open door. "Hey, Walt. I've got a story for Jenny."

"She's busy. We're all busy. How soon can you write the Erickson piece?"

"Today, but there's more to that story."

"Yeah, Sam says she thinks these other cases are linked."

Sam nodded.

"You're not alone. The cops think so too."

"Not surprised. Four missing—one of them dead. That's a hell of a coincidence in this town." Walt leaned back in his chair.

I did a double-take. "Wait... four missing?"

"And one dead. Thought that one would get more of your attention."

"I knew about that one already." The conversation wasn't going as scripted.

"How?"

I drew in a deep breath, then spoke, "The dead body was found in the yard at my mom's house."

"That's what we call 'burying the lede,' Dave. You've skipped the best part—what the hell is a body doing in your yard?" Walt asked.

"Beats me. But the police asked me the same thing. Over and over."

For a change, Walt seemed stunned into silence. "The police questioned you?"

"I found the body. It's their job." I sincerely hoped that pointing this fact out would convince Walt there was nothing unusual about them asking me some questions. At least until he found out who it was.

"So which one was it?" he asked.

"Reynolds did most of it. And Adams."

His eyebrow rose. "I meant, who did you find? Erickson, Cervelli, Lewis, or Elliott?"

"Wait. Who's Lewis?"

"Dexter Lewis. He's the fourth one who went missing. Coworker reported he walked off into the woods during a work shift Saturday and never came back." Sam tapped the pad on her lap.

"Where was this?"

"Northeast side. Lewis works for the power company and was trying to get the lines back up. Said he had to take a leak."

"This is the first I've heard that." Something clicked in my overly tired brain. "When Saturday?"

"About six p.m.," Sam interjected.

Right in the middle of my interrogation. No wonder the prosecutor didn't want to hold me. Relief flooded through me.

"Wait, he went to take a leak in the middle of a thunderstorm?"

"When you've got to go, you've got to go." Walt shrugged. "You found one of the others?"

"Not exactly." I blurted, "It was Ralph Walther. Police had been looking for him too."

"Isn't that...?" Walt's face took on a greenish tinge, and it looked like he would be sick.

I nodded. "Somehow, Walther ended up under some leaves in a corner of my mom's backyard—based on decomposition, it must have happened within days of the crash." I was getting back on script now. I wasn't lying, not even a little, and I'd spent half the night convincing myself that when looked at from a certain point of view, there was no reason to wonder if I'd had anything to do with it.

"So, the guy who accidentally killed your mom ended up dead in her backyard?" Walt asked. My script had failed spectacularly. Now Sam looked like she was the one who was going to be sick.

Jamie poked his head into the office, oblivious to the awkward silence. "Hey, Walt, coroner says they won't have an ID on that body for a few days. But he says it's not any of the missing people." He looked around and licked his lips, a nervous habit he'd developed a year or two before. "You want that in the story on the web?"

At first, we just stared at him. Finally, Walt said, "Not yet." His voice was more quiet than I had ever heard it. "Give us a minute, please."

Jamie ducked out, and Walt motioned to Sam. "You too."

"Right." She slunk from the room, eyes averted. I closed the door and sat, facing Walt, whose fingers were steepled under his chin.

"I know it looks bad," I spoke fast. "But the police questioned me and let me go, and given how much those guys hate me, that's saying something."

"Who else knows they questioned you?"

"I haven't exactly announced it to anyone. My neighbors probably know — the cops searched my place."

He nodded, and I wondered if he realized I meant my apartment neighbors. I decided not to enlighten him.

"You're dangerously close to being part of this story," Walt murmured, a register I wasn't even aware he had.

"It's a small town—a coincidence," I said. "A hell of a coincidence. Or maybe it's not a coincidence, and maybe it's a setup. I mean, if somebody wanted to kill that guy, it'd be pretty easy to throw suspicion on me, wouldn't it? Maybe they're covering their tracks."

"But who else wanted him dead?" he asked. It was a damn good question. "Or maybe somebody's trying to get you out of the picture. Hell of a way to do it."

I blinked. Why would anyone want me out of the picture? The only guy who'd ever seemed to have a grudge against me—aside from Adams—was the one now lying in the hospital morgue.

I wondered then about Mike Elliott, who had so rudely dismissed me from his front porch. But no, that didn't make sense; Walther had been dead for weeks by the time I'd gone to Elliott's.

What about Adams? Surely, he'd love to put me away for something. But then, anyone at the crash scene—including one Blaine Reynolds—knew about the threats I'd issued. Nobody else did unless they'd been gossiping.

"Like who? Adams?" I asked, hoping to sound casual.

Walt's gaze sharpened.

"I mean, he's never liked me, not since… well, you know."

Walt had been a reporter then and had covered my case. He was one of the few who seemed to believe me about another car being involved. Freelancing for the *Post* had been his idea.

"That doesn't make sense," he growled, volume starting to come back. "Adams is a cowboy, but I can't see him killing somebody just to frame you. You said they were looking for him? Walther?"

"Yeah. Walther hadn't been seen since his initial court appearance. He didn't show up for his next court hearing, and his lawyer hadn't heard from him in days."

"So, he was gone a month?"

"The lawyer said he hadn't seen him since..." I checked the calendar. "The eleventh of October."

There was a knock at his door. "Enter," Walt said.

Jenny walked in.

"Grab that calendar you started," he barked before she could say anything.

She returned a moment later with a current three-month calendar page that the ad representatives used. Several dates were circled in red, with names written into each box.

"So, October Fourth this year, the Elliott woman goes missing," Walt said. "Then the Cervelli kid disappears a little over a week later on October 10. And now, you're telling me that Ralph Walther disappears on October 11 or soon after. That's three in a week."

Jenny started to add Walther's name, then hesitated. "Wait, isn't that the guy...?"

Walt and I said "yes" in unison, and Jenny's eyes widened, but Walt continued. "And then nothing until November 12, when the teacher walks away from the school."

He slid his finger from October to November. "And then on November 16, Dexter Lewis walks off." He looked up at Jenny. "What are the odds we hear about another one soon? Three in a week again?"

"Nobody's reported anything," Jenny said.

"The family reported Walther. But they didn't have to. Cops were already looking for him." Walt tapped the calendar again. "Maybe it's just a coincidence, I don't know. Any new arrest warrants issued, anybody else you know the police are looking for?"

Jenny shrugged. "They've always got random people they're hunting. Burglary suspects, things like that."

"Keep digging. Back to Dexter Lewis. What do you have on him?"

Jenny looked surprised. "Well, not much. I was more focused on the body. Which, if it's Lewis—"

"It's not," Walt and I echoed again.

"It's Walther," Walt added. "But that's still off the record. We need the cops to confirm."

"But don't ask about him yet," I added. "I probably wasn't supposed to share that. I don't know if his family has been told."

"I know you've got questions, Jenny, but I'll fill you in later," Walt said. "For now, get to the crime scene and see if you can find anything out."

"Well, about that. Neighbors said they saw things happening by a house on Pine Street, but there's no sign of police tape or anything. Everything looks normal."

"It does?" I couldn't hide my surprise. Tim had insisted someone would tell me when they were done with the house. "232 Pine?"

"Yeah," she said, looking uncomfortable. "That was your mom's house, wasn't it? Court records still show it belongs to her."

"Takes time to catch up," I mumbled.

Jenny looked from me to Walt.

"Okay. Jenny, focus on whatever you can get from the cops about the body and what you got from the neighbors. And, sorry, Dave, have Sam get a picture of the house," Walt said, then raised his voice slightly, though the whole newsroom could hear him without that effort. "Jamie, give what you got from the coroner to Jenny, then you write up what you have on the new missing guy and the rest of them. Jenny, give Jamie what's on this calendar. And Dave, you write up the Erickson piece. After that, you're off this story until things settle down."

Our assignments parsed, we broke apart like players after a conference on the pitcher's mound. But for all the space everyone gave me, I felt like when I returned to my position, it was on the wrong field.

CHAPTER TWENTY-TWO

L ynwood had already been buzzing about Felicia Erickson's disappearance. When news hit about Dexter Lewis, the buzz became a loud drone. It increased to a roar when news of Walther's body broke, even without a name publicly released — police said they had to verify the identity — and by the time the papers hit the newsstand the next morning, it seemed no one could talk about anything else.

Though the paper hadn't mentioned it, it was no secret the body was found at Mom's house, and I saw my name crop up on more than a few social media threads. People wondered which of the missing people had been found dead; curiously, Ralph's name didn't come up. He must not have had many friends. I almost felt sorry for him.

Almost.

Police finally confirmed his identity on Thursday, and then the speculation about my role started in earnest. Walt tried to tamp down the worst of it, but it was no use. On Friday, Walt did what I had suspected he would do at the beginning of the week. He suspended me with pay and told me I could return when my name was clear.

I was thankful he said "when," not "if." At least he still seemed to believe me.

It didn't help when one of the TV reporters asked Chief Adams on camera if I was a suspect in Walther's death, and he hadn't denied it. His direct quote was, "We're keeping all of our options open, and that's certainly a history we're taking a tough look at."

I was glad for the time off. I couldn't do anything on the missing persons' story due to my perceived involvement, and it was more than a little difficult to focus on the mundane work of high school basketball. The one game I'd covered had been awkward as hell, and George Barlow made it worse. I caught him staring at me several times, suspicion written on his face.

Of course, being home wasn't much better. I was never that close to my neighbors, but now they all seemed to avoid me. My weekly poker game with some old friends from high school had been mysteriously canceled too. I wondered if I would need to move into Mom's house just to escape.

With nothing else to do on a Friday night, I went there and ordered a pizza. A rerun of a cop show played in the background while I wandered through the house, straightening up where the police had left things a mess.

Next, I went to the basement—Dad's old wooden workbench still sat against one wall with hammers, screwdrivers, wrenches, and other tools neatly hung from a pegboard above it. His old drill, belt sander, and circular saw were there too. Mom had used all of them when the occasion called for it, and so had I, but we always referred to them as Dad's tools, as if he would come back for them eventually.

It was a nice hope.

I sank onto the wooden barstool and ran my hand across the workbench. Even when it was in use, it was always dusty, and now that the house had sat empty.... The air around it always smelled of oak, sometimes more strongly than others, and today was one of those times. Dad had loved working with wood, whether it was building furniture or carving unique shapes. He told me once that as a firefighter, he saw how ugly wood got when burned, and he felt it was his duty to remind himself and others how beautiful and useful it could be.

I had just turned six when Dad disappeared. He'd gone hunting one day, which was odd because I don't remember him having a rifle, a bow, or anything like that in the house. It was a Saturday night.

At the time, Mom told me that out of the four guys he'd gone hunting with, one was injured, one dead, and Dad was missing, but people were looking for him. There were no helicopter searches in those days, but I heard someone say later that they used dogs. It didn't matter. They never found him.

For years, Mom and I talked about him as if he would come home someday. She apparently just said that for my benefit because she had him declared dead when I was thirteen. A year later, on a Christmas Eve visit to the Firehouse, I found a glass case in the lobby that included the names of deceased firefighters. Dad's name was included, listing the year of his death as 1994. The year he'd gone missing.

That's when I stopped treating the firefighters nicely when they did things for me. As far as I was concerned, they had given up. Somewhere along the line, I realized it might have been backdated, but I can be stubborn when I want to be.

I twirled a screwdriver and gazed around the room. A gaping rectangle opened into a crawlspace that ran under the back half of the house.

I used to hide from my parents as a kid—for some reason, I thought it was hilarious—and they would "search" for me. A few months before Dad went missing, we played, and I wanted to find a place where it would be hard for him to locate me. So, once, I overcame my fear of the dark and went into the crawl space. There was a short old iron door at one end, and thinking it led to the outside—I decided to open it, run to the back door, then hide upstairs.

But the door was firmly closed. Dad found me soon after, and while it was usually a fun game, this time he was so angry his face turned white—mad as I'd ever seen him, and he'd spanked me and told me never to go there again.

And I hadn't. The entire basement was off-limits for my hiding game. Even after Dad went missing, I feared going in there because I didn't want him to get mad at me when he came home and found out I'd disobeyed him.

A distant sound caught my attention, and it took a moment before I remembered there was a pizza on the way. I put the screwdriver down and left it and the memories of my dad in the dark.

CHAPTER TWENTY-THREE

I was on my third slice of pizza when one of the onscreen detectives figured out why the latest victim had been out on a particular road at night. It reminded me that I still didn't know why my mom had been out the night she died. And I still had no idea what she wanted to tell me.

I retrieved the stack of folders I had moved to the storage room—freshly outfitted with a new lock to replace the one the police broke—and stacked them on the coffee table. I started with Mom's address book, flipping through and comparing her best friends' home addresses against a Google map to see if she might have been visiting any of them. When that didn't turn up anything noticeable, I went back to the beginning, plotting everyone in her address book.

Most people lived in Lynwood proper, and since Mom had been driving north back to town, I felt I could rule them out. There were only eight who lived outside of town. Two lived north, and two more lived east; I ruled them out, as well. One lived south, but 98 was far from the most direct route from her house to town, so I ruled her out too. That left two in Columbus and one who lived south of I-70. None of the names were familiar.

I wrote down the numbers and addresses in my reporter's notebook anyway. It wouldn't hurt to start checking around.

An entry on the next-to-last page of my notebook caught my attention—"Ralph." I picked up my phone from the coffee table and scrolled through my voice messages to the one Ralph Walther had left.

The number matched one of the unknown ones from Mom's address book.

I put the phone down, hands shaking. Walther's number hadn't been in Mom's phone, but it was important enough for her to note it in her address book. I couldn't imagine why.

I wanted to grab Mom's phone to see if she had contacted him before, but it was still in the box of her belongings at my apartment.

I switched off the TV — determined not to sleep on the couch again — and strode up the stairs. Then I placed the folders, most of them unopened, back into the storage room and locked it. I paused outside my old bedroom door, considering the space I'd spent so much time in as a child. The bed was small for me now, and a fine layer of dust had gathered. I knew I needed to clean to rent the place, but I doubted Allison was still interested since a body had been found. I wondered again whether the police had questioned her about her visit.

I walked the broad hallway, passing the empty third bedroom and the top of the stairs to get to the primary bedroom. I removed my clothes, turned down the sheets, and slid under.

I frowned — I was missing something important. It shouldn't have been that hard to figure out what Mom wanted, and while I admittedly hadn't tried very hard until now, I was surprised I hadn't discovered it when settling her estate. I thought back to the dream I'd had the first night I slept on the couch after she died and the notebook full of her passwords and other important information. Surely something there should have given me a clue, but it hadn't.

And then there was the whole suspected-of-murder thing. I wondered if I'd ever be able to recover from that, at least in Lynwood. Maybe it was time to move out of town. Between the money Mom left me, and what I could get out of the house, I'd have a good start. There didn't seem to be anything left for me here. Would Walt take me back at the paper, even if Cam Adams walked into the *Post* and swore on a Bible that I was innocent and a nice guy to boot? Would any of my friends want me back at the poker game or hanging around with their families?

And after all, it's not like I had family here. I had a few failed relationships — more than a few, I guess — and nothing to show for any of them.

Unbidden, my thoughts drifted to Allison and what might have been back in high school and even what might have been last week before Ralph Walther had once again so rudely interrupted my life. Logically, I knew she was in no place to think about dating, with her husband having just killed himself. Even so, we reconnected in a way I never thought possible.

Somewhere along the line, the daydreaming drifted into an actual dream — I was chasing Ralph Walther with a baseball bat. Every time I nearly caught him, he'd hop into that awful red pickup and speed away, impossibly watching me through the back window with that clown-face grin of his. I found myself wandering the street away from Lynwood Elementary, looking for Felicia Erickson, but this time, it was snowing, and I slipped and fell on the metal door embedded in the sidewalk, making a bang that echoed up and down the street.

Then the road changed, and I was walking south on Wilson Street toward Heyward Manor, the old family homestead Ezekiel Heyward's family lived in, and there was a light on. In the dream, this didn't surprise me. The house had long been the source of urban legends for mysterious lights, creepy sounds, and a wide variety of other ghost stories. I knew the stories were all bogus, of course, but the light was on in the dream, and it made perfect sense to me. I walked to the door, produced a large key from my pocket, and inserted it into the lock.

It clicked repeatedly, but before the door opened, it shattered, replaced by the ceiling of Mom's bedroom. As the snowy street disappeared, I found myself in the familiar bedroom while the clicking continued. The bedside clock read two-thirty-two, and I rubbed my bleary eyes. The clicking sound seemed to be coming from somewhere in the room, maybe from the closet.

I fumbled for the lamp switch and turned it on. Leaning up on one elbow, I sought the source of the noise.

The door to the closet was closed, but the knob rattled. It twirled back and forth as if manipulated by a small child who didn't know how to make it work. I glanced toward the door into the hall, confirming it was still closed, then slowly sat up and slid from under the covers.

As soon as my feet hit the floor, the knob stopped moving, and silence reigned.

I sat still for a full minute, then two, while I worked up the courage to stand, pad across the room, and extend my hand for the doorknob. Again, I hesitated, then finally reached forward, grabbed the knob, spun it, and opened the door in one smooth motion before I could talk myself out of it.

I hadn't expected something to jump out at me, so I screamed like a little girl when it did. I had no sooner processed the falling vacuum cleaner than I was stunned by the blackness beyond it. Still half asleep, I expected a closet full of Mom's clothes, the way it was when she lived here, but since I had already moved that stuff out, the closet was almost empty.

Except for the vacuum cleaner, which now completed its fall with a muffled crack and a thump as it hit the shaggy carpet. It had tipped over and fallen against the door, and when I opened it, gravity completed its work.

Trying to slow my heart rate, I backed up, lifted my phone from the nightstand, and turned on the flashlight. I approached the vacuum with caution due a sleeping rattlesnake. It remained blissfully lifeless on the floor, and the light revealed nothing else lurking in the closet, inanimate or otherwise.

I lifted the vacuum and examined it. The machine's fall from the closet had popped one of the attachments from its holder, but otherwise, there was no apparent damage. I snapped the attachment back into place, shoved it into the closet, and turned it so that if it fell again, it wouldn't fall on an unsuspecting person. Then I slammed the door, strode back to bed, and moved to turn off the flashlight.

My thumb had nearly found it when I heard a telltale rattle-bang coming from downstairs.

CHAPTER TWENTY-FOUR

I dragged on a pair of jeans and opened the door to the hallway, standing at the top of the stairs for a moment, listening intently for any sound of an intruder. Then, I flicked the hallway switch. Enough light spilled for me to see that no one stood at the bottom of the stairs or near the front door but little else. I crept down, a step at a time, angling my phone's flashlight to reveal as much of the lower level as possible.

The flashlight wasn't built for range, and I vowed to get a good one for the house soon. The stairs creaked under my weight as I descended to the bottom, where I switched on the sitting room light, turned left, and moved into the dining room, turning on that light as well. As expected, the room was empty, apart from the oversized dining table and the china cabinet against the far wall. The entries into the kitchen and office were dark, though moonlight glimmered through the window over the sink.

Again, I paused to listen. The house creaked faintly in the wind, and I could hear the furnace running in the basement. I went down the left side of the room, around the table, toward the kitchen entrance. I reached the far wall, where I could look straight into the office, and made out the rolltop, yawning open like some too-wide jack-o-lantern mouth. I stepped forward and stretched into the kitchen to switch on that light, and it, combined with the dining room light, did a fair job of illuminating the inside of the office. After a glance to ensure no one lurked in the kitchen, I stepped forward and switched on the office light.

Everything was exactly as I had left it, aside from the desk. From there, I ducked through the narrow door into the kitchen. The back door to the yard remained closed and locked. The door to the basement, however, was partially open. I didn't usually leave it that way, but perhaps I had when the pizza guy rang the bell.

Every nerve pulled taut through my body, so perhaps I could be forgiven when the phone in my pocket picked that moment to vibrate. I dropped it and jumped back, forgetting the step into the small mudroom leading to the back door. The phone clattered to the floor, and I fell backward, my head hitting the wall and the base of my spine crashing into the hardwood floor. A snow shovel I had left leaning against the wall seemed to gouge my leg as I hit it, then went tumbling into the door. Lights exploded in my head, and the jolt shot an agonizing, slow arc up my spine, spreading to the rest of my body.

I shook my head, blinked, and tried to stretch my back and hips to work out the sudden pain. When my vision cleared, I looked into the kitchen, gasping for breath.

My phone was on the floor in front of the stove. Beyond that, the door to the basement was firmly closed.

My fingers explored the spot where I'd hit the shovel, high on the back side of my left leg. It was tender, but it didn't feel like it was cut. Gingerly, I pulled my legs under me and, holding onto the doorframe, dragged myself to my feet. My backside was already sore, and I felt forty years older as I stepped awkwardly into the kitchen. I touched the back of my head and winced, then opened one of the kitchen drawers, looking for anything I could use as a weapon.

I settled on one of Mom's rolling pins, then, stifling a groan, retrieved the phone. I swiped across the screen to see why it had vibrated and found a random news alert.

Grimacing at my stupidity, I yanked open the basement door. When no household appliances or people accosted me, I went through, switched on the light, and made my way down, holding the rolling pin in front of me.

It didn't take long to determine there was no one in the basement. The crawlspace was as empty as ever, and the only place large enough to conceal even a terrier was behind the washer and dryer, but that held nothing larger than dust bunnies and a stray sock I missed in the cleanup.

I breathed a sigh of relief, then wondered if an intruder could have fled the basement for the front of the house when I had fallen, closing the door behind them. But no, I would have heard something. The door must have shifted somehow when I hit the wall or floor. I duck-walked my way back up the stairs and quickly went through the rest of the house. By the time I was finished, my adrenaline was fading, the pain was worse, I had broken a sweat, and every light and door was open in the house.

Aside from the open rolltop, there was no sign that anyone else had been there.

Morning found me with a throbbing headache, an ugly purplish bruise where I'd landed on the shovel, and a stiffness and soreness in my lower spine that made me wonder if I'd broken my tailbone. Three ibuprofen and a full breakfast made a small dent, and walking through the entire house again helped to loosen knotted muscles. The shovel had cracked, though, and a careful inspection of the rolltop in the light of day revealed nothing more than polished surfaces and empty drawers.

I closed it again and locked it this time. As I put on my jacket, planning to go to the hardware store and my apartment, the phone rang.

It was Allison Van Buren.

"Hello," I answered tentatively.

"Hey. Hope I'm not disturbing you. Is this a good time?" She sounded nervous, as if she half-expected me to hang up. I wondered how I would feel in her position, calling a murder suspect.

"Yeah, sure. Now's fine," I said, slipping my jacket back off and sitting gingerly on the couch. I hadn't called Allison as expected because I figured she would no longer be interested in the house or me after the previous week's events. "Sorry I didn't get back to you. Things have…."

Have what? I had no idea what to say next, but she relieved me of the need.

"It's okay. I saw the news," Allison said, and my heart dropped. "I can't imagine the week you're having. But listen, I know you couldn't hurt that guy, let alone kill him, okay?"

I nodded. Of course, she couldn't see it.

She continued. "Dave, the police talked to me. I'm pretty sure they know you didn't do anything wrong. He wasn't even injured. They think he drank until he passed out."

"I'm sorry, what?" I managed. The last I heard, Reynolds and Adams were convinced they were letting a murderer walk out the door.

"Yeah. They kept asking me if I had seen any empty alcohol bottles in the house when I visited. Or if you had talked about Ralph, or mentioned wanting to get rid of him, or said anything about knowing he's gone." It all came out in a rush. "I told them you hadn't, of course.

Told them you had agreed to rent me the place, so there was no way you could have known he was there."

I shifted on the couch, lying down to ease the pressure on my tailbone. "They really said that?"

"Yeah. They were pretty frustrated when they left."

"Who was it? From the police?"

"Oh, it was… a funny little guy with glasses… I've got his card… Blaine Reynolds," she said.

"Funny is one way of putting it, I guess."

She must have heard the bitterness in my voice. "I don't mean funny in a good way. He was rude. Acted like he'd caught me breaking a school rule or something."

"Yeah, that sounds right."

"You know him?"

"Uh-huh. Reynolds interrogated me too. But we didn't like each other long before that."

"Oh." She didn't seem to know what to do with that information, so she brushed past it. "He brought another deputy with him, Eric something. He didn't talk much."

"Tall guy, big mustache? Young?" I thought I remembered seeing him a time or two.

"Yeah, that sounds like him. Said he wasn't going to shave it all month. Some charity thing, I guess."

I'd heard of the fundraiser but couldn't remember its name. A lot of police officers were doing it. An image of Reynolds in a handlebar burst into my head, and I couldn't help myself; I laughed out loud.

"What? What's so funny?" she asked.

147

"Sorry... I was picturing that mustache on Reynolds," I said and explained what I could remember of the charity. Her laughter made my headache feel better.

"Anyway," she said, still giggling, "I wanted to tell you what happened, but I wasn't sure if I should do that. They didn't specifically say not to, but I figured they wouldn't be thrilled about it."

"Your secret's safe with me, and I appreciate it." I meant it. "As you might guess, they're not telling me a damn thing, and Chief Adams is making out like he's about to break down my door and arrest me anytime someone asks."

"I'm sorry you have to deal with this on top of everything else," Allison said. I sensed she had something to add, so I waited. "And... well, it seems silly to bother you with this now, but... I wanted to find out if the house is still available."

I gasped.

"I know, it's a bit weird, with the body and all, but it was outside, not inside, and I probably wasn't going to use the garage anyway, and... well, I'm not superstitious or anything," she trailed off. "I just thought, since I saw the tape was gone... if you'd still like to rent it, I'd like to take you up on it. I can't keep staying on my friend's couch, and Chase is getting really tired of the floor." She took a deep breath. "To be honest, I think they want me to move back home, but I just... I can't do that."

"I understand. I, uh... well, I haven't gotten the paperwork yet because I figured... well, it doesn't matter. I will. But look, if it's urgent, you can stay here tonight."

There was a brief pause, during which my words cycled back through my aching head.

"I mean, I'm at the house now, is all. I don't mean with me!" I blurted out. "Sorry, realized how that sounded."

She laughed weakly. "I knew what you meant... I was just..." I could almost hear her groping for words. "That would be great if we could move in, even temporarily," she finally managed. "Thank you so much."

"No problem," I said, glad she couldn't see my red face. "Come over any time. I was about to run some errands, but I can wait if you want to come over now."

"Actually... could we? That would be so awesome," she said. "I'll bring lunch."

CHAPTER TWENTY-FIVE

L unch was a sack of burgers and fries from Betty's Burger Barn. Like the last time we'd met, Chase stayed quiet initially, sitting at one end of the dining room table, focusing intently on his burger. Allison had bought me the meal she'd seen me with the day of the funeral—a double cheeseburger, fries, and a chocolate milkshake.

"I can't believe you remembered that," I said, probably for the third or fourth time. "I didn't even remember." I popped a fry in my mouth.

"Well, you had a lot on your mind, didn't you?" I found her smile somehow soothing.

"Yeah. Well, so did you," I said, and Allison nodded, smile fading. I held up my milkshake in a mock toast. "Here's to better memories."

She tapped her paper cup against mine. "And to happier days ahead," she added. Her gaze held mine for a moment. Chase slid his plate back.

"Right," I said, taking the cue and standing up to gather the paper plates. Most of the dishes were packed upstairs, but I had left paper plates and cups out for pizza or take-home meals. I thought Allison might have blushed but resolved not to find out, mainly since I was probably doing the same. She busied herself with wiping down the table where our plates and cups had left marks.

"So, how come you aren't moving in here?" It was the first thing Chase had said beyond "hello," and I wasn't remotely prepared to answer.

"Chase, that's rude," Allison said.

"No, it's okay," I cut in. "We, ah, have a no-BS policy, after all."

They both looked at me blankly, then Chase caught on and laughed. "Oh, yeah. We do, Mom. It's okay."

I smiled at Allison, who looked more perplexed than ever. "I guess he didn't tell you we chatted briefly at Betty's that day. You had gone into the ladies' room."

"No, he didn't." She looked from him back to me. "Sounds like you covered a lot."

"Just the important stuff," I said, hoping she wasn't too offended. "Life sucks, people spew BS, other people know it's BS, and that sucks too. Does that about cover it, Chase?"

He nodded enthusiastically, clearly happy to be part of a conversation that included a hint of profanity.

"As long as you don't talk about... BS," she said, attempting to be stern with Chase but unable to hide the wry grin.

"I promise." He sounded so sincere that I almost apologized for using that language with him, but then they both burst out laughing at some private joke.

"Well, I'm glad that's settled." I dumped the last of the paper cups and plates into the trash. "To answer your question, Chase. I guess it's because I still think of this as my mom's house, not mine. And I don't know that I would feel right, just yet, moving into her house. Does that make sense?"

"I guess so. I don't want to return to my dad's house, either."

I wondered how Allison reacted to that but kept my attention on the boy. "No, I don't suppose you do. So, this way, you can move into my mom's house, and it won't be strange for you."

He nodded. "Thanks. Where's my room?"

"Well, that's up to you two, but you are welcome to use my old bedroom if you like. Remember it?" I laughed.

"Yep. It looks out over the street. Thanks, Mr. Kendrick!" He turned and bolted for the stairs, eager to check it out.

"It's just Dave," I said to his back, but if he heard me, he gave no sign.

"You handled that well." Allison sat. "I'm sorry if he was too blunt."

"That's okay. Better than holding it in, I think." I sat across from her.

"He's done a lot of that."

"How's he holding up? And you?"

"I don't know. Sometimes, Chase seems fine, and others he's just quiet for hours. Thinking, I guess. I don't know," she said. "And I'm okay. I have to be. For him."

Her face was at odds with her words — something in her expression told me she wasn't okay.

"And what about you?" she asked before I could think of anything to say. "As if you didn't have enough going on, now this police business?"

"Keeps me from overthinking, I guess." I don't know why I said it because I had too much time alone with my thoughts. "I've been trying to figure out what happened and not getting very far."

She looked confused. "What, you mean the... guy out back?" I thought she'd been about to say "body."

"Well, that and what Mom was up to." Her confused look reminded me that I hadn't shared her text message or anything else with her. Or anyone else. "She texted me just before the crash, saying she had to see me that night. It sounded urgent. A short time later, the scanner went nuts, and it ended up being her in the crash. I still don't know what she wanted."

"Oh, my God," she breathed. "That would drive me insane. You don't have any clue?"

"Not really. And I don't know why she was even out on 98. She almost never goes out at night, and certainly not out of town. She doesn't like driving after dark. And all her friends are here in Lynwood."

I had been sitting with my hands folded in front of me on the table, and now she half-stood and leaned across it, putting her hand over mine.

"I hope you're not beating yourself up over not seeing her before the crash." Her eyes locked on mine.

Until that moment, I hadn't realized that was what I'd been doing. Logically, there was nothing I could have done, but some part of me wondered if things would have been different if I'd left the office and gone straight to meet Mom. Of course, given where she was driving, the odds were I wouldn't have found her even if I had tried.

But logic doesn't always assuage guilt, and I found myself squeezing Allison's hand.

"I don't know. I can't help but wonder if there was something else I could have done. I mean, I know there's not, but still." Her eyes told me she understood all too well, and I wondered if she was thinking about Luke.

"It's not your fault." Her voice sounded as much a plea as reassurance. "We can't always control things."

"No," I agreed. "We can't." I patted her hand once, and then she drew back to her seat.

I had no idea what to say next, and I could tell she didn't either. "Thanks for the tip on what the police were asking, by the way," I said. "I figured they might move on when they let me back in here so quickly, but it's good to know anyway."

"Well, they could still tell you that, I think," she said, her smile widening. "Better than leaving you in limbo."

"Ah, the chief's enjoying that too much to let it drop this soon." She looked curious, so I went on. "He's never forgiven me for the accident I had right after high school. He doesn't believe somebody else ran me off the road."

"Oh. Right. Is… is that what happened, then? I never heard much about it."

"I'm not surprised. The police didn't believe me, so the newspaper never reported it. People tended to write it off as an arrogant, drunk kid." I shrugged. "I wasn't drunk, but I was stupid enough to drink, and I was arrogant. Can't blame them, really."

"You weren't arrogant."

"I was. I thought I would get out of town, play ball for a living, make millions of dollars, and never see Lynwood again. It never occurred to me that I might not make the majors, let alone that I might not even end up signing a contract."

"Well, you were good. I mean, I'm no talent scout or anything, but you were far better than anyone else around here. And obviously, they thought you were good too. Tenth round out of high school's great!"

"Thanks." I felt a little thrill as I realized she remembered when I had been drafted. I told her what happened the night of the accident, blurting it out in a rush. Finally, I stopped to take a deep breath.

"And, of course, Erin was Chief Adams' daughter," Allison said.

"He ended up at the crash scene, I heard later. As far as he's concerned, I should have been killed too." I shrugged. "Maybe he's right, I don't know. But he never believed me about a second car."

Chase picked that moment to pound down the stairs. "Mom, can we bring my books? There's not a lot of room on the shelves, but I can put some there."

"We have plenty of time to work that out, Chase. Don't worry, okay?" Allison said.

"What are you guys talking about?" Chase sat down.

"Old times." I laughed. I couldn't believe I'd told her everything. I hadn't talked about the night of the crash in so long; it almost felt like I was revealing it for the first time.

"Oh. Wait, did you used to know each other?" Chase asked.

Allison and I looked at each other. This time, we both laughed hard.

CHAPTER TWENTY-SIX

I spent the next hour helping Allison and Chase haul the things they'd had jammed in their trunk into the house and showing Allison all the property's quirks—including the step down before the back door. And she, in turn, helped me haul the folders and a few other important items out to my car.

"You have no idea how much it helps to have the place already furnished. I mean, we have furniture, but I haven't decided how much of it I want to keep." Allison sat on the living room floor, hooking up a Wii video game system for Chase. She'd taken care to point out that it did not have a bunch of online shooting games.

"It's no problem," I said. "You'll have to forgive Mom's old-lady tastes though."

She concentrated on which wires to plug in where for a minute. Then she said, "I wonder if I can ask a favor. I know I have no right, but..."

"I'm happy to help," I said.

"The thing is, I haven't been back to the house since I grabbed some stuff a couple of days after." She shot a glance at her son. Chase was sitting on the couch with a book, but I wasn't convinced he was reading. Then she continued, "I don't want to go alone."

"Sure. Of course. But I'm surprised you didn't get one of your friends to go before now."

"Most of my friends were Luke's. Even Lisa and Pedro—Pedro worked with Luke for a bit." Allison shrugged. "They've been so kind—but they treat me like I'm going to break or something."

"They think we're already broken," Chase said. "They want to put us back together."

"Yeah," Allison wrung her hands. "I couldn't face going to the house with them either. And I don't want to make Chase go back."

I glanced at Chase, but he didn't look up—it was as if he hadn't spoken moments earlier.

"Well, yeah, I'd be happy to come along," I said. "Happy" didn't really describe it, of course. I suddenly envisioned a suburban little house with a flat-screen TV, couch, two recliners, and a body on the floor, blood sprayed everywhere. I was sure the place had been cleaned, but the image persisted.

"Thank you." She went back to plugging in wires. "There, that should do it." Her voice was a bit too loud. "Want to try it, Chase?"

"Maybe later," he said. "I'm reading."

I felt like I was intruding, but I didn't want to leave. Despite the circumstances, it was the most normal I felt since before Mom's crash, and I didn't want it to end. Still, I thought it would be best to let Allison and Chase settle into their new surroundings in private.

Leaving Chase to his book, I led Allison back into the kitchen. "So, I'll work on getting a lease together in the next few days," I said. "I'm not worried about it, but just so you know. I also hope the police don't decide they need another look around."

"I'm sure they won't," she said.

"And here's a key to the rolltop desk. It's empty, and you're welcome to use it. I've been keeping it locked out of habit, and it sometimes falls closed when you leave it open." I'd rehearsed this in my head several times and settled on this line, even though there was no reason a falling top should require the thing to be locked as well as kept closed.

"One last thing—I moved the trash cans. They're right behind the house now, so there's no reason you or Chase have to go behind the garage."

"Oh. Right. Oh…," Allison said. "Is that where…."

"Can't even see it from the house," I assured her. "The only place he could have been and not be noticed."

"I didn't want to ask, but that's good to know."

"And… just let me know when you want to go to the house, okay? I… well, my schedule's pretty open. I'm on leave from the paper." Somehow, that hadn't come up until just now.

"You're kidding." Her face reddened. "Those bastards."

I found her anger gratifying somehow. "I was a distraction. And they're paying me until I come back, so I'll be okay."

"At least there's that." She looked at her phone. "I have Friday off. Would that work?"

"Sure."

"Thanks." She looked over her shoulder toward the dining room. "Do you want to come for Thanksgiving? I'll invite Pedro and Lisa since they've been a huge help, but I would also love to repay you."

It hadn't even occurred to me that the holiday was just a few days away. Mom always had me over for dinner, along with some of her former school colleagues, and they then played board games while I disappeared to Rusty's to watch football.

"I'd like that," I said before overthinking it. "Thank you."

After my escapades the night before, and the pleasant interlude with Allison and Chase, my research into Mom's whereabouts felt much farther away than less than a day.

On the short drive from Pine Street to my apartment on Hanover Street, I turned over my options on how to figure out what she had been up to. I wondered if she had used the map feature on her phone or if it contained any interesting texts. I also wondered about the search history on her computer. Her laptop rested next to me on top of a box of stuff I had taken from the locked room upstairs. I hadn't yet turned it on, having used my laptop to take care of the messy business of the ending of one's online public life.

I mulled over a stop at the grocery store but decided I was unwilling to face the stares of other shoppers. It would be pizza delivery again, but I worried how long it would take for such a diet to push me from a bit overweight to obese.

After dialing for delivery, I set the folders from the house, the box of mom's things, her laptop, and my laptop on one end of the coffee table.

Mom's phone was dead, so I plugged it in. Other random bits recovered from her wreck were also in the box—the car's owner's manual and insurance paperwork, an ice scraper, jumper cables, a handful of change, and a little bag of mints. She never ate the candies herself, but she'd offer her former students a mint. There was also a little notebook she used to track mileage. It was something Dad taught her, and she never dropped the habit, though she paid no attention to the results. I flipped through the notebook, hoping she had written something else, but it was just numbers. She also had a binder full of CDs. I skimmed these, didn't see anything unusual, and set it aside.

Mom never dated after Dad went missing. I asked her why once, and she said it was because, deep down, she hoped he would return one day. She knew it wouldn't happen, but she couldn't let herself give up.

I stared at the box for a long moment, then, with a sudden movement one might use to rip off an overlarge band-aid, I reached in and pulled out Mom's purse.

Mom had quilted the bag years ago, along with a few dozen others she sold at school sales. A few were still seen around Lynwood, but this bag was the original. Mom said she made mistakes on it and didn't feel right selling it. I had no idea what the mistakes were. It was blue fabric adorned with purple-and-red roses, the occasional green vine poking through. The crash had ruined it, of course. Mom's blood stained one side a dark red, so the blue and purple bits were nearly black. I shuddered and turned that side away.

I opened the bag and studiously ignored the faint, coppery smell while removing the contents.

For the size of the bag, it held surprisingly little. I found a hairbrush, a few tubes of lipstick, two more notebooks, a small canister of deodorant, and several pens. A bag of cough drops was wedged into one side pocket and a little packet of tissues in another. I found about two dollars in change and a small wallet that held her driver's license, credit cards, insurance and registration, and half a dozen photos, most of them of me. One was a familiar photo of her and my dad, taken just months before he disappeared. I had a copy in my wallet as well.

Finally, I found a little folder that looked promising, but it only contained coupons from various local supermarkets. I thumbed through everything, tossing them in the recycling bin.

I went to the notebook next. The first one contained random items — things Mom didn't want to forget. There was a grocery list — one pound chicken, two tomatoes, romaine lettuce — and phone numbers for the water department and the library. Flipping through, it felt like watching a slide show of the humdrum of Mom's daily life —

enough to be reminiscent of something but too little to trace any story from it.

I set that aside and picked up the second notebook.

CHAPTER TWENTY-SEVEN

T his notebook was old. It was a spiral-bound job whose darkened coils should have clued me to its age before I opened it. The handwriting was unfamiliar, and the notes seemed as random as in the first, but with less day-to-day stuff. This one had names and dates, streets, and strings of numbers that meant little to me. Some of them seemed familiar, but I couldn't remember the context in which I knew them.

It wasn't until I came across "Tom Walther" that the last names jumped out at me. Covering high school athletics, I had run across several surnames that permeated Lynwood after multiple generations had distributed siblings, cousins, and more throughout town. I found a Linscott and wondered if the man was related to Karen Linscott in advertising. I found "Calvin Thompson '66, Vol 143-78" and thought of my lawyer, Ronnie Thompson. I even found a "Walt Quinlan," but the date after the name was 1947, so there was no way it could be my editor. Perhaps my boss was a junior or a third or something. There was a Heyward, too—Obie Heyward. I found Barlows, Van Burens, and Figgins. Even Reynolds made an appearance.

I also found Kendricks: Josiah and Elizabeth, Levi and Elizabeth. I had no idea who they were. On the next-to-last page, I discovered names I did know—George and Josie Kendrick. They were my grandparents, though they died before I was born. I wondered where the others fit on the family tree, assuming they did at all.

The dates ranged back decades into the 1800s. The oldest were from the late 1860s, just after the Civil War.

Everything was written in black ink on paper that faded to yellow. But a few entries were underlined. The entries for "Eula Banks 4/17/83" and "Jimmy Nelson 12/20/82" were underlined in purple ink, like Mom used when grading papers, and "LP" was written in the margin. Walther's name, too, had been underlined, but no date was referenced. Below that, "Dalton?" and "Bruce?" were written in black ink, with the purple underline. George and Josie Kendrick were also marked. "LP" was written in purple on each of those pages, once per page.

I couldn't remember running across any Daltons or Bruces other than former or current NFL players, but Walther, of course, was quite familiar. And there were a couple of teenagers named Banks on the Lynwood football team. Jimmy Nelson's name rang a bell, but I couldn't place it. For that matter, two-thirds of the last names rang a bell, yet most of the full names were unfamiliar, like some of the Kendricks.

After the black ink stopped, the following pages were written in purple, and this time, it was Mom's handwriting. It looked fairly new as her writing had picked up a slight quaver in recent years, and this looked like it had that.

The first entry sent a chill down my spine. "Robert Kendrick, 10/12/94-3452" was written at the top. It was the date Dad had gone missing and was declared dead. Below that, "Victor Bruce, 10/16/83-3528" was added in with an asterisk. I had no idea what the last four digits were.

On the next page, Mom had written a short note.

"Bob, why didn't you put more in writing? I want to help you. I want to finish your work. But I need more. I need help. Please. I know you were trying to set things right somehow. I know you felt you couldn't tell me what you were doing, and I am trying so hard to forgive you." Her writing grew even more shaky as it went on. "I know you would tell me if you could. I'm scared. I'm scared for David. Why couldn't you tell me what was going on???"

If the raw emotion of the words wasn't enough, I saw two spots that likely marked where her tears had fallen on the page.

It was almost too much to process. I realized the previous pages must have been written by my father. I turned back to the beginning, ignoring the words but tracing the letters with my fingers. Small, blocky letters, made with short strokes, but pressed deep onto the page. So, this was how my father had written. Short, minimalist, with purpose, much different from Mom's flowing style. I thought of the few woodcarvings I saw him do and realized it was the same approach.

I couldn't keep tears from my eyes as I thumbed through it again, from the beginning back to Mom's note. I could hardly make out the words through misted eyes, but when I turned to the next page, they were more legible because they were larger.

Two words were written in my father's handwriting: "CALL DALTON." Both words were underlined. I wiped my eyes and turned the page again, but there was no additional writing in the notebook. I flipped back to the last page.

It had clearly been important to Dad to call Mr. Dalton, but he was apparently too familiar with him to bother writing down his first name. I stared at the message, wondering why Dad had left pages blank for Mom to fill in.

And then it hit me. The letters were not only underlined with purple ink. The letters were also written in purple ink.

I jumped from the couch as if it had bitten me. My breath caught in my throat, and I tried to back away from the coffee table and tripped, landing back on the couch. My eyes never left the page, with those big, blocky, bold purple letters staring at me.

I couldn't summon a coherent thought. Had Mom, feeling whimsical, decided to emulate Dad's handwriting? Had she shared the notebook with someone else who wrote the same way? Had my father somehow written the message from beyond the grave?

And who in the hell was Dalton?

The questions clattered around my brain like bingo balls waiting to be plucked and read out loud. I tore my gaze from the page and checked the cluttered mess of the table, seeking some clue that would make sense, but nothing did. And suddenly, the apartment felt very, very empty.

I needed to be around people. Without another glance at the notebook, the bloody purse, or anything else, I picked up my coat and car keys and left the apartment.

I called Tim and invited him to meet me at Lucky's, which billed itself as an Irish pub, but aside from a few Champions League banners scattered around and an endless supply of Guinness, was as American as any sports bar I've been to.

Arriving first, I snagged a seat at the bar, ordered a beer, and tried to calm my nerves by working out who "Dalton" was. It appeared that someone, not my mother, had written those words and had done it recently—certainly not thirty years ago when my dad disappeared.

It was a message meant for Mom, and the messenger—I refused to let myself contemplate who that was—must have thought she would know who Dalton was because there was no phone number. The name appeared earlier in the notebook—whoever it was had been around when Dad made his bizarre notes.

I tried to think of anyone in town by that name, mentally scanning rosters of area sports teams going back years, trying to place it, but nothing came to me. Rusty might know, or even Walt, but I wasn't ready to go to them.

"Where's mine?" Tim clapped my shoulder and sat next to me, and I waved to the bartender to bring him one. She complied without asking what he wanted. She'd played this game with us more than a few times.

"Surprised you called, with what's going on right now." He took a healthy swig.

"Surprised you answered, to be honest." In my haste to be around someone, it hadn't occurred to me that hanging out with a cop while under suspicion for Walther's death might not have been the smartest idea. But it was Tim, and for now, I thought I could trust him. He knew I wasn't a murderer.

At least, I fervently hoped so.

"No worries. It's off the clock. Just don't mention you-know-who, and we'll be fine." Tim took another drink, then asked, "What's going on? You sounded funny on the phone."

"Did I?"

He lifted an eyebrow.

"I just found something a bit weird, is all," I said.

"At the house?"

"What? Oh, no, no. Not there." I took a deep breath. "I've been going through Mom's things, trying to figure out why she was trying to reach me the night she... crashed."

"Right." He waved for the bartender.

I glanced down, surprised to see I had drained my first beer. "Anyway, I found this journal with lots of random items in it. I think it was my father's, but Mom's handwriting is there too. And, in the back, one of Mom's notes said, 'Call Dalton.' But I have no idea who that is."

"Hmm." He frowned. "I don't think I know anyone by that name."

"Me either."

"And that made you call me?"

"No, I... I don't know. I just suddenly needed to not be there? Needed to get out." I gave a nervous laugh.

"Ah."

The beers came—he still had half of one—and I studied a couple playing pool on the ornate table in the corner. Lucky's Bar, of course, was in one of Jethro Miller's books, with a legend of a ghost who was sometimes seen playing pool. The ghost was supposedly a former mayor of the city who had been shot to death, though the book glossed over the fact that he hadn't been killed there.

With a start, I recognized the man at the pool table—it was Mike Elliott, husband of the missing Robin Elliott. And his companion, a tall brunette in red leggings and a rather fetching blouse, drank and laughed. She swatted his hand playfully off her beer, and he got closer than necessary to help her line up a shot. She looked familiar, but I couldn't place her.

Tim followed my gaze. "Friends of yours?"

"That's Mike Elliott," I said. "And some woman who seems awfully friendly with him."

"That is interesting." Tim straightened his spine. "Doesn't seem to be missing his wife too much."

"Not really."

I tried not to stare but couldn't help myself. When Elliott turned toward the bar, I quickly shifted my eyes back to Tim.

"Great. I think I got caught watching him."

Before Tim could respond, Elliott came around the bar and right up to me.

"First, you show up at my house—now you follow me to the bar?"

"I came here on my own. Had no idea you were here."

"I've heard about you reporters. Can't leave people alone." He leaned into my personal space.

"We're just here for a drink, friend," Tim said in his best diffuse-the-situation voice. Elliott ignored him.

"I don't know what your game is, but you'd better stay away from me, you hear?" Spittle flew.

"Look, I went to your house to ask if you wanted to talk to us. You said no—we left—end of story. Us being in the same place is just a coincidence."

"Sure, it is." He moved closer.

"Man, what's your problem with me?" I leaned away from him.

"I just don't want some reporter bugging me, bringing cameras to my house. None of your damn business."

"We get it," said Tim. "Why don't you go back to your lady and your game, okay? Next round's on me."

Elliott glared at Tim. "Just keep him away from me. No more questions."

"None," Tim agreed, and Elliott stormed to the other end of the bar.

"What the hell was that about?" Tim asked.

I shrugged. "We went to Elliott's house a few days after Felicia Erickson went missing. Something he said got me thinking about the missing people, and since Elliott's wife disappeared, Sam and I thought we'd interview him."

"And?"

"He slammed the door in my face when we mentioned we were writing about the missing people. Told us to go away."

"That's it?"

"Yep." I shrugged. "I sure as hell didn't harass him and had no idea he would be here."

"Was she with him?" He nodded toward the woman with Elliott.

"He didn't invite us in." I shrugged again. "Maybe he just doesn't like media?"

"I guess not." He gestured over his shoulder — Elliott and the brunette were donning jackets, heading for the door.

CHAPTER TWENTY-EIGHT

We had a couple more beers before I felt like I could face my apartment again. It was barely dusk when I got home, and that night, I once again found myself on my couch, in a room dark but for the TV screen. It was just on for background noise.

A bottle of rum sat on the coffee table, along with a two-liter plastic jug of soda. I grabbed the rum out of habit, though I had strongly considered opening the bottle of Fontana's Finest that Ezekiel Heyward had left for me. In any event, the glass contained only soda and melting ice.

I flipped through channels, bypassing an X-Files rerun and finally settling on a Frasier marathon. I loved that show, but tonight, I wasn't focused.

Once again, my thoughts were scattered. When had Mom written in the notebook—had she done it when Dad was still alive? That made more sense. The purple ink looked newer, but that didn't mean it was. When had purple ink been invented? I groaned—I didn't want to know. And what about the quaver in Mom's handwriting that had only developed in the past couple of years? Maybe the tremor was caused by emotion—when she was upset, she wrote in the journal.

Yeah, that was it.

Except I knew it wasn't.

I wondered again what had happened to Ralph Walther and if he was related to Tom Walther. And those others—the ones with familiar last names but unfamiliar first names—everything was jumbled like puzzle pieces in a box. Where were the missing people—Robin Elliott,

Steve Cervelli, Felicia Erickson, and Dexter Lewis? Was Keith Erickson right about them all being connected? And had Mike Elliott killed and hidden them, starting with his wife?

I rubbed my face, feeling a wave of exhaustion—caffeine and the droning TV were no match for it.

The problem with sleeping on the couch was that it was not meant to be an all-night affair. It was comfortable enough for a few hours. But then I woke up, convinced I could find a sweet spot, and tossed and turned until five, when I admitted I was licked and went to bed.

It was the same cycle night after night. This time, as I tossed and turned, half-remembered dreams plagued me. I played basketball in one of them, dribbling back and forth, stopping, and shooting three-pointers. Sometimes, I made them, but more often, I missed. Birds swarmed, which the fans didn't seem to mind, and at some point, I went to the bench and accepted one of Betty's burgers, served on a phone book by a pink-haired girl with eyes as dead as Ralph Walther's. The birds were there for her, but I just said thanks, took a bite of the burger, and grabbed the ball.

When I dragged myself into the bedroom, I couldn't sleep. I missed something important but had no idea what it was. I finally gave up at eight, showered, threw my bat and batting gloves into the trunk, and drove to a Columbus sports complex. Perhaps getting out of Lynwood for a while would clear my head.

Few things are as therapeutic as time in a batting cage. Growing up, it was the only place I could tune out missing my father and the loneliness of my mother. Dad showed me how to hit a ball, and I decided I would keep at it because it made him happy when I succeeded.

And in a batting cage or a game, the intense concentration necessary to hit the ball, or field one, required me to block everything else out.

I took turns in the cage for an hour, then two, until my hands felt rawer than my bruised tailbone. In between turns, I made notes on my phone. I decided to look up Victor Bruce, Tom Walther, and the other names from Dad's notebook. I would also look up the other Kendrick names to see if I could track them. Mom had never mentioned Dad having siblings, but perhaps they stopped talking to each other.

I drove back to Lynwood via Route 98. As I approached the site of my crash first and then my mother's, I slowed. I had no idea what I was looking for or if I was even looking for anything — I just felt it was key to take it all in.

There was a little cross by the side of the road where I had crashed. I didn't stop but slowed enough to be able to read "Erin," printed in pink letters. After the crash, her family had installed a cross to mark the place where she died, but it had long since fallen over, replaced by the occasional flower. Someone had put up a new one.

I half-expected to see another where Mom died, but there was nothing — just an open stretch of road, curving to the left, with trees on the right, one of which bore the scars of the collision. I thought I saw a gouge in the dirt, but I drove by before getting a clear look. I resisted the urge to stop.

I spent the next few days looking up the names in Dad's diary but had no luck. None of them appeared to still live in Lynwood, nor did any people on various social media websites seem to have any connections to them.

The one exception was Jimmy Nelson. He didn't live in Lynwood anymore, but I found a website about him. Jethro Miller had mentioned

Jimmy when I interviewed him about his new book—I hadn't made the connection then, but now I remembered.

Jimmy Nelson lived down the street when I was a kid, still in kindergarten. He was a year older than me and a bit of a bully, but I played with him because there weren't many kids around. One day, he was dropped off by the school bus and never made it home.

I attended morning classes, so I wasn't on the same bus, but it was my bus all the same, so Mom freaked out. The disappearance made the paper's morning and midday runs, and the town went crazy trying to find him. A few days later, his body turned up in a field at the end of the street. I remembered some confusion because they previously checked there and hadn't found him.

The website that mentioned him was for a foundation dedicated to raising awareness of unsolved crimes involving children. It hadn't been updated in years, and a search on the secretary of state's website revealed that the non-profit ceased functioning six years ago. Still, Jimmy's picture smiled at me, and I couldn't imagine why I hadn't placed the name.

More digging revealed that Jimmy's parents, Stan and Lorraine, divorced. Stan moved to Cleveland, and his obituary hinted he had come to an unexpected end in 2008. Lorraine remarried—she was Lorraine Calcaterri now, a Fort Lauderdale, Florida, resident with two grown children. It appeared she had created the website and left it floating in cyberspace, apparently forgotten.

On Wednesday, I called Allison to find out what I could bring to Thanksgiving dinner. She asked me to pick up pies, as the ones she made burned.

"I hope you don't mind eating a bit late," she said. "Lisa and Pedro are going to Lisa's mom's, so it's just us. And Pastor Francis told me he was looking for volunteers for the homeless feast, so I said we'd go there at noon. You're welcome to join us if you like."

"I can do that," I heard myself saying.

"Great. Can we pick you up?"

"Sure." I tried to remember the last time I'd been a passenger in someone else's car. "You know where I live? Apartments on Hanover?"

"We'll be there at about quarter to twelve."

CHAPTER TWENTY-NINE

T hanksgiving morning dawned gray and cold enough for snow, though none was falling when I finally dared look outside. For the first time in what seemed like weeks, I slept soundly and for close to ten hours. I switched on the Macy's Thanksgiving Day Parade and did sit-ups and push-ups—a habit I'd been neglecting—before grabbing a shower and light breakfast.

It wasn't even eleven, so I settled in to watch the inane chatter on TV. Half an hour later it dawned on me that Allison might come up to get me, and I pictured her seeing the mess that was my apartment.

I then spent the next fifteen minutes hurriedly putting things away, particularly Mom's handbag, which I had left on my little dining room table. When my phone buzzed, letting me know she was downstairs, I had worked up a sweat equivalent to what I had done with my little workout.

I texted I'd be right down and then spent a minute catching my breath. On some level, I think I knew I was being stupid, but I couldn't shake the fact that I was nervous. This was a holiday, and there's no way it qualified as a date.

Did it?

I let that rattle around a bit as I clambered downstairs. Fortunately, I remembered the pies before heading outside and ran back upstairs to get them.

Allison's passenger seat was vacant, and Chase sat in the back. He waved as I approached, and I nodded before opening the door.

"Good morning! Cold enough for you?" I asked as I wedged myself carefully into the front and positioned the two pies between my feet.

"Oh, slide that back, David. I forgot how tall you are," Allison said, blushing. I found the release and adjusted the seat. It didn't help much.

"Mom said it's supposed to warm up later. Isn't that cool?" Chase said.

"Really? I haven't checked the weather report."

We bantered about the weather and the parade for the ten minutes it took to get to First Nazarene, where the homeless meal was being held. It was probably the happiest I'd seen the two of them, and it was wonderful to see.

"I hope you don't mind this last-minute change of plans." Allison switched off the engine.

"It's all right. Mom used to do this years ago," I told her. "I never went, though she sometimes asked me to. Seems like it's time."

The three of us walked in the side door and descended the stairs. Immediately below the sanctuary was a large hall for coffee hours after church and other community gatherings.

If it was a date, it wasn't like any I'd ever had. Pastor Francis assigned jobs — me restocking the food line, Allison in the kitchen, and Chase as errand boy — before I knew it, it was almost three o'clock, and we were cleaning up. We'd barely spoken the whole time.

———————

I carried the leftover turkey from the church, and as soon as Allison opened the door, warm spices surrounded me. "What's that smell?"

She laughed. "Ginger cookies. I made a batch before we left this morning. If you promise not to fill up on them, you can have a few before dinner."

I picked one up, bit into it, and chewed. "I may have a new favorite cookie."

"Why don't you and Chase go into the dining room and play a game while I get everything ready?" She pulled containers from the fridge—mashed potatoes, stuffing, corn, baked beans, and cranberry sauce.

I offered to help, but Allison insisted she knew how to reheat dinner, so I sat at the big dining room table playing double solitaire with Chase. Either he was very good, or I wasn't.

"Remind me to bring a chessboard next time," I told him after losing my third game in a row.

"I don't know how to play. But I'm pretty good at checkers." He smiled.

"No lie," Allison called from the kitchen. "He's got a real talent for games."

"So, I see." I laid the template for another game. "Maybe I should leave the chessboard at home, then."

"Unless you want to teach me." Chase looked up. "Mom doesn't know how to play, and none of my friends at school do either." He shrugged. "Or maybe they just don't want to play with me."

"Are you a sore loser or something?"

He rolled his eyes. "I don't lose. Ready?"

He thrashed me again.

"Sure I can't help?" I called out, smiling so Chase would know I was joking.

"Just about ready. Chase, would you set the table, please?"

Thankful for my solitaire reprieve, I headed to the kitchen to bring things to the table.

"Are you getting settled okay?" I asked. I'd been dreading the answer all week—I hoped the rolltop desk had been behaving itself.

"It's a big house, but still kind of cozy." Allison set a steaming bowl of mashed potatoes on a wicker hot pad. "Still getting used to all the old-house noises, but other than that, it's been great."

"Oh, yeah?" I set the plate of turkey, freshly heated from the oven, onto the table. "Anything in particular? The noises, I mean?"

"You know. The furnace kicking on, pipes banging, that sort of thing." We brought another round of dishes in, and I wondered how we would eat it all. "Actually, I wondered if you knew if there's anything loose outside the house. We've heard this rattle-bang now and then and can't figure out what it is."

"I told you, Mom, it's the desk." Chase was already sitting down, having set the table as fast as he played cards. "It opens at night."

Allison faltered, looking nervously at him, then me. "Chase, it's not the desk. Desks don't open by themselves."

"This one does." Chase didn't look particularly concerned. "Remember, I found it open that one time? When it was supposed to be locked?"

"I thought you opened it."

"You mean you hoped I did. But I didn't." Without waiting for permission, Chase speared a thick slice of turkey and dropped it on his plate. "It's okay. It's just a desk."

I watched him closely, but he didn't appear to be joking. "So, you're okay with a desk opening by itself in your house?"

"If that's all it does, sure. Maybe we have a ghost that likes to do homework. Maybe I should leave mine on the desk next time!" It came out in a rush as if he'd just thought of this brilliant idea.

"Yeah, right," Allison drawled, starting to heap her plate. "It does sound sort of similar," she said to me. "But I just can't believe the desk opens and closes by itself. It never happens when we're able to see it."

"Well, no. That would be scary." I grinned and hoped it sounded like a joke. "Honestly, I can't think of anything that would be loose. I can call Mom's old handyman, though, see if he can come take a look."

"I'd be happy to pay him," Allison said. "I wouldn't ask but it's woken me up a couple of times. That and the pipes."

I'd never heard the pipes banging before. "When did that start?" I asked.

"It's just every now and then. At least, I assume that's what it is."

I looked at Chase, but he didn't have a theory this time — at least not one worth telling around a mouthful of food.

I insisted on doing the dishes, then joined Allison and Chase, who watched football in the living room.

"Who's winning?" I sat in Mom's old recliner.

"The Lions. They're decent for a change."

We watched for a bit, all three of us taking turns on commentary — they both knew football well. It felt surreal. I watched football in this room on Thanksgiving for most of my life, but never with anyone but Mom and Dad before he disappeared. Sitting here with Allison, of all people, and her son, but not with Mom, left me with a mix of emotions that I didn't particularly want to pick through.

"You okay, Dave? You're quiet."

"Yeah, sorry. Just thinking. So, who's your team?"

"Steelers fans." She smiled. "Luke and I used to go to a couple of games a year. What about you?"

"Browns. If they were ever good, I'd be insufferable." I grinned, then fell silent.

"Sure you're okay?" she asked.

"It's just… it's different, watching games on Thanksgiving without Mom."

"Oh. Oh, Dave, I didn't even think of that—"

"It's fine. It's okay. I'm glad you invited me."

She nodded, then reached across the couch and took my hand, squeezing it.

"We're facing it, too, just differently."

"Yeah. No, I know, of course." I patted her hand and then let go, noticing Chase's gaze on our clasped hands. "It's good to be around someone who understands."

I stayed through the end of the first game and the second. We played cards and board games, half watching the screen. By the look on Chase's face, I could tell he was feeling a bit melancholy but didn't want to talk about it. I could relate.

When it was time for him to go to bed, I grabbed my jacket, but Allison asked me to wait. She came down twenty minutes later, and her eyes were red and puffy.

"Are you all right?" I asked.

"We were talking about Luke," she said. I didn't know what to say, so I hugged her. She was soon crying against my chest, and I held her for several minutes as she sobbed. Finally, she caught her breath and stepped back.

"Sorry." She sniffled and wiped her wet cheeks. "Didn't mean to lose control like that."

"It's okay. We all do it, don't we—lose control every once in a while."

"Yes, but you're... you know, you have your stuff going on. You don't need me crying on your shoulder."

"It's a bit refreshing to think about someone else for a while," I joked, and she snorted. "But seriously, I'm always happy to help you. I hope you know that."

She looked at me appraisingly for a moment, a look I remember her giving me once in high school when I asked her to the prom—only that time, it was without tears.

"Yes, I do," she finally said as she grabbed a tissue from the box on the end table. "You're right about facing things. And I think I need to too. Would you mind going to the house with me on Saturday instead? I've decided I don't want to go on 'Black Friday.'" She accentuated the phrase with air quotes. "It's time for me to move on. Get the things I need, put the house up for sale, and figure out my options. I can't do that with the house hanging over my head."

"Of course."

"Great. C'mon, let's watch a movie."

CHAPTER THIRTY

Friday morning marked the happiest I'd been to start a day in months. One movie had become two movies and an hour of chatting on the couch before I finally left Allison's. The whole time with her felt completely natural, like we'd been hanging out our entire life, and the only thing that stopped me from kissing her goodnight — besides fear of screwing things up — was knowing that she buried her husband not that long ago.

But maybe someday. Maybe someday soon.

I caught myself whistling while I scrambled eggs and laughed at myself.

"You're being ridiculous," I said to the room, which was, apart from me, empty. "Allison was your unrequited high school crush, and now you're trying to change history, but it's been a long time, and a lot has happened."

My attempt to temper my expectations wasn't having any impact. I took breakfast to my little table, pulled my laptop toward me, and opened a browser.

The *Lynwood Post* was still my homepage, and the top headline knocked my good mood out more effectively than any amount of talking to myself.

"Teen goes missing on Thanksgiving Day." The headline read, and I clicked on it. "High school junior fails to return from run." I scrolled.

"Brandon Kick, 16, left his house a few minutes after noon for a run. He was the top performer on the cross-country team at Lynwood High

School. He left the house to get a few miles in before Thanksgiving dinner but never returned. Police had searched his usual route but found no sign of him."

"Unbelievable." I scrolled up and stared at Brandon's picture. He was a lanky, sandy-haired kid with light freckles. I interviewed him before the season started, and he'd been the type of kid who predicted he'd win every race, but it wasn't arrogance. He was good, and he knew it. I'd been the same way at his age when talking baseball.

The paper's feed was displayed on the right, and the latest update was from Jenny—it brought my second jolt of the morning.

"A body was found in a field just north of town early this morning. Police were looking for the missing teen but said this was not him. #LynwoodNews."

I opened social media and pulled up the list of *Post* employees to see if anyone else had anything more recent, but Jenny's was the only update of the morning. While I watched, another came through: "Police won't say if the body is that of any of those who went missing in recent weeks. #LynwoodNews."

This time, Jenny included a link to a picture. The field was the one north of Lynwood Elementary School, where I had watched Blaine Reynolds and his cronies pick up a cell phone while looking for the missing teacher, Felicia Erickson. I felt sick to my stomach. What is happening in this town? I closed the computer and pushed aside the rest of my breakfast.

Footsteps approached my door, and I jumped when someone knocked. I was halfway there when I realized who was probably waiting.

I opened it anyway.

"Good morning, Mr. Kendrick. May we have a word?"

For the first time, I thought Blaine Reynolds looked tired. His wire-rimmed glasses still pinched his prim little nose, but his eyes were bloodshot, and his cheeks were paler than usual. The officer with him looked even worse—unshaven, with bags under his eyes.

"I suppose." I stepped back. "Come in."

Reynolds entered and gestured for the other officer—Franklin, his name tag read—to close the door after him. They stood just inside.

"I suppose you know why we're here," Reynolds said.

"You wanted to apologize for being rude the last time we spoke?" I knew I shouldn't antagonize him, but I couldn't help myself. "Or maybe to clean up the mess you left last time?"

"I need to know where you were between noon and two in the afternoon yesterday, Thanksgiving Day." He looked around and sniffed. "Let me guess. Here, by yourself, eating turkey, drinking beer, and watching football."

I laughed. "Actually, no. I wasn't here."

"Then where were you? Please be precise." Reynolds pulled a notebook from his pocket and made a show of clicking his pen.

"I hope you have other suspects." I shook my head. "I was at First Nazarene Church. I arrived shortly before noon and left right around three. And to answer your next question, yes, I have witnesses. Probably three hundred of them. I worked the Thanksgiving dinner for the homeless and needy."

Reynolds made his neat little note and then jammed his notebook into his pocket.

"You weren't anywhere on the north side of town?" he asked.

"First Nazarene is downtown."

"What was your relationship with Robin Elliott?"

That threw me. "I'm sorry, what?"

"Robin Elliott. How did you know her?"

"I don't. Why…" Then it dawned on me. "The woman who went missing. The first one. Is that who you found in the field?"

"Never mind that. How do you know Ms. Elliott?"

"I don't know her. As far as I know, I've never met her."

He pulled his notebook out again and wrote, "denies knowing victim."

He finished and looked up at me, waiting for me to elaborate. I knew his game and let him wait. Despite the gravity of the situation, it was almost fun to see him so frustrated.

"Very well, Mr. Kendrick. We will check your alibi, of course."

"Of course."

The two of them walked toward the door.

"Sergeant Reynolds?"

He looked over his shoulder.

"Look, I know you guys are working your tails off. The *Post* says it's the same field where you were looking for Felicia Erickson. If it's not her, I hope you can tell her husband soon. I'm sure he's a wreck right now."

He looked appraisingly at me for a moment. "Someone's already on their way to his house."

"Thank you."

The two left without another word.

I cleaned up the remains of my breakfast, channel-surfed for a few minutes, then picked up the phone. I needed to talk to someone, but calling Allison didn't feel right. After all, it was barely ten, and I'd only left her house nine hours ago.

Rusty answered on the second ring.

"It's a bit early for you, isn't it, Davey?"

I grinned. "Well, you know, it turns out I'm only a vampire when I'm working."

"You'd better come back soon, you know," he said.

"Not up to me, my friend. Are you in the office?"

"All hands on deck. Walt's rabid today. Can't blame him, really."

"Listen, I just had a visit from the cops."

He gasped.

"No, they're not arresting me," I said. "I didn't do anything and have an alibi to prove it."

"Thank God," he said. "I mean… look, I know you wouldn't kidnap people, but an alibi sure helps."

"Yeah, it really does. But listen… Jenny might know this already, but if she doesn't, you didn't hear this from me, okay?"

"What's that?"

"Well, I'm pretty sure the body they found was Robin Elliott."

"Not the teacher?"

"I figured it would be, too, but Reynolds asked me if I knew Robin Elliott. I asked if that's who they found. He didn't deny it."

"Did he confirm it?"

"It's not enough to print, but it's enough to maybe soften the reference to the teacher's last known location, you know what I mean?"

Rusty sighed, and I could tell from the loud creak he was leaning back in his chair, the way he did when he was stressed.

"Yeah, maybe. You know I've gotta tell Walt, right?"

"I know. I just figured he didn't want to hear from me today."

"If he did, he'd probably put you back to work," Rusty joked.

CHAPTER THIRTY-ONE

Three hours later found me sitting in the lobby of the *Lynwood Post*, summoned by my editor. I rarely came to the lobby for longer than it took to meet a source and bring them back to the office, but I figured since I was persona non grata, it was better for me to use the front door. The lobby was dingier than I remembered, with fading paint peeling in one corner over the door. The faux-brick floor had streaks of salt around the black plastic mat that had been placed to keep people from slipping and falling.

A wooden counter gave way to a linoleum top, upon which a small stack of today's paper rested, a bell to summon the desk clerk, and a bowl of lollipops. There was no receptionist behind the counter now — she had already told me she'd let Walt know I was here, then disappeared.

A line of framed copies of the *Post* blared headlines above the chairs lining one wall. There was one for the end of World War II, tattered at the edges; one announcing that Neil Armstrong had taken one small step for man; one showing the Challenger explosion; and one showing the Sept. 11 attacks.

I stared at them in turn, unseeing, wondering how Walt would justify ending my suspension. Or firing me. I couldn't imagine him wanting to see me for any other reason.

I was staring at the Sept. 11 paper when I saw it.

In the top bar, just below the paper's name, were three pieces of information.

The date—September 12, 2001. The price—50 cents, and a third line, one I'd paid no attention to because it meant nothing in today's world. Vol. 168, Ed. 241.

Somewhere in the back corner of my brain, I knew newspapers had always been cataloged this way as if the date itself were insufficient to track which edition was which. I suppose it had made sense in the 1800s when the system was inaugurated, but I had no idea why that was or why it was still in use.

The reason it caught my eye was the connection with Dad's notebook. Some entries were labeled similarly with "Vol," then a pair of numbers. Was it possible it was identifying the edition of the *Post* that carried some type of valuable information?

"Still remember that day?" Walt's voice boomed, and I jumped. I must have worn a blank look because Walt pointed at the paper. "Longest day I ever had. Hell, longest week."

"Yeah. Me too. Horrible." I glanced at the other editions. All of them included volume and edition numbers. Then, I focused. "You wanted to see me?"

"Come in." He looked tired, eyes almost glassy as he led me through the newsroom, where Jenny and Jamie were typing frantically. Neither looked up. I saw Sam down the hall in her darkened studio— it was always dark, regardless of what she was working on—hunched over her computer. She didn't look up, either. Only Rusty acknowledged my presence in the eerily quiet newsroom, giving me a thumbs-up as we went by. Walt led me into his office and closed the door.

"Thanks for the tip earlier—you were spot on. It was Elliott." Walt sat down—voice in the normal range for once. "I can't believe you thought to call us, what with everything going on...."

"I didn't do anything wrong, boss. And I'm still a reporter, and Reynolds is still an ass." I shrugged.

He nodded. "Be careful who you say that to. He could still be a pain in your ass."

"I know."

"For now, at least, the police do not consider you a suspect. Adams told Jenny — after a few questions — that you have a firm alibi for the kid's disappearance yesterday, so they don't think you had anything to do with the rest of them."

"They don't? Not even Walther?"

He shook his head. "Not even Walther. Police are now saying they think all these disappearances are connected, but they won't say how or why."

"That's... he said that? Wow." I closed my mouth to stop stammering, then tried again. "I mean, that's great for me, of course. I'm just surprised he would say that aloud, especially when it meant leaving me alone."

Walt shrugged. "Cam's an all-right guy if you're on his good side. I know you're not, but when it comes to law enforcement, he's at least fair." He kept his tone low. "He might not like you, but if he genuinely thinks you're innocent, he won't keep harassing you."

I didn't know what to say, so I waited.

"Anyway, given that, your suspension is lifted. I won't make you stay now, but Monday, you're back on."

I nodded slowly. "Thanks, Walt. I appreciate it."

So, just like that, I wasn't a suspect. I strolled to the car, twirling my keys, and wondered what else had developed. Surely, my alibi alone wasn't enough — though I also had a rock-solid alibi for Lewis' disappearance.

I was so intent on my thoughts that a man ran into me from the opposite direction. He collided with my left shoulder, spinning me to the right and making me slide on the gravel, nearly losing my balance. "Hey, watch where you're going," I said.

He faced me, and for a split second, I thought I stared at Ralph Walther's emaciated face and dead eyes.

I staggered backward into a car and grabbed at it for support. The man smiled, bent down to pick something up, and when he straightened, it wasn't Ralph. It was Mike Elliott. The brunette from the bar was with him.

"You could watch where you're going, too, you know." His tone was as sharp as his gaze.

"Um. Yeah. Sorry," I said. Elliott was unshaven and wore jeans and an awful Christmas sweater over his wiry frame. He looked as irritated as the first time I saw him. I wondered if he had an expression that wasn't angry.

"Is this how reporters get interviews? By bumping into people?" he asked, and the woman with him giggled. She wore a much more tasteful Christmas-themed shirt and put a hand on his arm to calm him. It seemed an overly familiar gesture.

"You've got no business bugging me," he protested.

"I work here." I pointed to the *Post*.

"Mike." The brunette tugged on his arm. "Not now. Not worth it."

Elliott glared a moment longer, then snorted and spun. "Stay away from me," he growled. The woman shot me an apologetic half-smile and followed him.

I remembered where I'd seen her before. The Walther Farms truck was parked in front of her house the day Felicia Erickson had disappeared, and the police had knocked on her door.

I walked on trembling legs to my car, let myself in, and sat. So many strange things were happening, and they all centered on Walther. I saw him as I passed in front of his truck on Lancaster Street. But had it really been him, or was my mind playing tricks?

"What the hell was that about?" I asked, then started the car and turned up the radio before anyone could answer me.

CHAPTER THIRTY-TWO

Twice more on the drive home, I saw Ralph Walther, though not as clearly as that first time. Once was just after I turned onto the street. I glanced in the rearview mirror, and he was at the wheel of a little Honda. Seconds later, he transformed into a woman in her 80s. Then, halfway home, I saw him jogging down a street with a dog on a leash. In moments, it became clear it wasn't him.

I locked the car and took the stairs two at a time to reach my apartment, praying I wouldn't run into another Walther in the confined hallway. Fortunately, I didn't. I opened my door, slammed it shut, threw the deadbolt, and dropped my keys on the table. Then I bent over, trying to catch my breath.

I've never been superstitious—never went in for ghost stories—though I'd heard plenty. Heyward Manor was the source of urban legends, most of which could be found in half the cities in America if you were of that bent. But between the rolltop desk at Mom's, the events of the other night, and now seeing a dead man around every corner, I had to wonder if maybe ghosts were real because that would mean that while I was sane, I was also haunted.

The alternative explanation was that I was losing my mind or, at the very least, dealing with some kind of post-traumatic stress, which scared me more.

Even though it was only three o'clock, I poured a drink, downed it, and another, before allowing myself to sit.

Things were happening so fast. Usually, my life is boring. I've had the same job for seventeen years—lived in the same apartment for eight. I've dated exactly three women since the accident, and none in more than two years. I watched the same shows, followed the same sports teams, and listened to the same music for as long as I can remember.

And I liked it that way. After losing out on my baseball career, I went into a deep funk and emerged through routine. First, it was rehab—I wanted my shoulder healthy again. I told myself it was for my baseball career, but part of me knew I would never play competitively again. Maybe I could have, but at the time, I was convinced my shot had come and gone—that I was damaged goods in more ways than one.

Of course, it didn't help that my shoulder never properly healed. Had my dreams panned out and being drafted led to signing with a major league team, I probably would have had access to far better physicians and resources than as an eighteen-year-old kid with no medical insurance. And, with superior care, I might have regained the ability to throw a baseball harder than your average fifth-grader. Instead, I could swing a bat without pain after six months, but that wasn't enough.

Then, I drifted into the newspaper job, and tracking high school athletes became my new routine. At first, I was hoping to cover the next top-flight athlete, the next Dave Kendrick—future superstar. It took years before I realized that my shot had been the best anyone would get out of little Lynwood, Ohio, and that made me even more bitter. By then, I hadn't played competitively in four or five years, and while I was still relatively young by baseball standards, it was too late for a comeback.

Especially with a bad shoulder.

My routine had sustained me since, but now it was shattered. Mom was gone, and I was alone in the world. And I was seeing phantoms.

Plus, I had reconnected with my high school crush at the worst possible time. As much as I wanted to explore that relationship, it wasn't possible or even wise right now. Neither of us was in a good emotional place to start.

I put that out of my mind. Now, what about Ralph Walther?

Why had I thought Mike Elliott was Ralph Walther? He didn't look anything like him, and yet I had been so convinced. The other two people, of course, were even more different than Walther. One wasn't even male.

Who was the mysterious brunette hanging around Elliott, who lived in a house near where Felicia Erickson disappeared? Was Mike Elliott involved in Felicia's disappearance? And why would this woman help him?

Then there was the matter of the truck—not Ralph Walther's pickup, but the one from his father's farm. I knew it was a large operation, but that coincidence was big. Was Mom's death somehow connected to the disappearance of Robin Elliott and Felicia Erickson?

Puzzling wasn't getting me anywhere—maybe I needed to focus on something else. I pulled out the box of Mom's stuff and opened Dad's notebook, flipping back to the pages where he had written names and numbers—the ones that had "Vol.," followed by a three-digit number and another number of two or three digits.

All of the volume numbers were lower than 168. And all of the edition numbers, if that's what they were, were under 308, which confused me until I remembered that there were no Sunday volumes for the *Post*.

Skimming through, I found twenty-one names with that numerical formula. Others just had dates. I entered them into a spreadsheet— names on the left, *Post* volume numbers in the second column, and dates in the third. In the fourth, I entered half a dozen that had what appeared to be a date but with a hyphen at the end, followed by a few more digits. In all, Dad cataloged fifty-five names in the notebook.

I entered Dad's name and Victor Bruce's, which Mom had written. The bottom line was devoted to "Dalton," with no other information available. I don't know why, but I highlighted his name. Dad apparently thought he could help with something. I once again wondered when that note, "Call Dalton," had been written, and once again, I decided that Dad had to have written it while he was still alive.

I rubbed my face, determined not to ask Google when purple ink pens that exactly matched the ones Mom used had been invented.

By the time I had finished, light was fading from the day. I considered comparing my spreadsheet to the *Post*'s archives but realized that only editions after 2006 were online. None of the volume numbers listed were in the past thirty years, so I'd need to wait till the library opened. Both the library and the *Post* have old editions on microfilm, but I preferred the library because the *Post*'s edges blurred, and its machine wasn't connected to a printer. Besides, doing research at the *Post* would mean questions from a lot of people, ones I didn't particularly feel like answering right now.

That level of searching would have to wait, which had the side benefit of me not having to go outside to face potential Ralph Walthers again.

I would need to drive Allison to her old house in the morning. Chase would spend the time with a friend from school, which meant she and I would be alone for the first time since I'd run into her.

I cooked a meager meal of jarred spaghetti, washed it down with another drink, and eventually went to sleep. On the couch.

CHAPTER THIRTY-THREE

We arrived at Allison's house shortly after ten in the morning. I borrowed Rusty's old pickup for the day, even though Allison insisted she didn't have that much she wanted to take with her. Visions of Ralph Walther left me alone, thank God, but I'd been jumpy as hell since leaving the apartment.

We were halfway there before I realized I had no idea what condition the house would be in. For all I knew, the place hadn't been cleaned, and a detailed vision of dried blood and brains on the walls and carpet swam into my head.

Allison must have sensed my disquiet.

"I haven't been inside, but I had a company come over from Columbus to… to clean. That's what they do—I guess there's enough mess for a business," she said as I switched off the engine. "They sent me pictures. I don't think we'll be able to tell anything happened."

"Okay," I said, feeling better. "You ready for this? What do you want me to do?"

"Just… just be there." She grabbed my hand, squeezed it, then let go. As she got out, she quickly walked toward the front door as if hesitating would let her change her mind. I followed, trotting to catch up.

The place looked and smelled clean, although there was a hint of that sanitary odor normally reserved for hospitals and nursing homes. It wasn't a good smell.

We passed the stairs on the right and a very neat living room on the left and went down the central hallway, which opened into the kitchen.

A door on the left led to the dining room, which led back to the living room. To the right of the hallway were two doors leading to the basement and garage, and on either side of the end was a large sitting room with a couch, two recliners, a big TV, and the kitchen. A sliding glass door opened onto a large, shady deck.

Allison walked straight through to the kitchen, pointedly avoiding looking anywhere else. My gaze was drawn to the floor in front of the TV. The beige carpet was unremarkable, yet I was convinced that this was where Luke ended his life. I moved without thinking until I stood just before it, staring down.

"Dave?" The way she said it, I knew she had to have called my name more than once. Allison was white-faced, a stack of dishes on the counter next to her.

"Did… did they miss a spot?"

I shook my head. "No. No, it looks… normal. Looks fine."

"Then… how did you know…?"

"I don't… know." Cold sweat trickled down my back, my head was heavy, and it seemed like I was holding fifty-pound weights. I examined the carpet and then stared at the TV. His blood must have splattered, and I almost stepped forward to inspect it more closely before catching myself. I looked back at Allison, who hadn't moved.

"I'm sorry," I said and strode back to the kitchen. "I don't know why… I don't… I don't know."

Some color came back to her face as she slid plates toward me. "These go in the box." Her voice sounded hollow as she turned to empty the silverware drawer.

Neither of us spoke as we stripped the kitchen of useful implements, then moved through the dining room and living room.

Allison decided the furniture would stay. She didn't have room for it or the memories.

We went upstairs next, and by the time we were finished boxing Chase's board games, video games, and other toys, I was glad we brought the pickup. Then we tackled the small spare bedroom they used as an office. As Allison retrieved various files, she said, "I always liked this room. It was a good place for my hobbies—journaling, keeping up with social media, and genealogy." She grabbed both laptops. "I guess I'll have to see if Luke has anything on here that belongs to the distillery—did you know he was an accountant there?"

I nodded.

"He wrote too—just dabbled. Wasn't very good—didn't believe in capitalizing, spelling, or punctuation." She smiled.

It fit with the kid I remembered from high school. Luke had always been a jock—he played football, basketball, and baseball, chased girls, and occasionally did his homework. Not that he was dumb or anything—he had different priorities. He was one of the smarter guys I played ball with. Schoolwork just wasn't his thing.

"He was always more of a doer than a thinker," I said. "The rules of grammar probably bored him silly."

She shrugged. "Luke figured no one would ever read it anyway. But he did the same thing in his emails."

"He had so much personal charisma that he didn't need to impress that way."

"You think?"

"He was our team captain for a reason. He got along great with the rest of the guys. And a lot of them looked up to him."

She grinned. "Luke looked up to you too. Said you intimidated him."

"What?" Even though we'd started as friends, Luke had been somewhat standoffish toward me. I often wondered if he'd discovered I asked Allison out, but the attitude had been in place before that.

Allison turned to the display case on the wall, took down one of the bats, and handed it to me. "He always kept this — right next to his own."

I turned it over in my hands. The shiny aluminum had scuff marks, and the tape wrapping the handle had started to rot. Its weight matched that of my own bat, and as I turned it, I saw with a start there was a good reason — it had been mine once.

The memory came flooding back. The day before the championship game, we'd had one last practice. I had a few bats I used at the time, and this one had been relegated to a reserve for a month or two. There wasn't anything wrong with it. I'd just gotten on a hot streak with another one, and that's all it took.

As we were leaving practice, Luke asked me why I carried three bats. I shrugged.

"You think, after the game tomorrow, I could have one of them?" he asked. "If you're going pro, you won't need aluminum bats anyway."

"Yeah, sure."

And that was it. I didn't give it any more thought. The next day, we lost the title game. Luke borrowed one of my bats — this bat — and hit a home run. I hit one too, but they weren't enough.

On the bus ride home, he asked me one more favor. He asked if I'd sign the bat and promised he wouldn't sell it if I made the big leagues. I thought he was messing with me, but I did it anyway, hoping he'd leave me alone. And he did. Classes ended a week later, and I probably hadn't spoken to him more than half a dozen times in all the years since.

But he'd kept the bat, even though I'd never signed a professional contract.

"I had no idea," I murmured, gazing at the scuffed metal with a faded black-marker signature.

"He said he never saw a better hitter than you. And he played in college," she said. "He also said you'd do anything for one of your teammates."

I winced. "I'm not sure that's true. I was pretty arrogant then."

"Were you?" Allison's eyes widened, and I laughed.

"Oh, yeah. I was convinced I would be the next big thing in the majors. The next Frank Thomas, but with a better glove."

"Maybe you could've been, but that didn't make you arrogant." She shrugged. "Luke was jealous of your talent and maybe a little in awe of you, but he said you were always nice to him."

"Well… he was a nice guy," I squirmed. "And I was jealous of him, too." I put the bat back on the wall, wishing I'd kept my mouth shut.

"That's getting packed," she said. "Both of them. Computers and that family tree."

I nodded, glad she hadn't asked what I meant. We finished packing the room in silence and then went into the primary bedroom.

Allison wiped tears several times as she wordlessly gathered photos and mementos. She packed clothes and other personal items but left the furniture again.

More empty boxes were carried from the basement to be filled, then I backed the truck up to the garage, and we loaded it with boxes, filling the gaps with various tools and yard equipment.

"I think that's it." She pushed the tailgate up, trapping a battered lawnmower.

"At least for this trip." I winked. "Mind if I fill my water bottle before we go?"

"Of course not," she said.

I walked to the kitchen and filled it at the sink. When I turned to go, Luke Van Buren stood in front of the TV.

"Stay away from them." He glared. He looked real enough, but his voice was distant. It was like trying to hear the TV with the sound on low. "Stay away, or they'll be sorry."

He wore a suit, but the tie was loose, and the top button was undone, like he'd just gotten home from a long day. His slacks were rumpled, and his hair frazzled. And even more disturbing, he stood precisely where he killed himself.

"I... what... how..." I was vaguely aware that I dropped the bottle and was now clutching the counter, backing away slowly. The unreality of the situation was overwhelming.

"Get away. Stay away. Don't make it worse for them." Luke glanced toward the sliding door as if waiting for someone to appear. He spoke so quickly that I didn't think he was taking time to breathe. *Maybe he doesn't have to.*

"How are you here?" I finally managed.

"Everything okay?" Allison's voice came from the garage, and my eyes went wide as I turned to the door.

"Oh, no," I murmured. My reflection looked back at me from the TV. Luke Van Buren was gone as if he'd never been there.

"Dave?" Allison asked, her voice closer.

"Yeah. Just, ah, I dropped the bottle." I picked it up and wondered if I could walk with my knees feeling like Jell-O.

Allison's face appeared. "You okay? You look pale. Too many boxes?"

"I'm good." My legs held as I strode quickly to the door. "We'd better get that stuff to the house before the weather turns," I said, even though there was no rain in the forecast.

"Right," she drawled.

I nodded, and when she went into the garage, I stole one last look at the TV.

No one was there, but there were two faint impressions of footprints on the otherwise pristine carpet.

I ducked out and closed the door a little harder than necessary.

Neither one of us spoke as we drove back to Pine Street. I'd like to say I was leaving Allison alone with her thoughts, but the truth was, I didn't trust myself to speak. I couldn't tell her what happened, but I had to talk with someone. I briefly considered Rusty, but the last thing I needed was someone thinking I was cracking up just as I got back on the job.

I glanced sideways at Allison several times, but her face was turned away. Finally, I pulled up in front of the house but didn't back into the driveway. "You okay?"

She turned, and her cheeks were wet. "Fine." She wiped her face. "Sorry. It just... it almost felt like he was still there. Like he was going to walk in any minute."

"I can imagine," I croaked.

CHAPTER THIRTY-FOUR

After dropping Allison and her things off at my mother's house, I got in the pickup, drove around the corner, and parked two blocks away. "What in the hell just happened?" I asked the rearview mirror. I felt like I had to say it out loud to try and exorcise the trip. It didn't help.

Had Luke Van Buren really stood in his living room two months after he died? Was he a ghost? Or had I officially lost it? I knew Luke wouldn't have been too thrilled with me hanging around his wife, especially this soon after his death. Was my conscience powerful enough to send me that kind of message in such a stark way?

That had to be it. Imagining Ralph Walther all over the place was one thing since I'd found his body moldering behind Mom's garage. At least I was transposing his face over actual live people. But this—this was something different.

I didn't know what to do with it, so I decided to file it away for now and focus on something else.

After exchanging the pickup for my Oldsmobile, I stopped by the apartment long enough to grab my laptop and added an empty manila folder for printouts, along with Dad's notebook. Then I drove to the library. It would only be open until six, but I figured a few hours would get me started.

A librarian showed me the microfilm machine and the rolls upon rolls of thin black ribbon that held the entire collection of *Lynwood Post*s back to its earliest days. I wondered if the collection was complete.

After all, who could be sure someone saved every edition? I'd find out soon enough.

As I fed the first spool of microfilm into the machine, it occurred to me that I was doing precisely what Jethro Miller had advised — "Just go through your archives, man."

I started with the most recent, the entry for Eula Banks, April 17, 1983. Mom had written "LP" in the margin in her purple ink, and now it seemed obvious she meant "*Lynwood Post.*" One mystery solved. I found the proper roll, switched on the machine, and scrolled to April 17.

The story was on the second page. Eula Banks rated five paragraphs when her body was found alongside a county road just east of Lynwood. She was initially reported missing several days before being discovered, and there were no signs of foul play. She had likely died of exposure, and police promised an investigation would be conducted.

I scrolled through the next several editions, but Eula Banks was not mentioned again. I also scrolled through earlier editions and found a paragraph in the police blotter about Banks being missing. She was five-foot-five, weighed 180 pounds, and was Black. That was the entire description.

I removed the roll and took out the one for the end of 1982. This article was much easier to find, as I knew it would be.

The top half of the front page was devoted to the disappearance of Jimmy Nelson, age six. Unlike Eula Banks, Jimmy had been white and a child, to boot. I was sure both were factors in the increased coverage.

I read through the article, which held details I hadn't heard before. Jimmy and three other kids had been dropped off by a school bus at the usual spot on Elm Street, just a block from Mom's house on Pine. He had two blocks to walk home, which was not an unusual expectation in those days. The other three kids had reached home, but Jimmy, for some reason, had vanished. It was as though he had gotten in a car or been whisked away by aliens. Police, understandably, were focusing on the former option for all the good it did them.

Jimmy's body was found in a field. There was no immediate cause of death available, but it had been cold, and there was speculation he had wandered into the field to explore and got lost.

His parents weren't buying it. Stan Nelson was furious at the police for not having searched the field sooner and insisted that Jimmy knew his way around it since he often played soccer there with his friends. That much was true, I knew, having been one of the kids who would go down there to play. Mom or Dad usually went along because I was only five, but sometimes other adults were left in charge. My memory of who that was had faded, and I wondered if Stan or Lorraine had been among them.

I spent the next half-hour following the story, from changes in school bus routes and drop-off points to ongoing criticism of police procedures. I finally stopped scrolling when I realized I had gone past Eula Banks' story.

I pulled the spool and grabbed one from the first half of 1982. Dad's notes led me to Joshua Belisle, a college student who came home for a weekend in early March, went out to a bar with his high school buddies on a Saturday night, and never came home. The story, which ran a week later, mentioned that his friends had dropped him off outside his house, but he never made it inside.

I couldn't find any indication that he'd been found. I scrolled forward and found a brief item about Janice Olson, a hairdresser who was reported missing after she didn't show up to work one day. She'd gone missing on April 28, 1982, but the story didn't run until May 3. There was no further mention of her.

I kept going. The next one was Obie Heyward's, and this was a front-page story. Obie owned Fontana's Finest and one day had not shown up for work. A few days later, Obie's nephew from Wisconsin — Ezekiel Heyward — arrived in Lynwood to take over operations. I wondered when that had been made permanent. Obie's photo was included — he looked almost exactly like his nephew did today.

For every entry that had either a date or a volume and edition number, I found a story about someone who had gone missing. One case in the 1960s involved a teenager, and that was the only other one that drew significant attention. Twice, I uncovered follow-up articles indicating a body had been found. One turned up in an abandoned garage on Elm Street — the same street Jimmy had been taken from. Another, a car mechanic who disappeared in 1967, turned up in the same field where Jimmy was found. This one got more play because the head was missing from the body.

I entered what I found about each person into my spreadsheet, unease squirming like a snake in my chest. I stood, stretched, and paced in front of the microfiche machine, trying to banish the chill, both natural and unnatural, from my limbs. The library's hush felt funereal.

In the days before Dad vanished, he had compiled a record of people who had disappeared. And if the dates and volume numbers could be trusted, he'd gone back more than a hundred years.

I skimmed my spreadsheet again, looking for patterns. I was about to give up and return to the microfilm when it clicked.

The disappearances happened in clusters. Four, five, six of them within a year, then nothing for years. And every time, the last one to go missing was a Kendrick.

I wanted to go through all of them, but I was more interested in jumping to the editions where my grandparents had been named. I sat back down and found the film for Kendrick.

I skipped them the first time around because it felt like a separate chapter in my search. Or maybe I was just afraid. Now, I scrolled to a date in July 1975.

The house fire that had been credited with killing George and Josie Kendrick was impressive. A photographer captured enough smoke pouring out of the ranch-style house that it appeared to be trying to make up for an otherwise cloudless day. Two firefighters were holding a hose, guiding a stream of water through one of the shattered front windows. I squinted but couldn't determine if one of them was my father, who had joined the department a few years earlier. I sincerely hoped he wasn't at the scene.

The story said both occupants were presumed dead, yet only one body, that of my grandmother, had been recovered. Because of the intensity of the blaze, they hadn't found my grandfather yet. They didn't say it outright, but it seemed they believed the fire might have been set.

I scrolled a few pages further. The blaze was ultimately ruled arson, and while they hadn't found George's body, he hadn't turned up anywhere else either. There was speculation that someone may have taken his burnt body.

I kept scrolling. I didn't find anything more.

I found a spool from 1944. I learned that my grandfather's father — George Alan Kendrick senior — and his wife, Daisy, took a canoe for a paddle on the reservoir north of town. Somewhere in the middle, the canoe capsized. A pair of nearby fishermen were able to pull Daisy from the water, but she died at the scene. Of her husband, there was no sign.

Further scrolling led me to their obituaries. They'd had just one child, my grandfather, but the obit didn't clarify whether Senior's body had later been recovered.

While looking for more details, I stumbled upon another story of a person found days later. A woman who had disappeared shortly before my great-grandfather was found in a wooded area near Heyward Manor, and she was missing her head.

I moved to 1932. There, I learned that Elizabeth Kendrick, nee Caudill, had died in her sleep. Her son, George Senior, found her. Her husband, Josiah, had preceded her in death, but I needed to find another microfilm from 1912 to find out how.

It wasn't much help. Josiah Kendrick had gone fishing with friends in separate boats on a nearby lake. He fell in and was presumed drowned, and his body wasn't recovered. The account said his friends heard him call for help and heard the splash as he hit the water, but when they got to his boat, they found no sign of him.

I looked earlier. Josiah's parents, Levi Alan and Elizabeth Kendrick, had gone for what was to be a two-week stay with some of Elizabeth's relatives in Springfield, Ohio, in October of 1900. They were expected home the first week of November, but their return was overdue by two weeks. The relatives said they had left Springfield as expected just before Halloween.

I found nothing more about them.

By now, it was dark and near closing time, but I pressed on.

News accounts from 1866 were difficult to make out, but the headline wasn't.

"Captain's family slain," the headline bellowed. Then: "Captain missing, Negro implicated in tragedy."

I knew the tale too well—it was part of the Kendrick family lore. Captain Alan Eugene Kendrick of the United States Army, a Civil War veteran, and his entire family had been murdered. The presumed culprit was the escaped enslaved person who had followed my ancestor back from somewhere in the South. No one seemed to know the reason. I could well imagine that those who kept track of such things in those days felt like the reason was obvious—he was Black.

The story had been passed down not by Kendricks but by local schoolteachers who considered it their duty to teach about the town's historic, and at times wicked, past. I suppose it was to be expected, what with the ghost tours and all, but those were relatively recent trappings.

Then there were the ghost stories. Depending on who you talked to, Mary Kendrick, the captain's wife, still roamed the streets, looking for her lost children. Alan himself was said to haunt the house where the murders took place, looking for revenge on the escaped enslaved person, but, of course, there was no proof that Alan had died there.

I nearly yanked the scroll out, but having come this far, I decided to continue. I zoomed in.

"The family of Civil War hero, Captain Alan E. Kendrick, was found slain in their home on Monday, whilst the captain himself is presumed dead in a dispute with the Negro he rescued from the grips of slavery." Well, that was a twist—rescued?

"All four of the victims—Mary Kendrick, 33; Elnora Kendrick, 12; Eliza Kendrick, 10; and Matthew Kendrick, 7—were found stabbed to death and brutalized at various places around their home on Pine Street, two upstairs and two on the main floor. A note written by

Captain Kendrick stated that the Negro Isaac Cooper committed the crime and vowed his revenge.

The story went on to say that the bodies had been discovered by a neighbor a day after the family had failed to turn up for church and that the authorities believed they had been killed sometime Saturday night or early Sunday morning.

Again, I scrolled. There were further mentions of the murders, but no indication that I could find that either Isaac Cooper or Alan Kendrick had been seen or heard from again. Then I went back. Pine Street — our house.

I found myself shaking, and not from the chill air this time. Mom's house was the scene of a quadruple murder. Now, desks were opening by themselves. I had known that Alan Kendrick's family had been murdered but hadn't connected the murders to the house where I grew up. I shook my head — no ghosts had bothered us while I lived there.

Unable to stop myself, I scrolled one more time. It was the story I thought I knew so well, but I couldn't be confident after this shock.

I found the *Lynwood Post* dated Oct. 12, 1983, but the item I looked for wasn't there. Then I tried the following day.

"One dead, one missing in a hunting accident," this headline read. The story told of four men who went into a wooded area northeast of Lynwood for deer hunting.

While out in the woods, the men became separated. One of them was mistaken for a deer and shot. He was not being publicly identified until notification of next of kin. Another man, Victor Bruce, was hospitalized. A third, Robert Alan Kendrick — my father — was unaccounted for, and police were searching the woods. A fourth man was not injured and was being questioned.

I scrolled ahead to the date Mom had written for Victor Bruce. There, I learned that the man who had been killed in the woods was Roger Pelfrey, a local mechanic. I expected Bruce to have turned up missing, but he didn't. He left the hospital the day after the disastrous hunting trip, only to be hit by a car and killed the day after that.

And here was the fourth man's name, the one who hadn't been injured or gone missing.

The man's name was Dalton Adams. In 1983, he was a sergeant with the Lynwood Police Department. The block letters in purple writing seemed to swim before my eyes. "Call Dalton."

CHAPTER THIRTY-FIVE

I stared at the screen, heart racing, pulse beating in my temples. Why hadn't it occurred to me that Dalton was a first name? *Because who names their kid "Dalton?"* A light flickered. Flickered again. I glanced at my watch—closing time.

I stood, hoping to ask for a few more minutes, but my head swam, my vision blurred, and a wave of nausea left me clutching the back of the chair. I wasn't one for motion sickness, but scrolling rapidly through microfiche always left me feeling like I was on a sailboat in rough weather. I hadn't noticed it because of the discoveries, but now it hit me full force.

It took a minute for my eyes to focus, and then I realized that I didn't need the library to find Dalton Adams. I could Google him from anywhere or search property records.

Or I could ask Chief Cam Adams how they were related. They had to be in a town the size of Lynwood. I wondered if he would answer. Somehow, I doubted it.

I gathered my printouts, phone, and laptop bag and went to the counter to pay for the copies. At a dime a page, I spent eleven dollars and forty cents. I had planned to take them home to highlight the pertinent sections but couldn't face that prospect now. At least I had written a name atop each page.

Through sheer force of will, I made it to the car before searching for Dalton Adams' name on my phone but found precious little. Various information sellers offered to give me his name, address, phone number, criminal record, mother's maiden name, father's occupation, hair color, eye color, favorite color, and high school mascot for low, low prices that would have paid my grocery bill for a week. Or two. But none gave a free address or phone number. And, at any rate, I wasn't entirely surprised. Police officers were usually given unlisted phone numbers even after they retired. They deserved that much.

I went to the Truman County Auditor's website next. Phone numbers were unlisted, but property records were not. Unfortunately, I couldn't find Dalton Adams—or Cam, for that matter—as being property owners anywhere in the county. Which meant they probably used a trust to conceal their home addresses. Of course, it had been thirty years. Who knew if Dalton Adams was even still alive?

The temperature dropped faster than the sun, and tiny snowflakes started to fall. I started the car and drove to Betty's, getting my usual double cheeseburger and fries and taking them home, hoping they'd still be at least a little warm when I got there. I unlocked my apartment door and dropped the bag when I saw someone silhouetted against the far window.

Realizing I made a fine silhouette of my own against the light from the hall, I stepped to the side, but if the person noticed me, they made no move. Keeping my eyes trained, I fumbled for the light.

The man wore a zipped raincoat, jeans, and sturdy, battered work boots. The faded green baseball cap on his head bore the legend of Walther Farms. The face under the brim was shadowed but normal enough, and several days of growth darkened the chin and sunken cheeks.

Ralph Walther lifted an arm, reaching for me, and his mouth moved soundlessly. He took a step and tried another, but before the second foot hit the floor, he faded, the way mist coming from a boiling pot disappeared into thin air. Another half-step, and he was gone as thoroughly as if he'd never been there at all.

I trembled and gasped for air, then drew in more. The commuter bag's strap felt like a vice on my shoulder, and I slung it onto the chair. I took a tentative step forward, and while I didn't disappear, my legs threatened to give out—another step, then another. One at a time brought me to the living room space. Where Ralph—or whatever it was—had been standing. Impossible.

I barked a laugh. I'd just watched a man I knew was dead disappear from my living room, and I was worried about where he had been standing?

The rest of the apartment was empty of other beings, living or dead. Finally, I retrieved my cold dinner from the hallway and closed the door. Even that action felt dangerous, somehow, as if I was trapping myself in with—well, a ghost, I suppose. Or my imagination, which maybe was worse.

I wasn't inclined to think it was because I never could have imagined what it looked like the guy had been trying to say.

Which was: "Help me."

I felt like I was watching from afar as my body went through the motions of reheating the cheeseburger in the microwave and then sitting down to eat. I sat at the table instead of the couch because I wasn't ready to be that close. I wondered if I could ever sleep on the sofa again. The concept of sleep, in general, seemed like a bad idea, so, of course, a wave of fatigue rolled over me.

For the second time in a day, I'd seen a dead person. Luke Van Buren talked to me but vanished in the blink of an eye. Ralph Walther hadn't been able to articulate for some reason and misted out. Luke had at least been in his own living room. Ralph, to my knowledge, had never set foot in my apartment.

215

Tales of Lynwood's supposedly haunted past came back to me — the ghosts of downtown, the phantoms that haunted city hall, the legendary Heyward Manor, the roaming, murdered Kendricks, and the ghostly tour guide. I also couldn't forget the corny tales the locals made up for tourists about things moving in the old hotel rooms or the firefighter who still cleaned the engines. I'd heard a million of them, and they were entertaining for a while, but I'd gotten tired of them years ago.

And I'd never believed them, no matter how many people I knew who swore to the encounters.

I pondered everything I learned today. We had our missing persons cases in the past; that wasn't news. But I'd never known there were so many. And while I still didn't know how many people go missing per capita in most cities, fifty-five documented cases over one hundred and sixty years in a smaller town felt like a lot. And I was sure there were others that didn't get attention or that maybe Dad hadn't discovered in his research. It's no crime for an adult to disappear for a while or move away without telling anyone. In this era of social media and cell phones that report your every movement to a computer somewhere, it's hard, but even twenty or thirty years ago, it was easier. Take some cash from the bank, buy a bus ticket, and off you go.

If it hadn't been for the circumstances surrounding Dad's disappearance and presumed death, police might have thought he did exactly that, for all I knew.

I thought again of my ancestors. Of course, I'd known about Alan Kendrick's family, though the details had been distorted over time. His wife and four children were murdered, and he was missing, either taken and killed by the killer runaway enslaved person he had brought north or in cahoots with him — murderous brothers with very different backgrounds. Both seemed unlikely, yet they'd left no more clues than D.B. Cooper or Jimmy Hoffa.

I had no idea how I would feel about walking into my childhood home again, and it turned my stomach to think of Allison and Chase sleeping in it, unaware of its gruesome past. I vowed not to tell them.

The longer I contemplated, the more creeped out I became. I turned on the TV, found a basketball game, turned the volume low, and retrieved my cell phone.

Tim answered on the second ring.

"Hey, Dave, what's going on? Reggie and I were just talking about you."

"Really?"

"Reggie asked how you were, and I had to tell her I hadn't seen you since we had beers the other night. I wasn't sure whether you'd want to hear from a cop right now."

He had a point, and I told him so. "I know it wasn't personal. For you, anyway."

"Of course not. I know you're not a killer."

"A reassurance I never thought I would need, but thank you," I said.

"So, what's going on? Oh... hang on." Whatever he said next was muffled, and I could hear Reggie's equally muffled voice in the background. Then the sound cleared.

"You doing anything tonight? Reggie's worried we have too much pulled pork and thinks you must come have some."

"That would be great. I'd love to get out of the apartment for a while." I laughed at my understatement.

"Well, come over then. Be good to catch up."

"Be there in a few." I pressed end, stood, and grabbed my jacket and computer bag. On a whim, I picked up the box of Mom's things. I deliberately left the TV and the lights on. And I kept myself from looking back as I walked out, closed the door, and locked it.

CHAPTER THIRTY-SIX

I hadn't been fishing for an invitation when I called Tim. It hadn't even occurred to me I might get one, as I hadn't been to his house for several months—well before I was investigated. I called to ask about the missing persons cases, at least the older ones, to see if he knew about them. I didn't expect him to give me an answer. But now, in person, I figured I might have a chance.

I stopped at the liquor store and picked up a bottle of red wine for Reggie and two six-packs of beer for Tim and me, keeping my head down so that I could avoid looking at faces. On my way out, I glanced at the television security monitor. The face I saw was drawn and pale, almost haggard, and barely familiar as my own. I resumed averting my gaze as I returned to the car.

The black SUV parked next to me bore a variety of bumper stickers, most with a paranormal theme. One of them stretched all the way across the bumper and bore the familiar catchphrase from the X-Files: "The truth is out there." They added a little Santa sticker at the end. Cute.

I wondered if I'd figure out the truth in time to avoid becoming the latest in a long line of Kendricks to vanish into the ether.

It took me a few minutes to reach the Jepsons' subdivision on the west side. The houses were nice enough but lacked the charm of downtown or the city's older neighborhoods. Most bore the same lines and same colors, with only minor variations in shade or porch structure. Many of the residents here were commuters to Columbus.

I pulled into their driveway and found Tim waiting at the door.

"Didn't know you were bringing supplies," he grinned, relieving me of my burden. He guided me into the kitchen, where Reggie beamed, hugged me, indicated the wine, and said, "You really shouldn't have. But I'm glad you did."

"If the pork tastes as good as it smells, I'm paid back tenfold." It was true. One whiff made me realize just how badly I'd been eating lately, and I suddenly felt as though I hadn't eaten for days despite the stop at Betty's.

Reggie thrust a plate into my hands. "Pork's in the pot. Buns are next to it. Dig in."

I didn't fight. Two big sandwiches, a mound of macaroni salad, and a beer later, I was stuffed.

Reggie excused herself to clean up, leaving Tim and me to adjourn to their cozy family room.

"How are you holding up, Dave?" he asked. "You look a little rough."

"I've had better years," I said. "All of them, in fact."

"Sorry about the whole investigation thing. Our job to check."

"I know. Occupational hazard."

"Yeah." He took another swig. "For you, too, I suppose. Having to write about all this stuff when you're going through a lot."

"Yeah," I echoed. "Had some time off from work, but going back Monday, I guess."

Tim raised his eyebrow.

"It just feels weird. How do I go back to covering basketball and wrestling and scanning police reports while all this is happening?"

"One step at a time, I suppose."

I stilled.

He looked at me curiously. "Dave?"

Police reports. Of course.

"Hang on." I retrieved my computer bag from the hallway and pulled out my dad's notebook.

"What's that?" Tim leaned forward, and suddenly I wished I had checked this alone.

"Nothing. It's… well, it's a project I've been working on. For work."

"Work? I thought you were off?"

"A reporter never quits," I said, hoping he'd buy the bluff.

I flipped through the pages. More than half of the numbers were listed in a format that led to the *Lynwood Post*. "Vol. 112-72." Volume 112, Edition 72. But a good number had a different format—"68-4284." I tried matching that to an edition of the *Post* but couldn't make it work.

Because they were police report numbers, I would bet one of Reggie's sandwiches on it. But not two. They were that good.

Every night at work, I pulled the police reports and shot right past the number for the stuff that mattered—the date, the address, the offense. But on rare occasions, I noted one for Jenny or another cop reporter, and the easiest reference point was the report number. The first digit was for the year, "23" for 2023, and the second number was where the offense fell in the list of reports filed for the year.

I flipped through some more, closed the notebook, and looked at Tim. "You might be able to help me."

"With what? Your story? What is it you're working on?" He frowned. "Wait, is this why you called me?"

"Only partially," I said. "I also needed to talk to a friend."

"I heard you're talking quite a lot to a certain lady friend." Reggie walked into the family room, carrying two more beers in one hand and a glass of wine in the other. I took a beer gratefully and passed the other to Tim.

"Yeah, well… that's complicated. And I didn't think bugging her again would be a good idea."

"I'll try not to be offended that I was your second choice." Tim smirked.

"Sorry. I don't mean it like that, I promise."

He didn't look convinced. "So, what is it you're working on?"

"Can this be between us? No sharing with Reynolds or Adams or their goon squad?"

He sighed. "Dave, you know I can't promise that without knowing what you'll say. But as long as it's not illegal, I'll keep my mouth shut — if you promise to keep my name out of the paper."

My turn to wince. "I can't promise that, if something happens with it outside of this room. But if it's just talk, I promise."

Reggie looked back and forth in disbelief. "Glad you got that settled," she sniffed. "What's this all about?"

I looked at the two of them in their normal world and was envious. Tim looked smaller somehow without his uniform. I decided I had to trust them.

"Okay." I took a deep breath. And a drink. "I have a… well, a tipster, I guess… who's been telling me that this craziness we're dealing with — people going missing, people turning up dead — isn't unusual for Lynwood."

Reggie looked curious, and Tim guarded.

I pushed on. "This guy gave me a list. But it was just names and numbers, no details. I figured out that some of the numbers corresponded to editions of the paper, where stories were covered. But not all of them. The rest, I think, might be police report numbers. For cases where people went missing but never made the papers."

"Dave, people go missing all the time. We must get a dozen missing persons reports a month."

"I know, but how many of them turn up within a day or two? How many of them are troubled teens who run away, only to discover that it's dark outside and they want their mommies?"

"Most of them," he admitted. "But that still doesn't mean anything. I mean… what do you think it means?"

"I have no idea," I said. "I only put this together today." I paused, wondering if it was wise to reveal all the evidence in the bag at my feet. "Besides, there's more. When it's happened before, most of the people who disappeared have done so within a short time of… of one of my ancestors going missing."

This time, they both stared.

"Excuse me? Your *ancestors*?" Tim set his beer down.

"You know about my dad, of course. In addition to him, six other people died mysteriously or vanished within a few months of him going missing. I don't know for sure, but I didn't see any media coverage of those people being found." In truth, I had no way of knowing since I hadn't scrolled more than a week past any of the reports, but somehow, I knew it to be true.

"That was 1994. Go back a few years. 1975. My grandmother was killed in a house fire that was ruled arson. At first, they assumed my grandfather was inside, but they never found him. They later theorized he had set the fire and run off, but from what I can tell, he was never seen again. Five other people vanished around the same time. Two of them were found dead a few days later, and one more than a week after that. And in 1944, my great-grandparents went canoeing and capsized

223

on the reservoir. My great-grandmother's body was found, but not my great-grandfather's. Seven people went missing in the weeks before that. The same thing happened in the teens. And, of course…"

"Of course, what?" Reggie leaned forward — wine close to slopping out of her glass.

"The most famous missing Kendrick of all."

Tim murmured. "The soldier."

"Capt. Alan Kendrick's entire family was killed" — I left out where — "and he goes missing, either with the enslaved person he brought back from the South or maybe killed by that guy and buried somewhere."

We sat in silence for a long moment.

"So, Tim? Any idea if these current disappearances are related?"

He nodded slowly. "Now it makes sense."

"What does?"

"How badly the Chief wanted us to keep an eye on you, even before Walther's body turned up. If this sort of thing happened before and he knew about it, he'd want to keep eyes on you."

"Don't be too sure. Adams hates me."

Tim shrugged. "Hate is putting it strongly."

I let it go. "Are you any closer to figuring out what's going on?"

"Not really." He sat back and reclaimed his beer from the end table, taking a long drink and letting out a belch. Reggie winced.

"I can't tell you anything specific, of course," Tim said. "But they have similarities."

"You mean besides apparently beaming up to Neptune?"

"Listen. The missing people were in trouble for one reason or another, for one thing," he finally said.

224

"They were?"

"Yeah. Robin Elliott was under investigation for trying to hire somebody to get rid of her husband."

I thought that was pretty specific, but I kept my mouth shut.

"How awful!" Reggie blurted. "Well, that gives her husband a motive, doesn't it?"

"Maybe." Tim drained his beer. "The Cervelli kid was caught on video robbing a truck stop on the interstate. We didn't find out about it until two days after he disappeared. And Ralph Walther, you know all about him."

"Everyone knew I had it in for Walther, but who'd want to get Cervelli?"

"Who knows? Truckers are a tight-knit bunch. Or maybe he stole the dough for drugs and pissed off a dealer or something."

"And… what was the other guy's name… Dexter Lewis?"

"He had a couple of DV's," Tim said, using shorthand for domestic violence calls. "Minor injuries, but he was still with her."

"Then what about the teacher? She seemed squeaky clean." I thought of Keith Erickson, so desperately convinced of his wife's virtues.

Tim snorted. "Nobody could prove it, but there were rumors she was banging the school principal in his office." He shrugged. "Maybe it's not true, I don't know, but it's an angle we're looking at. And if so, we'd look at the principal, his wife, or Erickson's husband."

"And the kid? Brandon?"

"Selling drugs in school. He was in court two days before he disappeared. We wondered if he had quite literally run off."

"Don't you still? That was only two days ago."

Tim shook his head. "We have… well, we have reason to believe he was abducted."

My mouth dropped.

"You were going to find out tomorrow anyway. Chief's calling a press conference. You keep this to yourself till then, got it?"

"Of course."

"You'll also learn we found Cervelli a couple of hours ago. So that's three."

I felt like I needed another beer.

CHAPTER THIRTY-SEVEN

W e each had another drink. Reggie scooted forward, looking like she was going to ask more questions, but with a sigh, settled for another sip of red wine. I finally broke the silence. "So, listen. Can you get me the police reports? They're not current cases," I quickly added. "How far back do you keep records?"

"If the cases are closed, anything over ten years is long gone." Tim shook his head

"And if they're open?" I leaned forward.

"If they're open and that old, they're probably in the cold case files. From what I've heard, we have a pretty hefty storage area for those, more than most departments our size."

"What's in there?"

"I'm a patrolman. I don't get to play around in the cold cases or detectives' files." Tim shrugged.

I nodded. "But could you get in to see them?"

"I don't know if that's a good idea. I could lose my job, especially if I were to get caught."

I frowned.

I'm sorry," he said. "If I get a chance, I'll take a quick look. But I can't bring anything to you or make copies or anything."

I'd thought of something else. "It doesn't matter. I can't get the files, but the reports are public records. If they still have them, that is."

Tim turned a bit green. "You sure you want to wake that dog?"

"I don't have a choice. I have to know what's going on. I... well, it creeps me out, this whole ancestor thing. And... things have just been weird anyway. I have to do something."

"Huh?"

I wanted to tell him—I did. But I couldn't figure out how to say that I'd started seeing dead people.

"I'm just on edge, I guess," I said instead. "This is all... it's more death than I've ever dealt with. And I've had a bit of experience." I realized I hadn't even mentioned going to Luke and Allison's house and decided to keep it to myself.

I continued, "I'm not saying I will publish everything I learn, okay? Maybe not any of it. I don't know yet. It feels very personal with my dad and ancestors involved, and I need to figure it out."

"I'll help if I can. But I also think that maybe you being alone isn't a great idea." Tim leaned forward.

"I'm a big boy." My face heated as I remembered my reaction to running into the very dead Ralph Walther.

"I mean, maybe the Chief wants you watched because he's afraid you're a target."

"Or maybe I'm his target."

"I doubt it," Tim said. "Point is, either way, you might be a target. Maybe you get out of town—go stay with friends."

"I just got reinstated. If I bug off now, I'm out of a job."

"Stay here," Reggie interjected. "You can stay with us."

"I couldn't," I said. I didn't want Tim trying to talk me out of following my chosen course.

"Well, buddy, you'll have to for at least tonight." Tim waved a beer bottle. "We've both had too many, and while I might look away on a normal night, this isn't one of them. You can't drive."

I was trapped.

"Hope you don't mind the couch," he quipped.

"Nope. Not at all."

Sunlight evaded the closed curtains and pierced my eyelids like needles, spreading a dull ache through the rest of my head. The aroma of Reggie's coffee helped, but only a little. I managed to sit up just as Tim came downstairs in his police uniform, utility belt looking like a more menacing version of Batman's bag of tricks.

"Morning, sunshine." He grinned

"Why don't you have a headache, jackass?" I shot back, drawing a laugh from him.

"Water last night, painkiller this morning," he said. "You should try it."

"Could'a told me that last night." My mouth felt like it had been stuffed with cotton balls drenched in pickle juice.

"Coffee will help." Reggie waved me into the kitchen. I followed obediently, sitting at the kitchen island and accepting a cup. I wasn't much of a coffee drinker, but it suddenly seemed like a wise habit to start.

"Dave, I'm glad you called last night." Tim lifted his keys. "I've got to roll, but… just promise me, none of what I said goes beyond you, right?"

"Not till your chief tells Jenny, Walt, or whomever," I said. "I'm not back till tomorrow anyway."

"Take care of yourself—find someplace safe to hang out for a while."

I nodded. "I'll try,"

Reggie and I made small talk until I finished my second cup of coffee. Then I thanked her for dinner and the couch and drove home.

Once I was sure no dead people were waiting in my apartment, I drank a soda, swallowed two pain pills, and collapsed on the sofa. Mom's address book was lying on the table, and I stretched toward it, snagged it with one finger, and brought it to me. She had a number listed for a DA. Could it be?

My brain felt fuzzy, so I took a long, hot shower and felt almost normal afterward. I picked up my phone to try that number and saw a text message from Allison that must have come while I was in the shower: "Dave, please come over when you get this. It's urgent."

I called Allison's number twice, once as soon as I saw the text and again as I drove toward her house, but she didn't answer.

I pulled up behind her VW and bolted for the door almost before the car had come to a complete stop. The front door opened as I approached, and the look on Allison's face stopped me cold.

She didn't look angry but absolutely stiff, as if she were fighting to control her emotions.

"Chase, please wait upstairs," she called over her shoulder as she stepped back to let me in.

"Is everything okay? What's wrong?" I asked

She led me into the dining room.

The table was empty save for a small, ancient, black book whose leather cover was cracked and flaked. It looked more like a wallet—the back cover had a flap that came over the front, with a tongue that slid through a loop.

For the second time, my feet felt like they were encased in cement. I stared at the book and then at Allison. "What… where did you find that?"

"This is where I found it. Right here. Actually, where Chase found it."

"What? How did it get there?"

She didn't answer, and suddenly, her urgent message, not answering the phone, and demeanor made sense. She was making sure I hadn't been the one to leave it when she was not there.

"I've never seen that before, Allison. And I would never come into the house without asking you first. This is your space now, not mine."

Her lower lip trembled. Perhaps she did have a tell, but I didn't know what it meant.

She exhaled and seemed to shrink two inches. "I know. I just had to ask you in person."

"I understand." I was a little offended, but the mysterious appearance of an old-looking book was, to put it mildly, bizarre. "You're sure Chase didn't find it somewhere else?"

"I'm not sure of anything right now, but I believe he's telling me the truth," she said. I stepped toward her to pat her back, but she came closer and buried her face in my chest. With shock, I realized she was crying.

I wanted to ask what was wrong beyond the obvious. The book was weird but shouldn't have been tear-inducing. It looked innocent and ominous at the same time.

"I'm sorry." She stepped back and brushed a hand across her eyes. "It's just that things have been a bit strange here the last few days, and I haven't been sleeping, and I didn't want to tell you because it was nothing I could put a finger on, but this… this is too much."

I nodded. "What happened?"

"Noises. That desk keeps closing, even though we never have it open. And the basement." She shuddered. "It feels like there's someone in the house, even in the room, but of course there's not. Aside from things being moved, there's never been evidence that someone's been here. Until now." She indicated the book.

"Have you opened it?"

"No. Chase said it's creepy, and I agree with him. But I have a feeling I know where it came from."

"You do?"

She pointed toward the craft room.

I crept toward it, half-expecting Chase to jump out and scare me into next week. But the room was empty, save for a few boxes and the desk.

The rolltop was open about a third of the way.

"That's where it's been since we came down," she said. "Look inside."

She handed me a flashlight. I took it, knelt before the desk, and shone the light.

At first, I didn't see what she meant, but then I turned the beam upward. There was a small shelf, one I'd never noticed, above the track where the top would go. With the desk fully open, the front of the shelf was concealed, but with the top rolled forward, a person with a long arm could probably reach it.

Carefully, I slid my hand in and reached up, running a finger along the front of the shelf, displacing dust. I reached further and patted the entire length of the shelf. Nothing was on it, but it was certainly deep enough to have held the little book.

I snatched my arm back before the lid decided to slam shut, but it maintained its position.

"I've never noticed that shelf," I said. I studied the top of the desk, and now I could tell where there would be room for the hidden space. "I don't know how old the desk is, but it's been here for as long as I can remember."

"I've found that desk open more times than I can remember, and I've only been here a week," Allison said.

"It did that the day you and Chase first visited, but I thought I might have imagined things." I decided to keep the basement incident to myself for the moment. It never occurred to me that these things were more about the house than they were about me.

"I could tell something had you rattled. I thought it was just that you didn't know it was me coming to look at the house."

"Also a factor," I said. "I... well, it's not the first time I've felt rattled talking to you. In a good way," I added quickly.

She tilted her head to the side a bit and almost smiled.

"Whose book is it?" Chase stood in the dining room behind Allison, and she jumped at the sound of his voice.

"Don't sneak up on me!"

He shrank back.

She clutched the front of her shirt. "I'm sorry, I didn't mean to shout. I'm just... tired."

"You mean scared. Me too, Mom," he said. "Whose book is it?"

"Well… it's David's, I guess." She looked at me. "I mean, it was in your mom's desk. It's yours."

"We think it was, anyway," I said, but deep down I believed she was right.

"Can I open it?" Chase asked.

"No. It's old. You might damage it."

I couldn't disagree. It looked solid enough on the outside, but the binding might come apart the second I tried to open it. Still, there was no question in my mind that I would.

I sat in one of the chairs, my mouth dry, though thankfully, without the sour pickle taste. "Mind if I open it here?"

"I think I'd be offended if you didn't." She sat next to me. I couldn't be sure, but I thought I saw Chase roll his eyes as he sat in a chair at the end of the table, his back to the kitchen.

I lifted the book. I half-expected it to be hot, cold, or to crackle with eldritch energy, but it felt exactly like I would expect an ancient leather-bound book to feel. It crackled a little when I tugged the tongue free from its loop and more when I folded the flap back and opened to the first page.

The cursive handwriting was faded and slightly blurred, elaborate yet surprisingly legible, at least on the first page. It bore a date — August the 4th, 1867 — and a name. Levi Alan Kendrick.

CHAPTER THIRTY-EIGHT

A llison and I spent much of the day poring over my great-great-great-grandfather Levi's diary. It was slow going at first. Between the looping script and the random fading and blurring of letters, we disagreed a number of times on some of the words.

Still, Allison's earlier standoffishness was gone, and she was just as interested in the diary as I was. Chase initially acted intrigued but soon found a video game that called his name, and for once, Allison didn't regulate his time on it. Thus, we spent much of the time translating the archaic writing to the tune of what I later learned was a Lego City game.

I'm not sure what happened to actual Legos, which probably makes me old.

We quickly learned that, although there was a page for each day of the year, Levi had ignored that convention. At first, he crossed out the dates, but soon, he stopped doing it and just added the applicable date below the header.

The first entry was an introduction, and he established the habit of addressing the diary as if it were a living entity:

> August the 4th, 1867
>
> Hello, Diary.
>
> I have decided it is time to find a companion with which I can share my thoughts, and while there are few I feel I can trust, I hold no doubt that you, at least, will not judge me or try to tell me what to do.

Since my family was taken from me before I had seen my eighteenth year, many have felt they must do what they can to guide me into the future. They mean well, I reckon, but I find it suffocating.

It has been more than a year since that terrible day, and I can still feel them rattling around in this house. I would have moved if I could, but I have nowhere to go and, as yet, no significant income to make such a change. Now that my income is increasing, I feel as though I cannot leave them, even though they have left me.

I despair of ever seeing my father again, though I feel he must still be alive. It has been a year and a day since life as I knew it ended, and I became the bitter man I am today, diary. Father sent me into Lynwood to send a telegram, bank business, and when I returned, he was gone, the Negro with him, and my mother, sisters, and brother all dead.

I know Father would slap me for referring to Isaac as "the Negro." He insisted we refer to him as "Isaac" or "Mr. Cooper." I obeyed him, of course, and in truth, the man was kind. He didn't seem particularly smart, but he was grateful Father helped him escape his past and the bonds of slavery. "If you can save even one man, do it," Father said and told me that his father, my grandfather, the Congressman, had told him that before he went to war. The Congressman died before Father returned, but Father was confident he would have been proud.

Father did everything to help Isaac. He built a house with a grand cellar and helped him establish his business, as Isaac had a talent for the making of whiskey.

Diary, I will never understand what happened. Not only did Father leave me here alone to find the most horrible of things, but

Isaac walked away from us, too, and his business. His house sat vacant for months before Zachariah obtained the property. I have heard nothing of the fate of my father, not the merest rumor.

I have taken his position at the bank, of course, though some thought I would be too young. Father trained me well, however. At least he did that for me.

I will tell you more soon, diary. There is too much in my head to not share.

The following entry was about business at the bank, and Levi's musings, while eloquent and at times dark, were mundane. He did write about meeting Elizabeth Daventry, the woman who would become his wife. He also wrote about people he dealt with, including Zachariah Heyward, who had moved into Isaac Cooper's house. Zachariah also had a talent for brewing, for he turned out to be none other than the founder of Fontana's Whiskey Distillery. Levi had underwritten the loan that established the current site of Fontana's after it operated out of Heyward's cellar for several years.

What Levi didn't write about, at first, was his family.

About a quarter of the way through the book, in an entry dated March 12, 1871, he appeared to decide his father was dead as well.

Diary, as you know, I care little for recalling the date of my birth. After twenty-two years, it seems ludicrous to make a fuss. Elizabeth chooses to, of course, and I would not deny her the pleasure, though it still leaves me feeling empty.

My dear mother loved birthdays. Each year, she would come across the hall and sing to me. She sang so wonderfully.

Now, I cannot have that memory without also recalling finding her in my bedroom, her beautiful throat cut and bleeding—eyes unseeing. I do not want that memory, nor the memories of finding little Matthew at the bottom of the stairs, or Mary in her bed, or Elnora, sweet Elnora, savaged and dead in her bed next to Mary's.

My birthday conjures such horrible scenes that I cannot find happiness in the day, no matter Elizabeth's wonderful efforts.

Father has been gone for five years now. I expect he, too, is dead. I am just glad I did not have to find him with the others.

Every so often, Levi wrote about the murders, usually recapping the same details. I gathered all of his family had been stabbed to death. And from his descriptions, Elnora had likely been raped as well. Levi seemed convinced his father could never have done such a thing, but he had less faith in Isaac Cooper. In his writings, Levi spoke of striving for his father's fairness, but his writings also showed a virulent racist streak that grew with time. He even took to lambasting people whose skin was simply a shade darker. Again, Zachariah Heyward's name rose to the top:

"Mr. Heyward seems likable enough, and he is certainly popular, though I suspect he buys some of that goodwill as he is also generous with his drink. He does not look like he is from Ohio, or if Mr. Heyward is, he could almost pass for an Indian. He says he works outside a lot, and the sun darkens his skin, but I wonder if that's all it is and, if I am right, I wonder how he has so persuaded the townsfolk he is the same as us."

Levi's writings lightened up when his son Josiah was born and became less frequent. He often wrote that he intended to be there for the boy far longer than his father had been around for him.

The book's last entry was from 1882. In it, Levi recited little Josiah's joy over how Elizabeth treated him on his birthday. Levi himself, it seemed, had not gotten over his bitterness over his birthday memories, but he seemed genuinely pleased for Josiah and hoped his memories would be happier.

I checked my notes—Levi and Elizabeth had both disappeared in 1900. Either Levi had given up journaling, or there was another book somewhere.

Chase gave up on the game and returned to sit with us. "Mom, what's for dinner?"

Allison looked at her phone. "Wow. It's later than I thought. I was planning lasagna, but… I forgot to make it."

"That's my favorite. How could you forget?" He glared.

"I'm sorry, I got wrapped up in this. I'll figure something out," she said.

"Dad wouldn't forget my dinner." Chase stomped through the kitchen and out the door.

"He's never said that before," Allison whispered.

"This is my fault. We should have stopped earlier," I told her.

"It's mine. I should have… I forget sometimes what he's lost, you know? Too busy thinking about what I lost." She wiped a tear. "I should get him. I don't want him outside alone."

"I'll go. I know what it's like to lose a father." I stood. "Maybe I can talk to him."

"Thank you." She nodded.

I went out the same way Chase did. At first, I didn't see him and nearly panicked—finally, I spotted him sitting under the tree next to the garage. It was uncomfortably close to where I'd found Ralph's body, but he wouldn't have known.

I walked toward him. "I'm sorry I kind of took over the day."

"Okay." His voice was flat.

"Mind if I sit?"

"Whatever."

I sat a few feet away, let the silence gather, and then said, "I used to climb this tree."

No response.

"I used to hide up there after my dad disappeared. I didn't know my mom could see me from her bedroom window. Thought I was all alone."

More silence. I was about to try something else when Chase's voice drifted toward me.

"I didn't know your dad disappeared."

I sighed. "It's not something I talk about much."

"What happened? Did he... did he have to leave... the way mine did?"

"I don't really know. My father went hunting with some friends, and something went wrong. No one ever saw him again."

This time, he looked up. "Do you think he's still alive?"

I shrugged. "I guess not. I think he would have come back if he could."

"Mine wouldn't. He left on purpose."

Suddenly, he was on me, crawling onto my lap, sobbing. I put my arms around him and rocked.

When he calmed, I rubbed his back. "I used to know your dad. I don't know what made him do what he did, but I know he never would have abandoned you. He'd want someone to look out for you."

I gulped as I recalled what I'd seen in Luke and Allison's house — Luke's ghost, telling me to stay away from his family. Yet here I was, comforting them in turn, doing the exact opposite.

"I miss him," Chase said. "I just want him back."

"I know, buddy. I know."

"I shouldn't have been mean to Mom."

"She understands. But she might be getting worried. Maybe we should go tell her we're okay."

"Yeah." He hopped down.

I stood, and he surprised me by taking my hand. He looked much younger than his eight years as we walked to the back door. When we got there, he let go and led the way into the house.

He went straight to Allison, who was standing in the kitchen with a glass of water, and hugged her. "I'm sorry, Mom."

"I'm sorry, too, sweetie." She returned his hug.

I turned and stared out the window at the tree, remembering the grief I'd felt while hiding in its boughs. I knew it was time to leave the two of them alone.

Allison whispered something I couldn't make out. Then, louder, she announced that she was making spaghetti.

Chase asked, "Dave, want to play catch?"

"Sure," I said. "I don't have a glove here though."

"That's okay. You can use Dad's." He took off through the dining room and pounded upstairs.

"Um."

Allison's eyes glistened. "It's okay. With me, anyway."

I wasn't sure how I felt, but I didn't have time to consider the matter further. Chase was back—he tossed me an oversized first baseman's mitt and headed for the door. I flipped on the floodlight, "Be dark shortly."

I deliberately took the end of the yard with a view of the back of the garage so that Chase wouldn't. He had an accurate arm—I could catch almost everything he threw.

"Did you play catch with your dad out here?" Chase asked.

"I used to stand right where I am now, and he'd throw me ground balls." Though I was throwing sidearm—the only way I could do it these days—my shoulder still ached. I ignored it.

"Did your dad get to see you play?"

"I started the summer after he disappeared." I tossed the ball to him.

"That sucks."

"Yeah."

We traded several tosses in silence. Shoulder aside, the easy rhythm came back quickly, and I could have quite happily kept throwing longer.

"Why do you throw sideways?"

I laughed. "I'm a sidewinder, didn't you know?"

"A what?"

"I throw sidearm now. I can't throw over the top like you do." I demonstrated, slowly, what I meant, then sidearmed another one.

"A sidewinder." Chase imitated my motion and threw it several feet to my left. "That feels weird."

"It is." I retrieved the ball and tossed it in the air.

He camped under it and caught it one-handed.

"It's just like throwing overhand—you have to find the right release point." I threw again.

It took him several tries before he got one close enough for me to catch and a few more before he could do it consistently.

"See, now you have a new skill," I told him.

"Yeah. But I'm not going to use it." He reared back and threw his hardest one yet, and it hit my glove—Luke's glove—with a satisfying pop.

"Good idea."

The back door opened, ending our game, and we ducked inside for dinner.

CHAPTER THIRTY-NINE

It was after eight by the time we finished eating, and I wondered if it was too late to try that number and see if it led me to Dalton Adams. I decided to call as soon as I left, but once again, Chase had other ideas.

Emboldened by his previous double-solitaire success, he wanted to play a board game. He looked so hopeful when he asked that I couldn't refuse, and thus, I spent the next hour trying to understand a variety of games that certainly hadn't been around when I was a kid. Allison won one of the games, and Chase won the rest before Allison announced it was Chase's bedtime.

"Don't leave yet, okay?" Allison asked as she stood to usher a complaining Chase upstairs. I put away a game that consisted of tiles, little wooden blocks, and dice, then checked my watch. It was well after nine. I gave up on the phone call and examined the diary again.

The soft voices of Allison and Chase reading to each other echoed down the stairs—a loving familiarity that made me feel like an intruder—a sensation made stranger by the fact that I'd grown up in this house.

I was focused on one of the diary entries when I realized Allison was calling my name. I bolted to my feet, afraid something else had gone wrong, but when I reached the bottom of the stairs, I found her at the top, smiling.

"Chase wondered if you'd give him a hug goodnight," she said. "You really made an impression on him out there."

"Well, yeah, sure." I climbed the stairs, and she patted me gently on the arm as I went past.

"I'll be downstairs."

I thought her hand lingered a few seconds longer than necessary. I didn't mind at all.

As I walked toward my old bedroom, now Chase's, I wondered which of these rooms had been Levi's and which had been Mary and Elnora's. I thought of little Matthew's body at the bottom of the stairs.

Chase sat in bed, reading a book about baseball's greatest hitters.

"I didn't know you liked baseball *that* much," I said.

"I wish I could have seen them play. Dad was always talking baseball."

"He was a pretty good player." I ruffled his hair.

He nodded. "He said you were the best he ever saw."

I started. "He told you about me?"

"He had your bat in his office. Said you would have been a major leaguer, but then you got hurt."

I sat on the edge of the bed. "That was the plan, but sometimes life doesn't get the memo." I pointed at the book. "Who's your favorite so far?"

He frowned. "I don't know. I think Willie Mays because he could hit home runs and steal bases. Or maybe Mickey Mantle because he was a switch hitter."

"Both good choices. I always wanted to hit like Frank Thomas. But I wanted to field like Brooks Robinson."

"I haven't heard of Frank Thomas." He leaned toward me.

I smiled. "Chicago White Sox. I'll tell you about him sometime. But I think you're supposed to be going to sleep?"

He smiled, and his sheepish grin matched his mother's while his eyes favored Luke. I hadn't noticed that before.

I hugged him. Before I could let go, he asked, "Has this house always been weird?"

I drew back, holding his shoulders and looking at him. "Weird, how?" I managed.

"I don't know. Hearing funny things, seeing funny things. It's like all the spooky stories about Lynwood are true in this house."

I took a deep breath, then said, "I guess I used to notice things, but I don't know if it was weird. It's just how it was. But there was never anything scary or dangerous." I met his gaze. "Has there been anything scary or dangerous?"

He scrunched his face. "I just get surprised sometimes." He shrugged. "Anyway, Mom will get mad. I'd better go to sleep."

He pulled back, slid under the covers, and turned toward the wall.

"Sleep well. And listen, if you need to talk more about it, let me know, okay?" I stood.

He looked over his shoulder. "Okay. Thanks."

———————————

Allison was curled up on the couch, holding a mug of hot chocolate, and a wooden tray on the Ottoman held a second cup that I presumed was for me.

"Mom never let me have hot drinks in the living room." I winked and sat on the other end of the couch.

"Well, lucky for you, I'm not her." She kicked off her shoes and slid across the couch to curl up against me.

I chuckled. "Nice socks." They were bright red with a green elf extending a present.

"Part of my Christmas collection." She turned her foot right and left so I could admire them. "Wait till you see the others."

I put my arm awkwardly around her, and she snuggled against my chest.

"Thank you for your help with Chase today," she murmured.

"No problem."

I was acutely aware of where our bodies were in contact.

"What did you say to him? If you can tell me." She turned her head toward me.

"I told him I knew what it was like to lose a dad."

"Really?"

"Yeah. No one could relate to what I dealt with as a kid, and it felt like no one would ever understand. How could they? None of their dads vanished." Given all I had learned recently, I wondered if that was true, but I hadn't told Allison what I'd found, and this didn't feel like the time.

"Anyway, I figured he might want to know that I lived through it. It's different, but maybe not that different."

"Well, you got through to him in a way I haven't been able to."

"My mom probably felt the same way. She worked with kids for a living, but I couldn't talk to her much about any of it. She was as lost as I was, so it didn't seem like she could help me."

"How did you survive?" She rested her head back on my chest.

"One day at a time, I guess. I don't know. I still think about it." *Some days more than others.* "Sometimes, I would talk to him as if he were there. And when I had to work something out, I'd try to answer how I thought he would. Of course, I had no idea what he would have said, but it helped, anyway. He's sort of a voice in my head now."

I was surprised to see a tear trickling down her cheek.

"I'm sorry," I said, brushing it away with my free hand. "I didn't mean…"

She caught my hand.

"I'm sorry we… drifted apart after school," she said. "And I'm sorry we found each other again in such terrible circumstances. But I thank God we did because I don't know how I could have gotten through these last few weeks without you."

I had no idea what to say. Before I could come up with anything, Allison's lips were on mine, tentatively at first and then more firmly. Uncertainty, anxiety, disbelief, and pleasure warred, but as I kissed her back, everything faded. Well, all except the pleasure part.

We didn't take it any further than a few kisses, but we stayed on the sofa talking quietly, sipping the cocoa for a long time.

It was after midnight when Allison showed me to the door. "I… I wish you could stay… but Chase is in a good place, and I don't want to mess that up."

"I understand." Part of me really wanted to stay too. But more of me worried it was too soon, particularly for her. I donned my jacket, lifted my computer bag, and slid the diary inside. There was a blast of icy air as I opened the door. "Wow. The temperature has dropped a lot."

She lifted her face to give me another kiss. "That should keep you warm until you get home."

"Indeed it will." I shivered my way to the Olds.

CHAPTER FORTY

I started the car and cranked the defroster. It had been chilly while playing catch — in the high forties — now it was below freezing and windy. My lighter jacket wasn't up to the task. I grabbed the ice scraper to clear a thin layer of frost from the windows, got back out, and kept glancing at the house.

So much was happening that it didn't feel real. If anyone had told me in the fall that by December, my mom would be gone, Allison would be living in my mom's house, and I would be making out with her on the couch — well, to say I wouldn't have believed it would be an understatement.

And yet, here I was, with all of that true. And with a side of ghosts, if you please.

I approached the driver's side to get back in the car, but as I opened it, I noticed a dark blue, four-door sedan parked about halfway down the block. It was in shadow but was clear of frost. It was the kind of undercover vehicle police departments sometimes used.

I got in the car, feeling uneasy and wondering if I was jumping at shadows. I believed that possibility until I drove to the end of the street and headlights popped on behind me.

I turned right and then left, even though it wasn't the direction I wanted to go. The headlights followed. I went straight until the road connected with Montcalm, then turned toward downtown. Whoever was behind me wasn't concerned about downtown; the headlights stayed nearly a block back.

Either the driver was terrible at being unobtrusive or didn't care if I knew I was being followed.

With nowhere else to go, I drove home. I turned into my parking lot, but the car didn't—instead, it stopped about twenty feet past my driveway. By the time I got out, its lights were off. I toyed with getting back in the car and driving the other way to see what would happen but decided it wasn't worth it.

I also considered grabbing my baseball bat and going for a chat but ruled that out too. If it were the police, they'd be armed, and if it wasn't—well, even if I "won," I'd probably be seeing the real police soon anyway.

Instead, I opened the door, peering inside to make sure there were no figures, alive or otherwise, waiting for me. I locked up, turned out the light, and went to the window, but I couldn't see the mysterious car from there.

Maybe they were following me because they, too, wondered if I was in danger. Maybe Tim had even asked them to.

Or maybe they still considered me a suspect, no matter what they had told the *Post*.

Both were possible, but in either case, I could do nothing about it. I felt confident I hadn't been followed before now. The only thing that had changed was that Tim, at least, was now aware that I had figured out a deadly secret about my family's past.

I tried to sleep, but it wasn't happening—my thoughts swirled. Mike Elliott and his girlfriend. Walther Farms. Steve Cervelli, the robbery suspect. The cops following me. The fact that they were, even though I had alibis for at least two of the times people went missing. Were Reynolds and Adams still trying to pin this all on me?

I gave up, switched on the light, and padded back to the living room, making sure no spirits were lingering along the way. The coast was clear—I checked the window—my shadows were still there, probably wondering what I was doing up so late.

Let them wonder. I'd hate for them to get bored.

I opened the laptop and typed: "What the hell is happening?"

I entered the names of the missing: Robin Elliott, Steve Cervelli, Felicia Erickson, Dexter Lewis, and Brandon Kick. Reluctantly, I added Ralph Walther's name to the list and then my mother's, Elaine Kendrick, because they were somehow involved.

Then I typed: "Suspects."

Mike Elliott headed the list. I enumerated the reasons—he was the husband of the first missing person who didn't report that fact until the next day, and he had a new girlfriend who lived close to where the fourth person disappeared from.

The mystery girlfriend: Her new boyfriend's wife went missing, and she lived near where Erickson disappeared. Plus, maybe she had a connection with Walther Farms.

Who else?

Keith Erickson. Did he know his wife was cheating on him? It's possible — he did install the school's security system. And he was very quick to point a finger at Mike Elliott.

I typed Ralph Walther's name here, too, simply because he was one person I knew for sure had killed someone. But he turned up dead just four days after Felicia Erickson had disappeared, and given the state of the body, I was quite sure he hadn't been up to the task of abducting wayward teachers.

Other names flitted through my head. Jethro Miller's book sales would skyrocket with another wave of mysterious deaths, and he did have a new book coming out soon. Cam Adams was just enough of a cowboy to start taking out people he didn't have enough evidence to arrest. Hell, Walt Quinlan probably sold more papers thanks to all those headlines.

None of them seemed particularly likely candidates. I gave up on suspects and added a new header: "Motive."

There, I had nothing. Oh, sure, there seemed to be some for taking out each of these people. Mom had been investigating something. Robin Elliott supposedly tried to hire a hitman. Steve Cervelli held up a store. Ralph Walther killed someone, though since I was the only one who believed that as a motive, it was doubtful. Felicia Erickson may or may not have been having an affair. Dexter Lewis got rough with his wife. And Brandon Kick sold drugs.

All maybes. And most of those facts were probably not public knowledge, which made it highly unlikely someone felt the need to go after all of them.

———————

Nine in the morning found me exhausted and marching into Walt Quinlan's office at the *Post*. "I'm sending a public records request to LPD today. These cases are connected; there have been cases before, and I think the records will prove it."

"Welcome back," he quipped. "Good to see you. Hope you're doing well and ready to get back to sports coverage. Rusty needs the help."

"I'll help, of course. But I've figured some things out, and I need to pursue this."

"I can't have you covering this story, Dave. I know what Adams said, and you're back because of it, but that doesn't mean you're not connected. Hell, everyone in town knows you're connected."

"I'm sending the records request one way or the other. I can do it on our letterhead, or I can do it on my own." I still hadn't sat down. "If I do it through the *Post*, you'll get to see what I find. If I don't, you won't."

He tapped his pen on his desk. "What records?" he finally asked.

"Cold case files. Going back years. Decades. Some of them are about my ancestors. Did you know that all of my direct male ancestors have vanished without a trace going back at least a hundred and fifty years?"

The pen stopped.

"And they're not alone. Every time one of them went missing, many other people did too. Some of them turned up dead. Some of them... well, I don't know. That's why I want these records. I want a complete accounting, along with anything they figured out about the causes of death."

Walt still didn't say anything, but now I had his full attention. He waited.

I nudged the door closed and sat down. "One of the people who went missing was your grandfather, Walter Quinlan, April of 1965. The *Post* wrote that his wife reported him missing when he didn't come home from work at Fontana one day. Fontana said he clocked out as normal, but his car was gone, and he never came home. The car was found a week later at a truck stop along the interstate."

I'd never known Walt to stay quiet this long.

I continued. "What was the story? Did they decide he ran out on his wife — went hitchhiking to start a new life in California or Florida? Or did they finally find him somewhere?"

"Canada." Walt's booming voice was barely a whisper. "They said he'd gone to Canada. To dodge the draft. Grandma was pregnant, but he didn't know it. She didn't even know at the time."

He put the pen down and leaned forward. "Once police found the car, they stopped looking for him. They told Grandma she needed to accept that he'd left to avoid the draft and that maybe she'd see him when the war ended. Or maybe not."

"There's a police report."

"Well, of course, there was. She reported him missing."

"Someone saw that report many years later. Why would..." I hadn't considered what I would say until now, but how could I have missed it?

"Why would what?" Walt asked.

"Why would the police still have that report almost twenty years later? And how did someone who wasn't a police officer see it?"

Or any of the other reports, for that matter? Dad had all the police report numbers, and I guess I had just assumed that he, too, had wanted to see them, but that didn't make sense. He had known the report numbers and the names associated with them. That meant he had seen the reports himself.

But how?

I could almost hear Dad's voice screaming in my head. *Call Dalton!*

A bang on the door made me jump. Without waiting for an answer, Jenny burst in.

"Walt, police found another body. They're having a press conference in half an hour."

Walt half-stood, moving his eyes between me and Jenny. Finally, he pointed to Jenny. "Get Sam. Go."

She did, closing the door after her.

Walt sat heavily. "Are you saying the police never closed the investigation into my grandfather?"

"Seems that way, boss. I've got to make a call." I stood and opened the door.

"Dave!" I turned back. Walt looked as angry as I'd ever seen him, and involuntarily, I stepped back a pace.

"Get those records. Do what you have to."

I nodded.

CHAPTER FORTY-ONE

I'd submit the request, but first, I needed to try calling that number, and I couldn't do it from the newsroom. I needed privacy. I scurried through the break room and design area and out into the former home of the printing press. On the far side, the former press operator's office had been converted into a too-small secondary office for our circulation manager. His primary office was in the front of the building, but this was where the deals with freelance carriers were made, and the day-to-day books were kept. For the moment, it was as cold as it was empty.

I closed the door and opened my laptop and notebook. As I entered the number Mom had for "DA," I realized how silly this would turn out if Mom's DA turned out to be someone else.

It rang six times before someone finally picked up. "Who's this?" a voice rasped.

"Is this Dalton?" I asked.

"You called me. Who is this?" he shot back. I wondered if he still smoked or if this damage to his voice had been done in the past.

"My name is Dave Kendrick. You knew my father."

His ragged breathing told me he was still there.

"Mr. Adams, I'm sorry to bother you, but my mother called you before she died, and I know you were one of the last people to see my father alive. I need to talk to you. To see you."

"Why? So you can end up like them?"

A chill ran down my spine.

"I have a feeling I'm in danger anyway. Might as well have some answers."

Again, his breathing told me he hadn't hung up.

"My father was in danger too. He knew it. He knew about all the other people who had gone missing. Because you helped him. You showed him the cold case files."

"How do you know that?"

"Because you were his friend. Because he needed help. You're the only one who could have done that."

More breathing.

"I suppose you want to see them too," his rasp turned into a sigh.

"And to know what you told my mother two months ago. The night she died."

"Lose the tail first. Then come." He paused, then reinforced, "Make sure you lose that tail."

"How do you know I'm being followed?"

"I'm not dead yet. Call me when you lose them, and I'll give you the address."

The line went dead.

So, it was the police following me. Dalton had all but confirmed that. But how on earth was I going to get rid of them?

I left the office and went out into the previous press room. Adding to its perpetual gloom were grimy windows. I strode to one that overlooked the parking lot and rubbed a corner of one pane clear. My car made me a marked person. I spotted the beige sport utility vehicle that had followed me to the office across the street, with one person sitting in it. It was well below freezing, but there was no plume of steam from the exhaust—the engine was not on. Glare from the windshield and dust on the outside of the windowpane made it challenging to make out the person inside, but someone was there.

I watched for ten minutes. Aside from random movement inside the SUV, nothing happened.

There was no chance of getting to my car or any other without being seen. I needed a vehicle that wasn't here at the building. I thought about calling Allison but didn't want to endanger her.

Then there was Dalton's last name — Adams. An ex-cop. And the fact that Cameron Adams was the chief of police. Odds were that Dalton was Cam's father or at least an uncle.

I thought of the supreme irony of going to a man for help who could well be the grandfather of Erin Adams. I shook my head — I needed to face this alone.

Finally, an idea came to me. I made a call, wound my way through the twisting back rooms of the *Post*, and left through the loading dock, which was on the side of the building away from the parking lot. I was two blocks away and freezing before I realized I hadn't bothered to retrieve my jacket.

———————————

Half an hour later, I was in the cab of Rusty's pickup, heat blasting. I told Rusty I needed to get a few more things for Allison before I came back to work and that my car wouldn't start. I hated lying, but I would have hated involving him even more. He grew suspicious when I told him I would walk to get it from his house but didn't challenge me.

From there, I drove east, out into the country where it would be obvious if anyone were trying to tail me. When I felt safe, I stayed well away from Lynwood's perimeter, angling back to the west. I had no idea where Dalton Adams lived, but that was the direction Mom had come from, and instinct told me it was right.

I called Dalton, and he gave me an address to a road that intersected Route 98, south of where Mom had crashed. Bingo. Then he hung up — very chatty fellow.

His house was set back from the road in a copse of trees, and I was suddenly glad I had Rusty's brown pickup truck and not my blue car, which would have stood out. A small Christmas tree decorated Adams' front porch, but there was no other indication, at least from the outside, that a holiday approached.

I hauled my computer bag, now laden with my laptop, several notebooks, and the old diary, to the front door and knocked. Adams must have been waiting as the door opened almost immediately.

He thrust a thick manila envelope into my hands.

"There. Don't want them anymore. Go on," he wheezed.

I stared. "These are the records?"

"Yep." He started to close the door.

"But I need to talk to you. I need to know what you know."

"I can't tell you what I know."

"Both my parents died after talking to you."

"That should teach you something." He glared at me for long seconds, then finally stepped back.

"Come in, come in," he rasped. "Quickly."

I stepped in, and he slammed the door. Then, he turned and hobbled, assisted by a four-footed cane, into a small living room. I was convinced that this was Cam's father because he looked like an older version of the cowboy police chief. His wispy hair did nothing to conceal the age spots scattered on his dome, and his face and hands were wrinkled and leathery as if they'd seen too much sun. His hawk nose and piercing green eyes completed the image, and I wondered if Cam realized he might one day be as frail as this man before me.

The room was as rustic as the man. The walls were a faux-wood pattern that I associated with the 70s, which wouldn't have been out of place in an episode of the Brady Bunch. A large fireplace dominated one wall, and a very un-Brady-like deer head leered from above. It looked like a fifteen-pointer. A massive recliner was next to a wooden end table, and a couch stretched along one wall, facing the picture window. A TV was mounted on the wall just inside the door we'd entered through.

"Want a drink?" he asked—gesturing to the bottle of Fontana's Finest sitting on the end table. Two glasses sat at the ready next to it. He looked annoyed, as if he'd made the offer out of habit and regretted it.

"No, thanks." I couldn't believe this man, likely related to Erin Adams, would offer a drink to a man who would soon be driving.

He nodded as if he expected the response, plopped onto the recliner, and then poured himself one. "You've got five minutes."

I sat on the couch, clutching the envelope. "Look... Cam's your son, right?"

He nodded.

"Then I'm sure I'm the last person you ever want to talk to, and I understand that."

"And yet you're here."

I drew a deep breath, then said, "First, I need to say that I'm sorry for what happened back then."

He waved it away. "I don't want to hear that."

"Okay. Then... you were my father's friend, right?"

"Course I was. Bob was a good man. Would've been proud of you, up until... you know."

I winced. Dalton wasn't going to make this easy. I couldn't blame him.

"Forget about me."

"Trying to."

"Do this for my dad. For my mom." I lifted the envelope. "They were trying to find out why people disappear. Why my ancestors keep disappearing."

"They should have left it alone. Nothing they could do about it." He shook his head.

"But why? Especially when your friend vanished — why didn't you do something?"

"I couldn't!" He yelled. "You'll never understand."

"Then help me."

"That's the one thing I can't do." He let out a raspy breath. "You don't have children, do you?"

"I'm sorry, what?"

"You don't, do you?"

"Well... no. Why?"

He sat for a moment, his rasping the only sound.

"Your father left behind a son. So did his father and his father's father. At least that won't happen with you."

"Why did Mom call you?"

He pointed at the envelope. "Bob left her some message that I had these," he said. "It was hidden; she'd only just found it. She wanted to see them. Like a fool, I let her."

"So, she came here?"

"Night she died. She looked at those. All of them."

"What's in here?" I whispered.

"Cold cases. Stuff I investigated. Stuff from before I came on the force. And during. Stuff I could never let go. But I had to stop investigating them."

"Why?"

He shook his head. "Everybody's got a boss, boy."

"Was she leaving here when she…?" I couldn't finish.

"Said she was going to see you. I told her that was a bad idea."

"Why?"

"Because there's not a damn thing you can do. You can read what happened. You can know what happened. You can even know what's coming. But you can't do anything about it."

"Do you know why people have disappeared?"

He struggled to stand. "I think your five minutes are up."

"Do you know what happened?" I yelled.

He speared me with that gaze.

"I've known for a long time, and I'll take that secret to my grave. You, of all people, aren't going to change that. Now get out of my house. And forget you know who I am."

I had no choice. Out of spite, I opened the envelope and peeked inside. They were indeed photocopies of police reports.

"Satisfied?" he growled.

I stood. "Fine. Thank you for doing this much."

"Don't mention it. To anyone." He raised his drink as if a toast. "You can see yourself out. And drive safely."

CHAPTER FORTY-TWO

I stayed well below the speed limit and flinched anytime something bigger than a Jetta passed me on Route 98, which, though cursed in my family, was still the quickest way back to Lynwood. I passed the place where my crash had occurred, then the site of Mom's. Twice, I had to pull over and wipe the inside of the windows because I was breathing so hard, and I was afraid to try to perform the task while driving.

"Drive safely," Dalton Adams' last words were full of snark. Something made me not trust him. Well, besides being Cam Adams' father and Erin's grandfather, that is.

It wasn't yet noon. I couldn't turn up at the office with a stack of reports I had just told Walt I would request. I agreed with him — there was no way Adams would give me these without a legal fight. Besides, my shift didn't start until two.

There was also the small matter of my car still sitting in the *Post*'s parking lot, probably still being watched. In theory, I could stay off the grid a while longer.

My shoulders relaxed a little when I made Lynwood's city limits, passing the self-storage place, two fast-food joints that couldn't hold a candle to Betty's, and a strip mall containing the ubiquitous check-cashing store, discount grocery, and tobacco place. I turned short of downtown to ensure whoever was watching my car didn't accidentally see me and made a left toward Rusty's house, dropping off the truck and starting the cold hike back to the *Post*.

It took twenty minutes to get to my first destination — the Lynwood Police Department — to cover my tracks and drop off the public records request. I printed two versions, one on *Post* letterhead and one on my own, just in case Walt hadn't agreed. I passed the one on the *Post's* letterhead to the front desk clerk and beat a hasty retreat on the off-chance she would take it straight to Adams.

If Dalton's envelope was what he claimed, the move was completely unnecessary, but I had to go through the motions, at least for Walt's sake.

By the time I returned to the *Post*, I was shivering in earnest. The obscure door I left by was locked, so I made my way to the front, hoping my tail wouldn't see me. I ducked inside.

"There you are, Dave! We wondered where you went." Jenny sat at her desk, not typing madly for once. "It's cold outside. You should wear a jacket."

"I wanted the full experience in case I have to do a weather story later." I sat down and put on my coat. "Yes, it's cold."

"You might get that story too. You see the forecast? Big storm rolling in."

Of course, there was.

"I haven't been checking." I put my laptop bag on the desk.

"What's this hot lead? Walt's all excited but won't spill."

I wondered if I had overplayed my hand with him. I hoped it wouldn't be a problem.

"Just some rumors I need to check out. I'm hoping to prove if they're true or false. Until then, just rumors — and it could take a while."

She nodded. "Anything I can check?"

"I asked LPD for some cold case files. Doubt they'll give them over but have to try." I paused. "So, who was the body?"

"That fast-food kid. Cervelli. They found him up by the creek on the north end. Not far from where the teacher went missing."

"They say what happened?"

She snorted. "They said he appeared to have died of exposure. But they wouldn't call a press conference for that, would they?"

"Why did they?"

"They said they knew there was intense public interest in the cases and just wanted to calm things down."

"I'm sure that will work." I rolled my eyes.

She laughed, started to turn back to her computer, and then stopped. "Seriously, where did you go? Walt said you went to make a phone call, but then nobody could find you. You might want to find him — he was talking about calling the cops."

"You couldn't have started with that? Where is he?" I grabbed my laptop bag and stood.

"Production, I think. Or advertising. Maybe circulation."

"That narrows it down." I headed off in search of Walt.

He was in advertising, getting his ear chewed by Karen Linscott, whose work birthday party ending I'd wandered into right after Mom died. I waved, hoping to let him know I was fine, but he took it as a rescue attempt and excused himself, leaving Karen staring after him.

"Where the hell have you been?" he boomed, ensuring at least half the building heard. He stalked toward his office, motioning for me to follow.

"I told you. I had to make a call. When I was done, I needed to run down to the bank, bumped into my lawyer, and went to talk to him." I hadn't scripted the lie, but it flowed disconcertingly easily. "Then I stopped by LPD and dropped off the records request."

"I damn near called the police. You come in talking about a bunch of missing people, then promptly vanish. No note, no call, your car's still here."

I winced. I hadn't even considered someone might think me a victim. "Walt."

He stopped and turned.

"I'm genuinely sorry. I didn't think about it and should have told someone where I was going." I meant that, in a way, but there's no way I would have told the truth about where I was going.

"Just don't do it again, okay?" He turned and led me back to his office. I wasn't sure if I was supposed to follow, but he waved me in.

He sat. "You a drinking man?"

"What? No. I mean, sometimes, but not that much. Bad habit."

"I'll drink to that." He reached under his desk and pulled out a bottle of Fontana's. I'd heard a rumor he kept one in the office but had never seen it. "One drink won't hurt anything."

I narrowed my eyes — was he offering me a drink in the middle of the lunch hour?

"Sorry, boss. Can't touch that stuff."

He froze. "Why not?"

"I don't drink whiskey. Ever. Not since."

He didn't blink or seem to get it.

"Since my accident." I groaned.

"Oh." He lowered the bottle. "You sure? Just this once?"

"I'm fairly certain I'd decorate your office if I did. Thanks. Besides, I'm not on for a couple of hours. I've got some errands to run, and this time I'm driving."

He put the bottle and glasses back in their hiding place and motioned toward the newsroom. "They don't know I keep that here. Appreciate you not mentioning it."

"Of course." We sat in awkward silence. "Anyway, need to get to those errands. I'll be back at two."

"See you then." He turned to his computer screen and ignored me as I walked out.

Still carrying my bag and already in my jacket, I stopped at Jenny's desk. "I'll be back in a while. Let me know if the cops say anything about what I gave them, okay?"

"You'll be the first," she said. "Where you off to?"

"Just need to go over a few personal things before coming back in. Catch you later."

I didn't give her a chance to respond and headed through the usual employee entrance to my Olds. While I scraped the car's windshield, the beige SUV sprouted an exhaust plume.

He followed me the four blocks to the library. I decided to go there because I didn't feel safe at the apartment, Allison was at work, and I needed somewhere I could work alone yet be in a room full of witnesses. I reached the door and looked back. The SUV had stopped across the street and was already shut off. On impulse, I gave it a cheery wave as I entered the library.

As before, the brightly lit library calmed me with its clean lines, hushed sounds, and faintly musty book smell.

"Need to see more of our microfilms, Mr. Kendrick?" The librarian behind the counter, a frumpy woman in her fifties, was the same as the one I had paid for the copies on Saturday. Which, somehow, was only two days ago.

"Not this time. Do you have a table where I can spread out a bit?"

She thought for a minute. "Well, you could use the genealogy room as long as no one else comes in. But if they do, you'll have to share." She led me past the reference stacks to a small room tucked away in the back wall of the main room and flicked on the lights. "If you need help with the files, just let me know."

"The table will do it, thanks."

"Okay, honey."

I winced. I hated it when strange women called me "honey." They were the only ones who ever did.

Once again, I fired up the computer and then pulled out the manila envelope. I couldn't help but look at the files lining the walls, wondering if the genealogies contained further clues to the mystery I was trying to unravel. It would probably take me days or weeks to wade through it all.

I opened the envelope instead and started to read, becoming so engrossed in the reports that when my phone buzzed, I jumped. I marked my place and answered it.

"Where are you?" Jenny asked.

"What? I'm... I'm down the street." I glanced at my watch. It was quarter after two.

"You'd better get here quick. Walt's looking rabid."

"Right. I'll be there in ten. Tell him there's a long line at Betty's."

I gathered the reports, being careful to keep them in order, then I drove to Betty's, hoping the line was short, and placed my order while watching the SUV idle at the curb.

The reports I read raised more questions than they answered, but they answered a few. For one thing, I was now convinced that most, if not all, of the disappearances reported over the years were linked. For another, I was convinced I wouldn't sleep well for quite some time.

Dalton had delivered beyond anything I could have hoped for. Not only did I get the base police reports, which usually acknowledged someone had reported something but contained little other information, but he also gave me the investigative files for many of the cases. It wasn't everything, but it was a lot, including the officers' case notes.

I was only back to the 1940s, but one thing was consistent. When missing people turned up dead somewhere, it was usually days or weeks later. And the descriptions I'd read were strikingly similar to the condition in which I had found Ralph Walther's body — severely emaciated to the point of being shrunken, but with no other apparent marks or trauma on the bodies. A few even listed the cause of death as exsanguination, but others made it sound as though all the bodily fluids had dried up. This was consistent whether a person had been gone for three days or three months.

And almost all of them had turned up within a radius of about half a mile. I walked into the *Post*, still reviewing details in my head, went straight to my desk, and opened a map on my browser. The neighborhood was easy enough because Mom's house was in it. I didn't dare enter addresses but zoomed in to see the familiar landmarks — the fallow field at the end of Pine Street on the east, the river north of Lynwood Elementary to the west, and the distillery to the north.

Then I gasped. No wonder there were so many stories about it. The Heyward place sat right in the middle.

CHAPTER FORTY-THREE

J enny and Sam had prowled around Tremont Street north of Elmwood Elementary for a while, trying to figure out where Cervelli's body had been found. They finally got a neighbor to point to a stretch along the river, but since he'd been found two days earlier, there was no police tape, so they returned to the office.

Rusty was there, too, and had the little TV on his desk tuned to the Weather Channel.

"Storm coming tonight?" I hoped there would be snow. Snow meant ice. Ice postponed basketball games and wrestling matches. And that meant I'd have time to review more of the reports.

"You might have an easy night after all." The plan was for me to go to two different basketball practices for features and then to a wrestling meet.

"Bummer. Was looking forward to getting back into it," I lied.

"Bullshit," he said. "Your mind isn't on sports."

I shrugged. "It's not. But maybe it should be."

The snow started at around three, and since the forecast called for between four and eight inches, the cancellations soon followed. I was skeptical—Ohio weather often came with significant forecasts, only to drop a dusting unworthy of a powdered donut. Of course, we did get good storms, just not nearly as often as predicted.

I spent the next hour answering the phone and posting the latest cancellations to the website and social media accounts.

Since school districts sent all this stuff directly to parents via text, I sometimes wondered why we bothered. But then, it's what we had always done, so we continued to do it.

By five, Jenny and the others had filed their stories, and by six, Walt had read them all. Rusty had a project he was working on for a weekend package, so I was left to monitor the weather and post updates as needed.

The snow faded until it looked like nothing more than summer cottonwood tufts blowing in the breeze, leaving maybe an inch on the ground. Since it wasn't busy, I dove back into the police reports as soon as Walt and the others left.

Some cases ended with bodies, and in several instances, the cause of death was listed as exposure, but they were still suspicious. Others, like Walt's grandfather and most of my ancestors, were left open because there were mysterious circumstances, and no bodies were found. The files weren't chronological, so I kept stumbling across more recent cases. The report for my grandfather, George Kendrick Jr., listed him as a suspect in the death of my grandmother, but he was ultimately presumed dead in 1982, seven years after he went missing. I wondered how they decided to do that, given he was considered a fugitive.

The report was vague—the detective wrote that "other factors" led him to believe it was unlikely that my grandfather was an arsonist without spelling out what those factors were. I saw with a start that the detective had been Dalton Adams.

It was a year before my father's death. After that file, I found the one on my father's disappearance. It didn't contain much I didn't already know, but there was one major detail. While the news reports indicated four men had gone hunting, the police report said there were five. And the fifth was a name I knew well—Tony Gianini, Dad's fellow

271

firefighter. I pondered another trip to the back room for a phone call but couldn't leave the police scanner.

The rest of the report repeated details I had already read in the *Post*. Roger Pelfrey had been found dead, shot with a .38, in a wooded area just north of town. I rechecked the Google map and confirmed there was a wooded area just behind the Heyward place. Dalton Adams had said the five men had spread out but underestimated how dark it would get and lost track of each other. He said that Pelfrey claimed something was chasing him, and Adams had tried to help by firing a warning shot above the attacker. He said he hadn't hit anything, and the investigator had believed him.

Somewhere in the chaos, Victor Bruce had fallen and broken his collarbone, and Dad had wandered off. Faced with an injured friend and another scared silly, Adams and Gianini did what they felt best, which was to deal with what they had. Gianini stayed with Bruce and rendered aid while Adams got out of the woods and summoned an ambulance. They kept assuming Dad and Roger Pelfrey would turn up, but they never did. The next day, search parties combed the woods, which was when they found Pelfrey.

For some reason, no one ever questioned whether Adams had, in fact, shot Pelfrey or what had happened to the attacker chasing him, and I wondered if Adams had really given me everything after all.

Of Dad, they found no sign, nor did they find Pelfrey's mysterious attacker.

My phone pinged. Allison asked how work was going.

I texted: "All right. Dull. But I found out some stuff. A lot of stuff."

"Come over later, tell me?"

"Love to."

I checked the weather radar again and went back to the reports. There were a few from the early 1900s, but nothing older than that. For some reason, I had hoped they would have scrawled out reports from the 1800s, but if they had even written reports in those days, they weren't here now.

By the time I finished, it was approaching nine o'clock. Another couple of inches had fallen, but that was it — another dud.

I stood and stretched. I hadn't realized how hunched I was between reading reports and making notes on my spreadsheet.

"Some project you're working on," Rusty said. Marla had disappeared into the back. "I don't think I've ever seen you so quiet."

"Oh. Yeah. It's...." What was I going to say? "Something I'm working on for Walt."

"Sounded like he thought you had a story for him."

"I will, but it's not ready yet. Going to be a few days." I should have given myself more time. "Listen, don't tell him I was working on this tonight. I want to get it right and don't want him breathing down my neck."

"Good luck with that." We both laughed.

"You might as well leave. I don't think we're going to get much more snow," Rusty said. "If we do, I'll write it up. You look beat."

"And starving." I'd completely forgotten dinner. "You sure?"

"Yeah, go on."

Marla came back carrying a steaming coffee mug. "Is he chasing you out?"

I nodded.

"We've got the snowpocalypse covered." She chuckled.

"I won't fight both of you." I repacked the reports and stuffed them in my straining bag, then pulled out the phone and texted Allison, offering to pick up a pizza. She sent a thumbs up.

I put the phone in my pocket and found Rusty grinning at me.

"You've got someone to text at this time of night when you're getting off early, do you?"

"Who me?" I said.

"Hah! You're blushing!"

Marla turned. "Oh, did you meet a girl?"

"You two are terrible," I said. "I sure as hell can't tell you now. You'll have to wait until tomorrow. Or next month."

They were both still giggling when I left the room.

I got to the parking lot, waved again to my shadow in the blue sedan, and started the car. While it warmed, I called a pizza place and placed an order. I texted Allison again when I had the pizza in the car and was on my way.

In the thirty minutes since I left work, snow fell in earnest, and by the time I got to the house, it looked like another inch had fallen. The roads were starting to get nasty, but I didn't have too much trouble.

When I arrived, I was surprised to find the front door open and Chase standing there in his pajamas and snow boots, holding Allison's phone. I got out and grabbed my bag and the pizza.

"Hey, isn't it past your bedtime?" I yelled over the wind, which had picked up considerably.

He answered, but I couldn't hear what he said.

"What are you doing up? And why do you have the door open?" I asked when I got close.

"I don't know where Mom is," he said. "I don't think she's here."

CHAPTER FORTY-FOUR

C hase handed me Allison's phone. Juggling the box, I saw my last text had come in when I left the pizza shop, and it was the only one I could access without a passcode. That meant she hadn't replied. I checked my own to confirm.

I guided Chase into the foyer and used my hip to close the door. "She wouldn't leave you alone—she's got to be here somewhere. Allison?" I called out, walking toward the kitchen and putting the pizza box on the counter. She didn't reply, so I went back through the dining room. Chase shadowed me closely, wide-eyed.

"Allison? You're scaring Chase," I called, hoping my voice sounded playful. I led him up the stairs and checked her room, then the other bedrooms and the bathroom. Then, I checked the storage room, which was still dead-bolted.

I went down on one knee and looked at Chase. "Were you up here?"

"I was in bed."

"Why did you get up?"

His lower lip quivered.

"I'm not upset with you, Chase. But you have to tell me what you know, okay?"

At first, I thought he wasn't going to reply, but he finally murmured something.

"What was that?"

"I thought I heard you downstairs," he said. "I wanted to say hi."

"You heard my voice?" I frowned.

"I thought so. A man's voice."

"Could you hear what he said?"

"No. I snuck downstairs, but you weren't there, and Mom wasn't there. Her phone was on the couch." He rushed forward and hugged me, nearly knocking me off balance and sobbing, "She never leaves her phone."

"Chase, it's okay. We'll find her," I hugged him back, but I felt cold inside. This could not be happening. I could not have Allison come back into my life only to have her disappear, just like my father.

I picked Chase up and carried him downstairs. "Come on, buddy, we'll find her." We got to the first floor, and I set him down. "You're heavy, you know that?" I took his hand and led him into the living room, where the TV was still on, and a mug of hot chocolate sat on the end table. I checked—it was still warm. I poked my head into the sunroom next, but there was no sign of her there.

We went back into the kitchen via the craft room, which was empty. The desk was mercifully closed. I checked the back door, but it, too, was bolted. Then, I looked through the window. It was difficult to see through the wind-blown snow, but it appeared there were no tracks.

"Maybe she's doing laundry." I headed for the basement.

"I don't like it down there," Chase muttered.

"You can wait here."

"Don't leave me," he whimpered.

I took his hand. "I won't leave you, Chase. I promise. But chances are your mom is just downstairs and couldn't hear us. Especially with all that wind." It was howling, but it was unlikely that would matter to anyone in the basement. Chase looked just as doubtful.

"Let's go down slowly together, okay? I'll hold your hand."

"Okay," he whispered, and my heart broke.

I opened the basement door and switched on the light. At the last second, I grabbed Allison's flashlight from the counter, just in case. Then, I led the way slowly down the creaking steps.

The washer and dryer sat silent against one wall, and boxes lined the wall between them and the old workbench. We went around the corner to the section under the foyer and living room.

The crawlspace yawned, pitch black inside. Chase whimpered and pressed his body against me, squeezing my hand tight.

I switched on the flashlight and directed it toward the opening. Something looked wrong. I stepped closer. Chase was crying now.

The small wrought-iron door against the far wall, the one I had thought opened to the outside, was ajar. There were stairs several feet beyond the threshold that looked like they did lead up to an outer door, but between the wrought iron and the stairs was a gap on the left-hand side.

It was just wide enough to be a tunnel.

"Did you see that before?" I whispered.

Chase finally lifted his head, craned his neck, and gasped. "No."

I considered calling the police and wondered how fast they'd have me back in handcuffs. I didn't want that for Chase or me.

Then, an idea hit.

"I'm going to call a friend," I pulled my phone from my pocket and called Tim. Voice mail.

"Hey, it's Dave. Listen, can you come to Mom's house? We can't find Allison, and I don't want to call the chief. Need a hand. But please come alone, okay?"

I hung up and hoped he would get the message soon.

A distant sound made us both freeze. It happened again—a thud and then a faint cry.

It sounded like a woman. And it sounded like it was coming from the tunnel.

Chase sobbed. "Mom?"

"Chase, I have to check. I need you to wait here."

"No!" He grabbed my leg.

"I have to see if your mom is there."

"I'll come with you."

"That's not a good idea."

"You can't leave me," he cried.

I didn't want to leave him alone, but I couldn't stop him from following me anyway.

I scanned the basement for something I could use as a weapon and spotted a familiar box near the dryer.

I pulled out the baseball bat I signed for Luke in high school. Though it had been close to twenty years, the grip felt as familiar as a well-worn jacket.

"Okay. Come on," I told Chase. I climbed into the crawlspace and pulled him up after me, then shimmied my way to the opening. I paused when I realized the old oak smell I always attributed to my father's workbench was much stronger here. I was relieved to see that once I squeezed through the iron door, I'd be able to stand again. Stairs led down into the tunnel under the side wall of the house. There wasn't any light switch I could see, and it looked like we would be descending into a black pit.

"Grab my belt," I said. "I need to hold the flashlight and the bat."

The belt cinched painfully. Holding the bat in front of me like a sword and taking a deep breath, I started down.

CHAPTER FORTY-FIVE

T here were about twenty steps down before a landing, with more going down to the right, away from the house. "Stay close and stay quiet, okay?" I whispered over my shoulder. Chase nodded.

I stopped above the landing and leaned forward to peer around the corner. There were another ten steps down, then a dirt-floored corridor that went another forty feet or so before turning right. There was no light or movement.

I led Chase down, glad he had his snow boots on, at least. It was colder down here, and I knew he had to be feeling the chill. I slipped off my jacket and put it on him.

"Chase, if I tell you to run, you need to get back up to the house and call 911," I told him.

He nodded. Words seemed too much for him.

We traversed those stairs, and then I peeked around the next corner to find another set of stairs going down. We had to be close to, if not completely under, Pine Street at this point. I wondered if the city had any idea this was here.

Halfway down the set of a dozen stairs, I could see a corridor at the bottom. This time, there was light coming through a broad doorway. I immediately switched off the flashlight, hoping no one had seen us. Chase gasped, and I felt my belt tighten against my waist.

"Quiet," I whispered.

There was a low rhythmic voice.

I shoved the flashlight into my jeans pocket and gripped the bat handle with both hands, then crept to the side of the door. The light had to be coming from candles or something. It flickered. Shelves of casks stared at me like huge, blank eyes, blocking the view into the rest of the room. The walls were made of old brick, which arched and met like an ancient subway tunnel.

The oak smell was overpowering, and there was something else mingling with it—almost like oatmeal. The temperature, too, had risen from the low sixties to somewhere north of eighty.

Casks. The kind you'd find in a wine cellar. Or a whiskey distillery. I felt my stomach lurch. Had we somehow ended up in Fontana's?

I dismissed that thought—the distillery wasn't underground, and it wasn't this close. Perhaps this was someone's home brewery or something.

I moved closer. There were three rows of casks. Beyond them, cutting the back of the room in half and shielding the left corner, were three metal contraptions. The first stood on a low table and had a copper tube, maybe four feet high and three across, with a small copper pipe sticking out of the top. It widened as it led to a fatter, taller cylinder that rested atop a brick fireplace, which radiated heat. And beyond that was another metal tub with an open lid.

The chanting was louder now.

"What is that?" Chase whispered.

Glass bottles lined shelves against the far wall.

The voice droned, and I thought I heard a different voice whimper. Chase must have heard it, too, because he grabbed my arm. His pale face was terror-stricken. I rubbed his back once, then hugged him fiercely. "It's going to be okay," I whispered. "Hang on."

Candles were mounted on the walls and the floor, sputtering in grubby glass containers. The heat coming from that metal cylinder was almost overwhelming. I peeked between the casks and sucked in my breath.

There was a metal table, about three feet high, with a person lying on it. All I could see were the feet, but it was enough to make my heart drop. They were clad in brightly colored Christmas socks.

Gripping the bat, I ran as fast as I thought I could with Chase hanging onto my jeans, and for an absurd moment, I feared he would pull the belt free, leaving me to charge some unseen enemy with my pants around my ankles.

Allison's arms, chest, and feet were strapped to the table, a plain metal job with a lip running around the edges. She didn't appear to be fighting. Along the far side of the table was an indentation along the edge just inside the lip. Red liquid ran along it from her slashed wrist.

Fontana's owner, Ezekiel Heyward, chanted by her head, eyes closed. His trademark necklace dangled from one hand. The other held a dripping blade.

"Mommy!" Chase yelled. Heyward opened his eyes.

"About time. Shame you brought the boy." Heyward sneered, then raised his voice. "Close the door and get down here!"

A door slammed behind us.

"Chase, get in the corner." I hefted the bat.

"Uh-uh." Heyward turned the blade point down and held it over Allison. "Come closer, and I will finish this quicker."

Footsteps sounded behind me, and I turned halfway to face the new threat. A man with a matted mass of grey hair covering his head and face walked toward us. He carried a sword, the kind I'd seen in Civil War reenactments.

"Kill him. The boy too."

The man didn't hesitate; he raised the blade and swung it toward me in an overhand chop. I barely managed to get the bat up in time to block it. He stepped back and swung again, sideways this time. I parried with the bat again.

The man swung a third time and a fourth. I blocked both but feared that he'd get lucky and the blade would hit my fingers. If I didn't think of something quickly, I'd be missing more than just a few digits.

When he tried another overhead chop, I not only blocked but ducked to the side and, this time, launched my attack, swinging for his ribs. The bat connected with a sickening crunch. He didn't seem to feel it and made no attempt to defend himself. He swung again at me like an automaton. This time, I felt the tip burn across my thigh.

Heyward yelled, "You may hurt him, but he will kill you. He has no choice."

Luckily, the man wasn't skilled with the blade as he kept swinging it rather than trying to stab, which would have been harder for me.

Finally, he swung from my left side, and I blocked, turned, and slammed my left elbow into the side of the man's face. He grunted and staggered as the sword clattered to the floor. I completed my turn and was ready to swing again, but the man hit the wall and slid to the ground, holding his head.

"Nicely done, David. I knew I should have given him sword lessons," Heyward said. "Shame, too, it's probably ruined that blade. One of your ancestor's, I believe."

I turned to face him and gasped. Heyward still held the knife in his right hand, but his left forearm was wrapped around Chase, whose eyes were wide and fixed. The pendant still dangled from Heyward's left hand.

"Oh, do put the bat down," Heyward said.

"You're going to kill us all anyway. I'm not going without a fight."

He shrugged. "Suit yourself. You've already proven yourself stronger than your old man."

This was one curveball too many, and I gaped.

"What, you didn't know?"

Realization dawned slowly. "You killed my father?" Was that even possible? Was Heyward even old enough for that?

I thought of the photo from the 1960s of this man's uncle, who looked so like him. *Could it be…?*

His laughter brought me back to the present. "Of course, I didn't. I wanted you to know what it would be like to grow up without a father. And I wanted him" — he nodded toward the man still gasping against the wall — "to know that you were doing it and didn't really need him — well, much, anyway." He shrugged.

I felt as though he'd put a strap across my chest and squeezed it. I tore my eyes from Chase and Allison, bleeding but still breathing, and looked over my shoulder.

"It can't be," I said.

"Tell him your name," Heyward commanded.

"Robert Alan K… Kendrick," the man wheezed. "Lynwood Fire Department."

"Dad?"

CHAPTER FORTY-SIX

The man didn't respond. I wanted to look him in the eyes to see if it was really my father. But there was Chase. And that knife. And Allison, still bleeding on the table.

I growled at Heyward, "What the hell have you done? What are... why? What the hell is this?"

"Your great-great-hell-I don't-know-how-many grandpas took my daddy away from me. My daddy didn't care. He just left me. And now I make sure every one of his spawn knows exactly what it's like to have their fathers taken away."

His eyes glinted almost as much as the pendant in the firelight.

"So, I take 'em. And when they get old, I get rid of them and take their sons. But you couldn't get around to having any, could you? You went and killed your girlfriend instead. So, I wait. And now you've got this kid who thinks you're pretty cool." He shook Chase. "But instead, you've brought him down here. I guess my fun's over."

He spat. "It's fine. It's... all good, as they say. I was tired of hiding you Kendricks anyway, pretending my house was full of ghosts. They never had it better, free food and nice lodgings."

"Let him go," The man lying on the floor gasped.

"Who, this little guy? Nah. Not yet, Bob. Get David here a drink."

Groaning, the man — I couldn't think of him as my father — stood, holding his side.

"One of the new batch, please," Heyward specified.

Bob shuffled toward the bottles on the wall.

"Why is he doing what you say?"

"He's mine." He jiggled the pendant. "Too many drinks of my special brew. He'll do whatever I tell him. Just like all the others."

"Ignore him. You can fight… Dad." I wrenched the word through my tightening throat, still not quite sure I believed this raving lunatic.

"No, he can't," Heyward cackled.

I couldn't be certain, but the pendant appeared to glow brighter than before.

"Hand your son that bottle. Tell him to drink it. Tell him it'll be good for him.

Dad picked up a bottle and turned toward me.

"Chase. Chase!" I yelled. Chase's eyes snapped back into focus.

I glanced at his chest. "Sidewinder."

"Huh?"

"Sidewinder!" I repeated.

"You are just a little nuts, aren't you, Dave?" Heyward said.

Chase caught on. He grabbed the pendant from Heyward and ripped it from his hand.

Heyward howled as the chain scraped his fingers. "Give me that!"

Chase whipped the pendant toward me, sideways, just under Heyward's grasp. I took one step forward and swung the bat.

The bat connected with the mottled red and green stone with a metallic clink, and the pendant zoomed back the way it came, flying over Heyward's head and smacking into the stone wall behind him. Behind me, Dad gasped and drew a deep, rattling breath.

"No! My dragon blood stone!" Heyward screamed as he let go of Chase and picked up the pendant.

Chase rushed to my side, burying his face in my shirt.

Candlelight flashed from pieces of the shattered stone as they fell loose from the metal clasp.

Heyward whispered, "What have you done?" He lurched toward a door at the far end of the room. I let him go and rushed to the table, leading Chase by the hand.

"Allison! Wake up!" I fumbled with the strap across her chest, then stopped and unstrapped her injured wrist instead.

"Here," a voice wheezed. The man Heyward claimed was my father pulled his shirt over his head, wincing. He handed it to me. "Wrap it. Must stop... the bleeding."

I wrapped her wrist.

"Tighter," he said.

I cinched it.

"Now... go get... him." He pointed in the direction Heyward had taken.

"Why? I need to get her and you to a hospital!"

"He has... more of those. And a gun." He gasped again, and I wondered if his injuries were worse than a few broken ribs. "He'll... come back... finish us. Use that... mumbo jumbo of his... make himself young again, start all over."

"Start over?"

He nudged the bottle he'd put on the floor. "This stuff. Lets him into our heads. Makes us... do things." He wheezed. "Then he does this ritual, kills somebody, and melts the years right off him." He put a hand on my shoulder, his eyes steady on my face. My last shred of doubt fled.

"How?"

"No time. Go! Stop him!"

How can this be? I hated myself for injuring him.

"You have to finish this. I can't. I'll take care of them."

I nodded, retrieved my bat, and went to the door. My father told Chase to put pressure on his mom's wrist.

I looked back.

"Hurry," he wheezed.

CHAPTER FORTY-SEVEN

I went through the door, which led to another tunnel. This one had gas lamps mounted every twenty feet or so, which enabled me to run. I slowed before going around the corner and up the stairs in case Heyward was lurking. I didn't think I could stop bullets with a battered Louisville Slugger.

Two flights and three turns brought me to the bottom of another staircase that opened into a broader room. Here I slowed, barely peeking over the rim of the stairs to make sure the room was empty.

Unlike my mom's basement, this one had a trap door that leaned against the wall. More flames danced in lamps, and I wondered if this guy had a medieval fetish. I walked out into the broader area of what I guessed was the main basement and followed it to the only other way out, a narrow staircase leading up.

Knowing I'd be a sitting duck on the stairs, I took them two at a time, but unfortunately, my thigh picked that moment to remind me that it had been badly scratched. Wincing, I hurried as quickly as I could, trading stealth for speed. I pushed open the door with the bat, and when no one shot at it, I stepped into the room and let out a breath.

It was the kitchen of the Heyward manor house. The room was warmer than the cellar because the pot-bellied stove in the corner leaked light and heat around the edges and radiated out into the room. A steaming pot was perched on the stove as if dinner would soon be served.

A table was set for three. Perhaps the place was in use after all. Well, clearly it was.

There were three doors out of that room, and I tried to figure out the rest of the layout.

There was a dull thump somewhere above me. Part of me wanted to wait since Heyward would have to come back this way to get back to the wine cellar.

But the smarter part of me wanted to find him before he got that gun. Taking a chance, I started toward one of the doors. I tiptoed my way to the open archway, then slid through and to the side to avoid presenting a silhouette. I also vowed to stop watching so many cop shows.

This room was darker, and I had to adjust to the gloom. I took three steps toward the stairs when there was an ominous click. I'd also seen enough cop shows to know someone had just cocked a gun. I turned to my right. There, standing in the corner at the bottom of a grand staircase, was Ezekiel Heyward.

He didn't look good, even in the dim light from the kitchen, but his hand was steady enough. He appeared to be almost leaning against the wall and coughed a wet, phlegmy sound.

"How nice of you to leave everyone defenseless," he croaked.

"They've gone out the other way," I lied.

"Doubtful. Your father couldn't haul that girl. You probably killed him with those broken ribs. And the boy's far too small to help."

I cringed, hoping he was wrong about my father's condition but dreading him being right. He must have seen it because I saw his teeth gleam in the darkness.

I staggered backward. His teeth. That smile. That horrible grin. I'd seen it before. That night in October — Ralph Walther's face had been contorted into this grin, this malevolent smile that belonged to Ezekiel Heyward.

"You," I whispered. "It was you. You killed my mother."

"About time you figured it out." His voice sounded stronger. "She had to meddle. Had to go see her old friend Dalton, didn't she?"

He coughed again but kept the pistol pointed at me. I wondered if he could hit me at this range.

Then again, we were pretty close.

"And that bastard told her everything. Let her see the old pictures. She figured out it's been me all these years. Had to run off and tell you. Well, I couldn't have that."

"Ralph had no idea." I could hear the disbelief in my voice.

"Of course not. Walther fell asleep driving and woke in an ambulance, watching you fight to get to him."

"And then, what? You made Ralph drink himself to death?"

"Poetic, really. Another alcohol-related death to haunt your family." He cackled. "Oh, but that was fun. You were so *angry* when you saw him—well, me—smile. Now put the bat down."

"No."

"Boy, you put it down, or I'll end you right here!" He still had some power in his voice, plus I didn't have a lot of options. I set the bat down on its end, then dropped it. The clang echoed through the house.

"Back the way you came. Nice and slow. Neighbors are used to weird noises here, but I'd just as soon keep the gunshot in the basement."

"Why?"

"You'd rather be shot here?"

"Why shoot anyone? Why… what's this all about?"

291

"I told you. Revenge. Pure and simple. Oh, I figured out how to make some money off it too, but mostly, just revenge on your daddy, his daddy, his daddy, and my daddy."

"Huh?"

"Shut up and walk, boy."

I considered trying to kick the bat at him but knew it wouldn't do enough to distract him. I walked to the door — gave him the silhouette I'd denied him before. Then I saw my chance in the kitchen.

I dodged quickly to the side, ran through the door, and grabbed the handle of the pot that had been sitting on the stove, hoping like hell it was insulated, and swung it back toward the door just as he appeared.

He screamed, and a shot rang out as he staggered back out of sight. The pot hit him on the right shoulder and spun him back as I lunged for the door.

The next shot was deafening, and I felt something flash past my cheek. I stopped so fast I fell, my feet sliding in whatever had been in the pot, and for the second time in recent memory, I landed hard on my tailbone, then cracked my head on the floor for good measure.

A door slammed, and there was fighting in the room I had just left.

Dazed, I tried to scramble backward, and then I stood, wincing at the pain in my backside and feeling an embarrassing warmth down the back of my pants. I strode through the archway.

"Now, you turn on me?" Heyward screeched as he shoved at a second figure, who staggered.

I darted forward, dipped, and grabbed the bat in one smooth motion I'd never be able to replicate, and spun on a soup-slicked heel. Heyward raised his left arm, the one holding the pistol, and pointed it at the man he had shoved away — his secretary, John West.

I swung the bat one-handed, bringing it down hard on Heyward's wrist. There was a snap, and he howled with pain. Recoiling, he dropped the gun. I kicked it backward with one foot, still brandishing my bat.

"Enough," I said. I didn't need to bother.

Heyward's face was pale even in the poor light, and he gasped for breath. For the first time, he looked scared.

"Sir. Smash it."

West's voice, smooth and deep, almost made me jump. At first, I thought he meant Heyward, then the gun. Neither made sense.

"At your feet, sir. Smash it. Before he uses it again."

I looked down. Sure enough, there was another pendant, this one smaller than the one Heyward had used in the cellar. He must have had it wrapped around the gun or his hand. It glinted in the firelight from the other room. Or, perhaps, it had a glint all its own.

"Why?" I asked.

"He's been using stones like that to prolong his life. He steals life from the living," he said calmly as if explaining how the mail was delivered. "He kills them, and it makes him young again. He's been doing it for decades. Lots of them."

Something clicked into place in my tired brain.

"Zachariah. Zachariah Heyward," I whispered, and he moaned. "You... it's been you all this time? What is it, a hundred and fifty years?"

"He was born in 1849," West said. "His mother was a fabulous woman who didn't get what she deserved. His father was a bad man and has been punished for it ever since."

"You abandoned me!" Heyward shouted. Again, I was momentarily confused.

"You and your uncle would have killed me."

I looked at West in disbelief. "Are you saying that you are Heyward's father?"

"Yessir. I was Isaac Cooper in those days. Your ancestor helped me escape, and then I helped him escape."

My mouth dropped. Heyward took the opportunity to lunge at me, but I jabbed the end of the bat into his chest, driving him back against the wall.

"I'm sorry, sir," West said, and again, I wasn't sure which of us he was addressing. "I had no idea my spawn could be so evil."

I stared at Heyward. I remembered wondering if he had Native American blood in him, with his black hair and somewhat darkened complexion. Could he be half African-American? And was he really over a century and a half old?

Heyward leaned against the wall, but he wasn't sobbing anymore. In fact, he was whispering something.

"Sir. Smash it now." West instructed. His voice was much firmer, and I didn't delay again. I turned the bat, gripped the handle with both hands and slammed the head down against the pendant.

"No!" Heyward lunged forward, but there was no energy left this time. The gemstone crunched a moment before Heyward hit the bat, knocked it sideways, and fell over his precious stone.

He huddled there for a moment, trying to pick up the pieces with his good hand. Then he looked at me, and his eyes, little more than black pits in the gloom, shrank into his head. He let out a long gasp, then fell sideways, landed hard on his shoulder, flopped onto his back, and lay still. His eyes were open.

West said, "It's finally over." He put a hand on his forehead, took a deep breath, then another, and dropped to his knees. "It's finally over."

CHAPTER FORTY-EIGHT

I wasn't sure what to do. West was kneeling, holding his face in his hands, so I picked up the gun — I didn't know how to engage the safety but didn't feel the weapon should be left lying around, so I jammed it in my back pocket. Then I reached for my phone but realized it was in my jacket, which was on Chase in the cellar. Instead, I checked Heyward for a pulse. I didn't find one.

"Don't worry, sir. If he moves, I'll kill him myself," West said. He was standing again. "You okay?"

I was drained. My left leg ached from being stabbed by the sword, and my backside and head throbbed from the fall. The backs of my legs hurt, too, as I brushed my hands against my backside. They came away warm and wet, and I held them up in the candlelight.

I couldn't help it. Laughter escaped in a burst, then a flood.

"Sir?"

"Soup," I managed. "It's just soup. *Hot* soup, but soup." His blank stare gave way to a grin.

"I need to get a doctor for the people downstairs." I finally got myself under control.

"Did he hurt them?"

"One of them — he cut her wrist." I swallowed. "I hurt the other. He came after me with a sword because... because he told him to." I motioned toward Heyward's inert form.

"He made your father do many horrible things. Is he okay?"

"I don't know. I hit him in the ribs with this." I waved the bat.

"Let's get help. There are probably people upstairs who need it too. They won't be able to get out, even when they try."

"More? Who?" My eyes widened.

"People he's taken and hasn't... used yet." West spat the last two words, then lifted a cell phone from his pocket. He dialed, gave the operator the address, and covered the phone. "I'll get help. You go on down now, sir."

I started for the kitchen but stopped in the doorway.

"You don't have to call me sir. Please don't call me sir. I'm David."

He waved and continued to give the information to the operator.

The trip downstairs was at once harder and easier. It was easier not having to worry about a madman with a gun, but now that the adrenaline started to subside, the pain, particularly in my left thigh and right shoulder, was numbing.

Allison was extremely pale but awake. My father was too. Only Chase looked healthy.

I hugged Chase and Allison tightly. "It's over. I got him,"

My father leaned on the other side of the table, watching us, joy warring with pain on his features. I let go of Chase and Allison and went around the table.

"I'm... I'm sorry I couldn't get to you," my father said. "I've been... down here or in that godforsaken house all this time. And every time I thought he wasn't paying attention, he took control of me again. Made me do horrible things." He shuddered. "I was afraid to try again. I knew he'd make me hurt you or your mother. I had to stay away."

I wanted to hug him, but I didn't want to hurt him.

"We have to go upstairs," he said.

"Right. Yes. Someone's calling an ambulance."

"Who?" Dad snapped to attention.

"John West. He helped me…"

"John's a good man. But we need to get out of here quickly. Just in case." He grimaced. "After all, he's the one who taught Heyward this stuff in the first place."

We went through Heyward's basement again since that's where the ambulance was coming. It was a slow trek. I half-carried Allison up each flight of stairs. She felt so cold that I didn't want to let go of her.

My father fared a little better, but it was obvious that each step caused him pain. Chase did his best to help, holding my father's left hand and providing him with a sort of brace.

Together, we made our way to the basement, where I stopped long enough to call Tim, who had called twice and left a voicemail—this time, he picked up.

"I'm on my way, and I'm bringing the cavalry. Sorry, buddy," he said. "I called in and said I was doing a drive-by—they tried to wave me off, said you had a tail. I told them I was going anyway."

"It's fine. Really. But come to the Heyward place. That's where we are now."

"What? That's… somebody just called for an ambulance there!"

"They'd better get two," I said, then remembered Heyward's body. "Actually, make it three. Long story."

"This had better be good." I heard him call for two more medics. "Are you okay?"

"Been better. Listen, gotta go. Can't keep the phone at my ear right now."

"Put me on speaker, then. I'm not disconnecting."

"All right." I did, then shoved the phone in my back pocket. "Hope you can hear. Best I can do."

I thought I heard a muffled response but didn't bother to verify. I pulled Allison's good arm back over my shoulder and helped her slowly up the narrow staircase.

Flashing red lights mingled with the candlelight in the kitchen and were almost as welcome as the warmth. John West stood in the archway with a mop. He had cleared away the worst of the soup.

"Okay, boss?" he said. "They just got here."

"Yeah. Police are coming too," I said. "Just to be safe."

"Oh, yessir. They said they'd be over." An approaching siren confirmed it.

"John… look, I want to thank you for helping me. And please don't take this the wrong way, but I'd really appreciate it if you'd go first to the door."

"Yessiree. Happy to." He turned and walked past the body.

"Chase," I called over my shoulder. "Don't look at what's on the floor, okay?" I wanted to go another way around to spare him, but I'd have to rely on the dim lighting.

Tim met us at the door, along with two other Lynwood police officers. They had their weapons drawn, but Tim didn't. Beyond them, I could see another officer patting West down while still another covered them with a gun.

"Tim. I have a gun in my back pocket. I don't want it. But I can't put Allison down."

He nodded and kept his questions to himself as he came around me and pulled the gun from my jeans pocket.

"I don't know how to put the safety on," I said. "It's not mine."

"I've got it. Who else is here?"

"Allison's son, Chase, is behind me. With...." I swallowed again. "With my father. And John says there might be more people upstairs, locked up."

"I'm sorry, what?"

"I can't explain it myself. Medics first. Allison's hurt. So is Dad."

"Okay. Come out slowly."

"Only way I know right now, buddy." We eased down the steps, and Tim checked us, then Dad and Chase, ensuring no one else was armed. Then he waved a medic up.

"Anybody else?"

"Ezekiel Heyward. He's dead. Just in there. And the others upstairs. I didn't go there."

"Okay." Tim gestured to the officers. "You two, with me."

They looked at each other uncertainly, then up at the imposing place.

I nearly laughed.

"Don't believe everything you hear." I followed the medics who had taken Allison and my father to a row of ambulances.

CHAPTER FORTY-NINE

I didn't want to let either my father or Allison ride in an ambulance without me, but the medics were just as insistent I couldn't ride both rigs, especially not at the same time. Finally, I agreed to let Chase ride with his mother, with the promise that my father and I would be right behind them.

I sat gingerly on a bench on one side while the paramedic tended to my father, strapping him to a board and starting an IV. Dad looked even paler in the harsh lights, and I wondered when he had last been outside. In the daytime, anyway.

"How did this happen?" I asked my father. The question felt inadequate and absurd, but I had no idea where to start.

"He... he used that whiskey to get into peoples' minds," he said, his voice dry.

"But Fontana's sells thousands of bottles!"

"Only...." He coughed, winced, and closed his eyes for a moment. "Only the stuff from the basement. He called it his special brew."

I thought of the gift Heyward had presented to me. He'd used those exact words.

"Heyward... he had Dalton, see," my father continued. "I had no idea. I'd heard... I'd heard that Heyward had my father prisoner in the mansion, so I got some friends together to break in. Dalton said he'd come, but when we tried it... Dalton turned on us. He shot Roger, Victor got hurt, and Tony helped him, and then Dalton came after me. Ordered me at gunpoint into the house, where... Heyward was waiting."

The medic had been checking vital signs and busying himself with the equipment, but now he seemed frozen. "What on earth are you talking about?" he stuttered.

"Long story," Dad and I said at the same time, and that was it. Tears forced their way out of my eyes, and I squeezed Dad's hand too hard but couldn't help it. He squeezed back.

Dad said, "I was right. My father was there. Heyward… and Dalton made me sit with him, and Dad poured me a drink. I didn't know what it would do." Tears streamed down his face. "After that, he made Dad lay on that table… and he made me bleed him for his… his ritual."

"My God," I whispered. The medic's mouth dropped, but by then, we were nearly at the hospital.

"Son." For a moment, Dad's voice recovered its strength, and in that one syllable, any last bit of doubt I had about his identity was finally quashed. "I may not have much longer. I…" He faltered again, but only for a moment. "I want you to know I love you, and I'm so proud of you. I've always been proud of you."

The ambulance screeched to a halt at the Emergency Room. The back door opened, and the shaken paramedic climbed out, then turned and unlatched the clasps holding Dad's gurney in place.

"C'mon, Dave, you can stay with him," the paramedic said. I finally registered his identity — it was the guy I'd knocked down trying to get at Ralph Walther the night my mother died.

"Hey. I'm sorry about…"

He waved it off and then, with the help of the driver, wheeled Dad's gurney out. I followed them into the emergency room in time to see Allison being wheeled into one of the little rooms. Chase wasn't allowed inside, and a nurse was trying to persuade him to sit in the waiting area.

"Chase!" I called. "Come here, come with us."

"Dave, he needs you," Dad said, his voice fading. "He can't come with me either."

"And neither can you," said a nurse. "Trauma three," she told the medics, who dutifully headed in that direction.

"Dad, I'll see you soon." I kissed him on the cheek. "Hang in there."

"Okay. Help… the boy," he said.

They reached the trauma room and closed the door with what felt like a disturbing finality. I turned to find Chase still at his mother's door, trying to peek inside while a nurse held him back.

I went over and put an arm around him.

"Chase, let them do their thing. Your mom's going to be okay," I told him.

He resisted me at first but finally let me lead him to the waiting room. We sat side by side on chairs that may have once been comfortable but now had lumps from supporting too many varied bottoms. My tailbone and legs hurt, and I wondered if the soup had been hot enough to leave burns.

I lifted Chase's hand and squeezed it. He squeezed back. Hard. We watched as four more ambulances pulled up. Dexter Lewis was in one of them. Brandon Kick was in another. And Felicia Erickson was in the third — looking worse than any of the rest, as pale as death with an oxygen mask over her face.

The fourth carried Ezekiel — Zachariah, I corrected myself — Heyward, with no urgency. I presumed it was him, anyway. His face was covered.

Chase's eyes grew wide. "Who are those people?"

I could barely process it myself, let alone begin to explain it to an eight-year-old. "The last one is the guy we saw," I told him quietly. "He's dead now. He took the others prisoner."

"Did he kill them?"

"No, but I think he was going to."

"Were they people who were missing?"

"Yes."

He was quiet for a minute.

"He was going to kill Mom, wasn't he?"

"I think he was. And the rest of us, too, probably."

"What bullshit," he said.

I laughed and hugged him. "Yes, it really is."

With a start, I suddenly wondered if Luke had drunk some of Heyward's "special brew." *He did it to himself. Said he had to.* Those had been Allison's words when she told me Luke had killed himself. A chill ran up my spine, and I held Chase tighter.

Yes, he'd gotten to Luke too.

"Did you kill him?" Chase asked when I finally let go.

Had I? I'd only hit Heyward's wrist, but he appeared to start going downhill before that as soon as the first pendant was smashed.

"I'm not quite sure," I told him. "I don't really understand what happened."

"I think we hurt him when we smashed his necklace," Chase said matter-of-factly.

I smiled. "I think so too. Good throw, by the way."

"Good hit."

Eventually, a nurse got around to checking my injuries. I needed stitches on my thigh and had first-degree burns on my legs, along with a lump on my head that they couldn't do anything about aside from giving me a couple of acetaminophen. She let Chase stay with me the whole time.

CHAPTER FIFTY

Allison's nurse came out first, inviting both of us back to see her. Chase bolted forward. "I'll check on your father," the nurse told me, reading my expression perfectly. I thanked her and followed Chase.

Allison still looked pale, but not as bad as when they put her in the ambulance. Her lank hair seemed to stick to the pillow, but she smiled weakly as Chase ran in. He managed to contain himself just in time and hugged her gently.

"Hey, honey. Why are you crying? I'm okay." She gave him a big hug.

"That man was going to kill you," he said, his voice muffled. He finally let go and kissed her on the cheek, then hugged her again.

"Takes more than that," she whispered, but I could tell from her expression that she knew the truth.

We took turns asking each other what happened. Allison said she went into the kitchen to get plates for the pizza I was bringing when she heard a sound from the craft room. She didn't have time to investigate before someone grabbed her from behind and stuck something over her face. She didn't remember anything else until waking up on the table with Chase and my father tending to her.

Chase and I took turns filling her in, and I apologized profusely for not knowing about the secret tunnel under the house.

"So Ezekiel Heyward used some sort of black magic to keep himself young and to get people to do what he wanted?"

"When you put it that way, it sounds perfectly reasonable," I said, and for the first time since we came in, Allison laughed. "It does sound crazy. But my dad went from trying to skewer me like a kebob to teaching Chase how to treat your injury just like that." I snapped my fingers.

"And then there was John West. He said he was trapped the same way, forced to do whatever he was told. And so was anyone who drank that special whiskey. Fontana's Finest."

"That could be a lot of people.

I nodded, remembering the bottle Walt kept in his desk drawer and the drink that Dalton Adams had on his side table during my visit. Both of them had offered me a drink. I shuddered as I thought of what could have happened if I had accepted.

"I'm sure he offered it to plenty of influential people in town," I said. "I remember reading about how Fontana's survived Prohibition by reclassifying their whiskey as a 'medicinal supplement.' I wonder now who he gave some of that drink to back then."

We were quiet for a moment, each lost in our thoughts. Chase still hadn't gone more than five feet from his mother's side.

"Luke must have had some," Allison murmured.

"What?"

"When he… did what he did. He worked late that night. Normally, he told me, but he didn't let me know that night, and I was upset with him because of it." She swallowed and reached for Chase's hand, holding it tightly. "When he got home, he was pacing. He went in the basement, and when he came up, he had the gun."

The noises of the hospital seemed both hushed and jarring.

"I asked what he was doing, and he said, 'I had to work late. He made me work late and is making me do this. I have to do it.'" She swallowed again. "I thought he meant work had gotten too much for him—which was weird, he'd always liked it there—but now I wonder if he was referring to Heyward. Maybe Heyward made him stay late and actually... made... him do what he did."

Chase was crying now, and Allison pulled him close. Both of them were in tears before long, and I wanted to melt into the wall.

"I'm sure you're right," I managed. "Maybe you two should be alone for a few."

She nodded, and I ducked out, shaken. If Heyward could actually force people to kill themselves—then it was no wonder he escaped notice for so long. After all, he made Ralph Walther drink himself to death.

I remembered again the grin he flashed me in the manor, how it so closely resembled the one I had seen on Ralph Walther's visage the night he killed my mother. He had been innocent, after all, just another of Heyward's victims.

Walther had been holding a liquor bottle when I found him, and I had no doubt it was Fontana's Finest. He called me to apologize, and when I didn't pick up, he went to my house. Perhaps Heyward meant the bottle for me, a peace offering of sorts, and when I wasn't where he expected to find me, he made Ralph find a quiet spot to drink it all down.

Heyward himself gave me a bottle. Walt Quinlan and Dalton Adams both offered me drinks. I now realized that if at any point I faltered, I might have taken Dad's place imprisoned in Heyward Manor.

I suddenly felt very cold. I had wandered and realized I was just outside the room where they'd taken my father. No one seemed to be paying attention, so I pushed the door open.

Hospitals had a way of making even the strongest people look frail, and Dad wasn't strong at all. Stringy gray hair covered his scalp, cheeks, and chin, and his eyes were sunken. A tube carried air into his nose, and another protruded from his left arm, which was hooked to an IV. He was skinny, unnaturally so, but he appeared to be sleeping peacefully. His skin was the color of mayonnaise in the antiseptic light.

I covered his hand with mine. His was cold and clammy.

"Dad?" I whispered, and suddenly I was six again, wondering where my daddy had gone, why he hadn't come back to see me or take me to school or play catch with me or tuck me in at night. Now I had the answer — he hadn't been able to — but that old ache flared bright in my chest. I dropped to my knees, holding his hand, and cried like I had as a little boy.

How long I knelt there, I don't know. One strong emotion seemed to trigger another, and they combined to knead my exhaustion into a crushing force. I felt like I could just lay down on the floor and sleep until my father awoke.

"Son?" His voice was so dry I almost didn't register the sound, but then he gave my hand a faint squeeze. "David... Is that you?"

His eyes, which were vacant while he was doing Heyward's bidding and bright afterward, now looked yellow, rheumy, and wet.

"It's me, Dad," I said as I reached to hug him, just briefly. "You're in the hospital, and they're going to help you get better. Then you can come live with me, and we can catch up."

He smiled. "I'd like that very much, But I fear my time is nearly up."

"It can't be. I just got you back," I said.

"I know." He squeezed my hand, and it scared me to realize that he was trying to squeeze tightly, but I could barely feel it. This was the same hand that had no difficulty swinging a sword a few hours ago.

"How's your leg?" he asked as if he'd been reading my mind.

"It's fine. I'm glad you're not good with a sword."

"I was... holding back a bit." His voice faltered, and I wanted to call a nurse for some water but didn't want to get thrown out. "He forced me to do many bad things, but I was able to fight just enough. Sometimes, I could resist in little ways, like when I snuck into our house."

"I'm sorry I hurt you. Are your ribs okay?"

He chuckled, then winced. "Always knew you had a good swing. I've been sick for months. Heyward has been healing me, keeping me alive. Using innocent people to do it. I hope he rots in hell."

"Too good for him," I said. "What do you mean, sick? Have you seen a doctor?"

"No. Heavens, no. He couldn't let anyone know I existed. John's the only one who knew."

His eyes fluttered as if he couldn't stay awake.

"What do you mean you snuck into the house?"

"I came in at night sometimes, through the basement. Just to be near you and your mother." He took a labored breath. "Even left your mother a note when I saw she was still trying to find me."

"You wrote 'call Dalton' in the notebook!"

His eyes widened. "She told you?"

"She found it, and later, I found it," I said. "Dalton didn't want to do it, but he gave me the information to figure out the Heyward place was key to what was going on. I wish I had figured it out sooner."

He smiled again. "All the same, I'm glad you did. He wasn't ready to try his ritual with that girl, but I think you forced his hand."

I wasn't sure whether that was good news or not.

"How did you get that desk to keep opening until we found Levi's old diary?"

"What?"

"The rolltop. It kept opening and closing, sometimes when I was just in the next room. And finally, Allison found Levi's diary. Did you hide it in that desk?"

"I have no idea what you're talking about. Who's Levi? What diary?"

"Levi Kendrick, son of Alan Kendrick. The Civil War guy."

"I don't know..." he coughed. "Anything about that. But that house always had its ghosts."

I held his hand, listening to him breathing.

"This is okay, David. I'm glad it's over. I know he can't get you anymore. I love you, David."

"You're going to be okay."

The door opened, but I ignored it.

"Dad. You're going to be okay." He smiled again at me and, this time, didn't fight it when his eyes closed. He'd fallen asleep.

"Who let you in here?" A man's voice, low but firm. I turned to face a doctor in scrubs and a white jacket.

"Nobody. It was open, and I had to see him, just for a minute."

He looked as though he wanted to scold me but opted against it.

"It's all right," he said. "We were going to find you soon anyway. We were hoping he would recover consciousness before we did."

"He was talking a few minutes ago. He just fell asleep."

"What did he say?"

I wished I hadn't revealed that information. "He said he'd been kept as a prisoner for years." I chose my words carefully. "He said he'd been sick for a while."

He nodded. "That appears to be the case. But before I go, I need to discuss his identity. You said this is your father, missing for thirty years. How can you know that?"

"He's my father. I'd know him anywhere."

He gave a patient smile. "But the last time you saw him, you were, what, five? Six? Seven?"

"Six." I was frustrated, but the professional in me understood the skepticism. "I'm sure. His eyes, for one thing. And he said things that convinced me."

The doctor gave me a long look and finally nodded. "Good enough for now," he said. "We'll need to do a DNA test. It's not that I don't believe you," he added quickly. "But it's not about me, really. I'd treat him regardless. But for other purposes, your father is legally dead, and if he wants to reclaim his life, he'll need evidence."

"Right." I hadn't even considered that. I remembered reading about a person in another country who had been declared legally dead, even though he had moved to another country without telling anyone. He'd returned and appealed to a judge, who had upheld his death inexplicably.

"More pressing right now," the doctor's voice interrupted my thoughts, "is his condition. He is in advanced liver failure and doesn't have long to live without drastic measures."

"How drastic?"

"A transplant, for one thing. Which will be very difficult to obtain given your father's legal status and which we couldn't do at this hospital anyway. But he also has pneumonia, as well as three cracked ribs and severe internal bleeding from blunt force trauma to his side and chest."

I nodded slowly, feeling nauseous. "He was hit with a baseball bat."

The doctor—Warwick read his jacket—gave a start. "Well, yes, that is consistent with what we saw."

"So, what happens now?"

Warwick took a deep breath. "I've already reached out about a possible liver transplant, but as I said, without him having been on any list and without a proper legal identity, it's highly unlikely we will be successful in the time your father has left. We will do all we can, but you should prepare yourself for the possibility that your father may not recover."

My mouth was as dry as Dad's had sounded. "How much time does he have?"

"It could be days, a week or two. It could be hours."

I looked at my father. I didn't want to believe what Warwick was telling me, but I couldn't deny just how bad he looked either. "Can't I give him part of my liver?"

"You can certainly be tested to see if you're a match, but to be honest, I didn't expect him to wake up. I'm not sure he'd survive the surgery."

We stood in silence while he updated his chart, and I willed my father to heal.

I headed to Allison's room to tell them where I'd been and that I needed to go back.

"You okay?" Allison asked as I opened the door.

I choked up. "The doctor. He, ah, he said my dad is in liver failure. And has other issues. Says he...." I wiped a tear away. "Says he may not make it."

"Oh, Dave. I'm so sorry," she said. I could tell she wanted to get up.

Chase did it for her. He ran over and hugged me fiercely.

"Thanks, bud," I said, hugging him back. "You take care of your mom, okay? I'll be back as soon as I can."

CHAPTER FIFTY-ONE

F our days had passed since the ordeal in Heyward Manor, and aside from a few bruises and various aches and pains, I was back to normal—physically, at least. Emotionally, I was exhausted. I'd spent every day by my father's bedside, talking to him when I could but mostly just watching him sleep and fight.

It wasn't going well. I needed a break, so I asked Tim to meet me at Lucky's.

"It's the most bizarre case I've ever seen." Tim followed that statement with a swig of his beer.

I sipped a soda. I had no stomach for alcohol after all that had happened. "You don't normally have hundred-and-seventy-five-year-old men abducting and killing people?"

Tim looked sidelong at me. "I know that's what that guy West says, but come on — that's not possible."

I shrugged. "Neither is my dad being alive."

"True."

"So, what's the story?"

"Off the record, right? Adams would kill me."

"Off the record."

Tim took another fortifying swig, then put the glass down.

"West's story is that Heyward was looking for fresh blood for some scheme of his. And he had to abduct people, so he wanted to pick people who others wouldn't miss, or people he thought someone else might have a motive to get rid of."

"What, so he took Robin because he thought Mike would get the rap?"

"Pretty much. She really was under investigation for hiring a hit man."

"Jesus. And Cervelli?"

"Petty thief out late at night. Easy mark."

"How is that easy?"

"West wasn't clear on the details other than to say he wasn't directly involved." Tim shrugged. "He just knew about it but didn't report it because he believed Heyward would kill him."

That much was probably true. It seemed West had decided to keep his mind-control theory to himself. "And Ralph?"

"Well, that's where it starts to get weird. West claims that Ralph had done some work for Heyward in the past and that Heyward thought police might connect the two of them while investigating your mom's death."

Heyward himself had told me he made Walther crash, but that seemed a stretch.

"A Walther Farms truck was near the school when Felicia Erickson went missing. Was Walther involved in that too?" I asked.

"Ah, so you know about the truck. No, Ralph wasn't around — would have been dead by then, of course — but another Walther Farms employee was in the area. One Mike Elliott."

"So the girl I kept seeing him with was in that house."

"Turns out that's his step-sister. We think she and Elliott somehow got Felicia to follow them into the house and play dumb if anyone knocked on the door. We did, but only because of the truck — we didn't know it was Elliott's at the time. When she played dumb, Reynolds fell for it."

"Why did they abduct Felicia?"

"We don't know that they did. She left the school on her own and met up with Elliott in the parking lot, but then he walked away in a different direction than her."

"Wait, you knew all along it was him?"

"Not at first, but when we figured it out, we knew we had to get away from that 'mysterious stranger' crap. Another one of Reynolds' bright ideas. So instead of just saying we had a person of interest or something, Reynolds put out a vague description that didn't help anyone."

"Okay. So if Elliott left one way and Erickson left another, how do you know they ended up together at Elliott's sister's place?"

"Well, the truck, for one. And we found Erickson's lesson plan tucked under the couch, the same one she'd gone to her car to retrieve in the first place. She says she left it intentionally to leave a trail."

"She talked to you? Why did she say she left?"

Tim shifted uncomfortably. "Well, that's just it. She said she doesn't really remember. She remembered going out, and then she met Mike, and he told her she needed to walk down the street or she'd be sorry."

"That's it? She'd be sorry?"

"Like I said, her account wasn't great. She doesn't remember walking four blocks but remembers meeting Mike at the door. And then she doesn't remember how she got from there to Heyward's place."

"It's a short walk across the field. Maybe half a mile."

"She doesn't remember it. And she was in heels, so you'd think she would."

I thought of Ralph Walther's phone call to me — how he insisted he didn't remember being at the crash scene, even though he knew he was.

"And what does Elliott say?"

"Not much. Lawyered up immediately. Mostly, Elliott says he doesn't remember what happened to Robin or Felicia."

"And the others? The electrical worker and the high school kid?"

"They're not much help, either. Lewis said he suddenly felt the urge to walk into the woods and did, and then blacked out. The kid remembers running all the way to Heyward Manor but doesn't remember why he thought it was a good idea. It sounds like he let himself in and went straight to the room where we found him without knowing why he was there."

We sipped our drinks in silence. The sounds of the bar were the most normal things I'd heard in a week, yet I felt I was a thousand miles away.

"So, when did he kill Elliott and Cervelli?"

"Not sure. And we don't know how their bodies ended up in that field because we'd searched there before. West claims he doesn't know, but I'm not sure I believe him."

"And… did you find their heads?"

"Yeah." He shuddered. "Elliott's was in that still down in the wine cellar. Heyward was distilling a human head, the sick bastard. And Cervelli's was in a freezer in the kitchen."

CHAPTER FIFTY-TWO

I didn't see John West again until two days later. Allison and I took Chase downtown for the annual Lynwood Winter Festival. Shapesville teemed with vendors selling Christmas ornaments and other holiday-themed trinkets under heated craft tents, along with photo booths and, of course, Santa Claus. Allison and Chase were in one of the tents, painting a globe to hang on their tree at home, and I took the opportunity to find a bench at the edge of the square to watch people pass back and forth, reveling in their families.

"This is a hard time of year for some of us." John West's distinctive voice caught me by surprise, and without asking permission, he sat next to me.

"Harder for some than others," I said. "Always has been."

He nodded.

"I'm surprised to see you out and about."

"Powerful people suddenly remembered the mighty questionable things they did while 'under the influence,'" he explained. "Once I reminded them I was far from alone in the things I did—and could prove it—they were more than willing to lose the details to history."

I cocked my head. "You didn't..."

"Give them more special brew? Of course not," he said. "But all those years, Heyward had me keep track of his dirty deeds. He couldn't even remember them all. I always hoped I could use it to put him away. Turns out, it just saved me from going away myself."

"Safer to have him dead than locked up."

"Indeed."

A child of about three squealed as he ran past, chased closely by another a year or so older. Both had red and green scarves that trailed.

"How's your father?" West asked.

"He passed last night." I studied the crowd, watching the revelry, wishing I could feel any of it.

"I'm sorry, David."

I pretended the cold was affecting my eyes, dabbing them with a corner of my sleeve. "I just don't understand why."

"He'd been ill for some time."

"I know..." My voice trailed off as I remembered my last conversations with my father.

In his few waking hours, my dad explained that his father's disappearance had devastated him. In trying to find him, he dug around, chasing rumors, until he figured out there had been clusters of disappearances in which his ancestors all seemed to have been involved. He noticed the connection to Heyward Manor much faster than I did and decided that the rumors of strange lights and sightings might mean people were living at Heyward Manor—or were being kept there.

But he hadn't known about the people in Heyward's web or been able to prove that Heyward was behind it all. He confided in his friends and convinced them to break in to see what was going on for themselves, thinking his father might be inside.

Most hadn't believed him, but one, a police officer—Dalton Adams—had. He was convinced by the mountain of evidence Dad built and took it further, finding copies of the cold case files.

Just before the raid was to occur, Heyward got wind of it and, through another officer under his sway, was able to get Dalton Adams to drink Fontana's Finest. When the raid happened, Heyward took mental control—Adams shot one of the men and was supposed to shoot the rest but was interrupted. He took Dad at gunpoint into the mansion, where Dad was locked up together with his father. Then, my grandfather—under Heyward's influence—shared a bottle he "stole" from Heyward. Heyward instructed my father to kill my grandfather as part of the ancient ritual that made Heyward young again.

My father never understood why our family had been targeted.

West interrupted my train of thought. "My son wanted revenge. Revenge on me. Revenge on your ancestors. Revenge for being born."

"But who did anything to him?"

West rested his elbows on his knees and interlocked his fingers.

"I suppose I did."

I waited for him to explain.

"Zachariah Heyward—that's his real, given name—was my son. But no one was to know that, see, because it was forbidden. His mother was white, and her family owned me."

"How horrible."

He nodded. "I was enslaved in South Carolina with my mamma. She was born in Africa—lived in the Caribbean before being brought up north. She taught me… things."

He cracked his knuckles and continued. "The Heywards owned the plantation. Ezekiel and Helene. Zeke was a hard man, but Helene was sweet as could be. French girl. Zeke would travel, and when he was away, Helene sometimes let us come into the house and have proper food. We became close. Too close."

"And you had a son."

"It was a disaster in the making. Helene and her husband weren't 'friendly,' so the child couldn't possibly be his. Plus, we didn't know what the child would look like. So, the next time he went on one of his trips, Helene loaned me a rifle, and I and a few others snuck out after him. We made sure old Zeke never came home."

My eyes widened.

"Now, I ain't sayin' it was right. But Zeke... he was a hard man. He'd killed other enslaved people for less. I was convinced that not only would I be killed, but I feared for Helene and the baby. And Mamma promised she could make sure no one ever knew what we had done."

"How?"

"She was a practitioner of an old religion. Hoodoo, some call it. She used it to heal people, mostly, but she also used it to make people keep secrets. Keep people who knew about the Underground Railroad from sharing things they shouldn't. One little drink was all it took, and all who took it took it willingly. They didn't want their owners to be able to succeed in torturing information from them."

The shiver that ran up my spine had nothing to do with the cold.

"So, the baby was born, and Helene's brother-in-law Joseph moved in and took over the plantation. Joseph was worse than Zeke, but Zachariah's skin was light enough that he was only slightly suspicious about who the real father was. He took care of the boy, but he beat Helene. He was an awful man."

"Then, some of my friends found Alan — Captain Kendrick, your ancestor. He'd been injured and captured but had somehow escaped a caravan headed to that prison at Andersonville. They found him and hid him. Mamma helped him get healthy."

"Why did you leave with him?"

"Zachariah was a teenager by then. He overheard Helene arguing with Joseph. Joseph hit her and told her he was going to take the plantation by birthright since Zachariah was his brother's son. Then, Helene blurted that Zeke wasn't the real father."

"Oh, no."

"His suspicions must've come roaring back, and with Zachariah's swarthy skin, he made the leap to deciding she had slept with one of us enslaved people. So, he did what he thought was right."

"What was that?"

"He killed her. Zachariah ran to find out who his father was."

"Were you there? How did you find out what happened?"

"Found out later from a parlor maid — us workers were invisible to the owners. Like a piece of furniture." He shook his head. "At the time, I didn't know what had happened to Helene. I thought Zachariah was playing a game — a dangerous game — when he arrived at our shack. I knew that if I said any such thing, my life would be forfeit. Then later, when I heard Helene was gone...."

West cleared his throat. "Well, I got scared. For me and for Zachariah. I didn't know where the boy had gone after I told him I didn't know who his father was. And Kendrick was well enough to leave, so I decided to go with him. Because of Mamma and her friends, I knew if I could get to the Underground Railroad, we'd be safe. Traveling with Kendrick gave me a cover — if we got caught, I could pretend he was my owner."

"And that worked?"

"I'm sitting here." He smiled. "It was a close thing, sometimes. We soon got word that someone was following us, trying to find us, but we didn't know who. I assumed it was Joseph, who had a financial incentive to get me back."

"But it was Eze... Zachariah."

He nodded slowly. "He didn't catch up till about a year later. Where he was in between, I don't know. While I worked on the plantation down south—the Fontana plantation—I learned how to make whiskey from an enslaved person who learned from Zeke. But then he died, which meant I was the only living person who knew the recipe that made the plantation profitable. That's the reason I thought Joseph was trying to find me. By then, Kendrick and I had dug the wine cellar."

"So, you were going to set up your own distillery here."

"Did set it up. You're looking at the founder of Fontana Fine Spirits, though I never would have called it that myself. I was going to call it Cooper's Whiskey. The first batches were still fermenting when Zachariah showed up."

Right then, I decided to buy every one of Jethro Miller's ghost books to study them. "Is that when he killed the family?"

"When Zachariah arrived, Alan and I were the only ones at the house. He forced us downstairs at gunpoint, tied us up, and then tortured us. He was furious with Alan, who he saw as a race betrayer, for daring to help me escape. Then he decided he needed to make sure Alan's family was orphaned, the same way he'd been orphaned. But he wanted Alan to see it happen, so he took him prisoner. He snuck upstairs, thinking to kill Alan's wife, but ended up killing everyone except the one boy who wasn't home. Somehow, he decided that was even better."

"Did he even have an endgame at that point?"

"Still revenge. But he had fun befriending Levi, the boy. Zachariah built his house over the second entrance to the cellar that Kendrick and I had previously built. Zachariah and Levi made the tunnels nice and long, so they could use them as a Railroad escape. Or at least that's what Zachariah told Levi. Levi financed the whole thing through the bank."

"He was controlling people even then?"

West gave a sardonic laugh. "Only through his charm, at that point. I was locked in the cellar with Alan. Heyward would come down and tell us all about it. He was a master manipulator. He used Levi against Alan, and he used Alan against me."

"How?"

"He figured out that I was healing both Alan and me. It was a stupid thing to do, but I thought Alan was going to die. He put a gun to Alan's head, and I finally admitted that I could heal people." He turned to face me, and I saw the pain in his eyes. "It never occurred to me that he could actually learn it since he was half white."

"But he did."

West nodded. "Frightfully fast. Soon, he pushed that knowledge farther and farther. Mamma must have died by them because I was able to tell him about how Mamma was able to make people keep secrets. After he tortured me, of course."

He said this so matter-of-factly that it chilled me more than anything else he'd said.

"Mamma said the brew was only for helping people keep whatever secrets we were tasked with protecting. Maybe that's what it was, but Heyward… he made it more. He made it so it gave him total control over someone. And when he couldn't figure out how to make people drink it, he dreamed up the whiskey idea."

"And for that, he needed you."

West nodded. "Unfortunately, I drank his potion without knowing what he was up to. He didn't bring us much, you see, so we ate and drank what we could. Once we did that, well, he could loosen the reins.

All he had to do was keep us out of sight. So, when he finished that mansion, he built secret rooms and tunnels so that he could entertain guests and, at the same time, keep us tucked away. Years later, when Levi had a family of his own, Zachariah got ahold of him too. And got rid of Alan. He's been doing that ever since."

"And the age thing? How did he pull *that* off?"

"He just kept pushing." West shook his head. "Healing requires a bit of blood. Not enough to cause harm, but enough to give a bit of life back to a person. It takes time, but it's effective, sure enough. Heyward was patient in some ways but not in others. He got in a fight once. Oh, this was maybe ten years after he finished the mansion. I don't know for sure. Anyway, he hurt his hand pretty good and wanted it healed fast. He used Alan's blood, nearly killing him, but it worked."

I realized my jaw was hanging open, but I couldn't seem to lift it.

"With that success, he decided to see what else he could do. Used a few of his 'friends' to catch the fellow he had been in the scrap with — brought him down to that cellar, and decided to find out what would happen if he didn't just use some of his blood but all of it."

"My God."

"It was a terrible thing to watch. And when Zachariah was finished, damned if he didn't look as fresh as a schoolboy." He sighed. "Over the years he figured out that the younger his victim, the younger he could make himself. I watched him go from sixty-five to twenty-five overnight."

"But surely people noticed!"

"That first time was a bit of a scramble. But by then, Zachariah had me working for him in the distillery since nobody dreamed Isaac Cooper was still around. He had me tell people he'd gone away on business but that his nephew from New York had come to keep an eye on things and that his word was as good as the original Heyward's. He'd changed so much, no one would have believed it was still him, but there was, of course, a strong family resemblance."

He shrugged. "A few months later, he told everyone that he'd received word that the original Heyward had died, shot by bandits or some such foolishness. But since by then he had shared his special whiskey with any number of town leaders, it was child's play to ensure a smooth transition to his new identity for the distillery, the house, and pretty much anything else he wanted."

"He didn't get everyone."

"Not everyone drinks, and not everyone drinks whiskey. You're a case in point. And some people he didn't think were important enough. So, he found other ways to get them to do what he wanted. Chief Adams, for example."

"Really? He left Cam alone?"

"Oh, he tried getting him, but Cam doesn't drink. Hasn't since his daughter was killed. But Cam knew Zachariah had some hold over Dalton. I don't know how, but he kept Cam in line with good old-fashioned fear."

"So Cam's hate for me is all his own."

West nodded. "I'm afraid so. He'll never believe that someone ran you off that road."

I blinked. "Wait... he..."

"I don't know anything for sure. But I do know that Heyward told Dalton to report that there was no evidence of another car, so the fault would be entirely yours."

I couldn't breathe. I flashed back to that night, driving, laughing, seeing the headlights dart toward me, swerving to avoid them. "Why would he try to kill me?" I gasped.

327

"Like I said, I don't know that he did. Maybe he just saw an opportunity to make your life more miserable." West sighed and, for a moment, looked ten years older. "The longer it went on, the worse it got. He could distill whiskey in a way that gave him control over the decisions of people who drank it, like whether or not to leave a room. But soon, he wanted to be able to make someone take more drastic actions. And the blood potion wasn't enough for that."

"The heads?"

He nodded. "He would distill a batch with a severed head hanging inside."

I clasped my hand over my mouth, afraid I'd be ill.

"And you didn't even drink it." He chuckled.

We sat in silence for a few minutes. Allison and Chase were still painting baubles. They were as happy as I had seen them in recent times, but every once in a while, a shadow would flit across the face of one or the other.

"Luke. Did he do that to Luke?" I asked.

West nodded heavily. "Luke walked in on Heyward at a bad time. When he wanted to control more than a person's thoughts, he had to shut himself off a bit. Luke walked in while Heyward was controlling the fella that crashed into your mom. He didn't know how much Luke had seen or heard, so he forced him to go home and finish himself off."

"And all these missing people, he just needed them to brew more whiskey?"

"He was planning to use the kid to make himself younger again, but then you forced his hand by going to Dalton, so he grabbed your girl instead — to lure you in."

"So, he knew I went to Dalton?"

"The control thing isn't complete — sometimes people are able to break through, do things Zachariah wouldn't want when he's not paying attention. Like when the Walther boy called you, which meant he had to go. Or when that teacher tried to fight the urge to walk away, Zachariah had someone nearby to ensure she didn't."

"Elliott."

"Yep. But even if Zachariah didn't notice it right away, the betrayal somehow registered in his brain, and then he'd make the offender tell him what he'd done. Once he'd transformed you, Dalton would've been next on his hit list."

There was another lengthy silence.

"What will you do now?" I asked him. "Now that you're free of his influence?"

"Satisfy a dream, I think."

"What's that?"

"Go to Scotland and learn from the distillers there. As it turns out, somewhere along the line, Zachariah named me his beneficiary. It was quite the joke, see. He knew he'd never die, but every time Zachariah signed off on a bank loan or financial document, he'd put me down as his beneficiary to rub my nose in it, to show me how invincible he thought he was."

"You own everything?"

He nodded. "Mansion, distillery, branding, all of it. One hundred percent. Already found a buyer."

"Thank you for telling me all this."

"You're welcome. I trust you won't go spreading it around. Nobody would believe you."

"No, I suppose they wouldn't." I thought of Jethro Miller, but he had enough stories.

West stood. "I'd best be off. Looks like your new little family will be done soon."

I stuck out my hand. "I wish you well, Mr. West."

"It's all thanks to you, Mr. Kendrick. If it weren't for you, I'd still be a slave to my son."

"One last question then."

He paused.

"How are you still around? After all, you were Zachariah's father. Shouldn't you have died when the amulets were smashed?"

He laughed. "There are stronger powers at work in this universe than the paltry ones I told my son about."

Without another word, he turned and walked away, merging with the crowd. I watched until I felt Allison's arm slide around me.

"Who was that?" she asked. "He looked familiar."

"John West. From Fontana's," I said.

Chase gasped. "From the mansion?"

I nodded. Before Chase could ask something else, I pointed toward a food truck. "Enough of that for now. I think I owe you two a hot chocolate."

About the Author

Jim Sabin graduated from Whitmer High School in 1991 and then attended Ohio University, Athens, where he obtained his bachelor's degree in Journalism, graduating in 1995. He worked in newspaper journalism for decades, both reporting on various local beats and editing local newspapers.

Jim was an award-winning newspaper reporter and editor for twenty years in Ohio, and drew on his past experiences for inspiration for some events in "The Missing." He saw first-hand how missing persons reports are often met with apathy at all levels; He had also seen how something unexplained and scary whips a small town into a big fervor.

In 2017, he returned to his alma mater, Ohio University, to work in Media Relations.

Before his death, Jim lived in Canal Winchester, Ohio, with his wife and younger son, Alex. He also spent as much time as he could with his older son, Chris. Family was his bedrock, and he left an impact on all those lucky enough to know and love him.

www.ingramcontent.com/pod-product-compliance
Lightning Source LLC
Chambersburg PA
CBHW030640260626
47157CB00007B/2422